# The Inseparable Gang of Happy Girls

## Volume One

### J.C. Pacheco

ISBN-13: 978-1-7340366-0-2

To my mother, 'G', 'K', and 'S'

# CONTENTS

# 1 SPINNING OUT OF CONTROL

**Gemma—London—Spinning out of control**

PRIMROSE HILL
October 2018
She stripped off her clothes slowly. First, she took off her white blouse, then her dark blue skirt. She stood in front of the bed clothed only in her white bra and panties. She looked at him, and then she moved her hands up to her bra and took it off.

She now stood in front of him. She was beautiful. She really was. She had nice hips, a flat stomach, large breasts, and a flawless complexion. She didn't smile. She breathed slowly. There were four plastic beads sewn onto the front of her white panties. They looked like pearls. She looked at him.

He stood in front of her. She scanned over him with her eyes. The room was dimly lit by a lamp in the corner. And the street lights cast a dim light into the second floor window of the bedroom. He was 51 years old, but he looked at least 10 years younger. A strict exercise regimen and a lifetime without alcohol, cigarettes, or drugs had kept him looking much younger than he really was. He was hardly a good catch, but he had the one thing she really needed: **money.**

He knew exactly what she was thinking: 'How did I end up here?' He really didn't care what she was thinking at that point. He wanted her.

She sighed. Okay. This was her fate. She inserted her thumbs into each side band of her panties and pulled them down. She stepped out of them and then stood back up. There. She was totally naked. She stood naked before him.

This woman was beyond anything he had ever dreamed of having. Now she was standing in front of him.

She was 40 years old. Her named appeared in Burke's Peerage. She was 'an Honourable'; the daughter of a British baron. Her mother had been the daughter of an army colonel. She was also divorced. Her ex-husband had managed to bankrupt them both before he left her to face ruin all alone. Creditors had taken their house in Notting Hill.

An Oxford University graduate, her degree in French Literature was of little value. Her lineage had gotten her a job as an editor at a fashion magazine, but a declining circulation had led to budget cuts and layoffs. She was a middle-aged white woman. What did she know of the young urban youth culture which now pulsed through London? Nothing. She had been replaced by a rude, shabbily dressed and dreadlocked 24-year-old girl, a fashion design graduate from one of the UK's third tier universities.

Jobless and virtually unemployable, she moved in with one of her friends from her elite boarding school.

Her father, the 8th Baron, an aged retired army major, was a heavy drinker. He smoked too much and spent his days in his bedroom. He had had a mediocre army career. He had retired, failed at business, and now lived off his modest army pension in a cottage that was located near the former family pile in Sussex. The family seat had been lost to *his* debts two decades earlier. The Edwardian cottage was the only thing that had saved him from homelessness.

His wife had already passed away, and his son, the future 9th Baron, had moved to Hong Kong. He was involved in finance or real estate. The 8th Baron wasn't really sure. His son hadn't spoken to him in decades. He had been a distant and indifferent father. The children had never interested him.

Six months had passed since Gemma had lost her editing job at the magazine. She was desperate. She had no family she could turn to. She needed a new man to take care of her.

Gemma's past and her father's scandalous lifestyle had made her a social pariah, and an embarrassment to be seen with, or employ. The American millionaire had been introduced to her by a former boarding school and Oxford classmate who felt sorry for her. 'Get any man you can, Gemma.'

So now, Gemma stood naked in a near stranger's bedroom. She wanted to die. This was her only way out? *This was how she was going to survive?*

'Lay down,' he told her.

Gemma climbed onto the bed and lay flat on her back.

She was beautiful. The American couldn't believe his luck.

He climbed into bed and then spread her legs. He pulled her body towards him. Gemma was trembling. She was afraid. The American got on top of her. She could feel his full weight. She could feel everything. She wished she could be numb. But fate would not be that kind to her.

Afterwards, Gemma got up and sat on the edge of the bed. She felt sick. Her head was spinning. *How had she ended up in this place? Why had she been abandoned to this fate?*

'I love you,' he said.

'I love you, too,' Gemma lied.

The American crawled towards her again. Gemma exhaled slowly. The American grabbed her and pulled her towards him. Gemma, completely defeated, could only think, 'Okay. Once more.'

The American had other plans. After a lifetime of dismissive glances by beautiful women, he wanted to do something to Gemma she had never had done to her before. The American could sense she was completely unaware of what was about to happen to her. Something stirred deep inside him, something dark and brutal.

3

Gemma was not only a beautiful woman. She was the very embodiment of a stratum of society that looked down on him, treated him with derision, and used him for their own purposes. Now, Grey, the American outcast in London, had one of them. She was like a beautiful caged animal. She was completely under his control. Grey felt power surging through him. He looked at her perfect face, flawless skin, and glossy brown hair for a moment.

Earlier that evening, while at dinner in one of London's most expensive restaurants, Grey felt himself falling deeply in love with her. This was the first time he had felt anything like it. It was almost unsettling to someone like Grey.

Grey knew that Gemma felt uncomfortable with him. She was probably embarrassed to be seen with him in the restaurant. The highborn Gemma was well known to the 'London Set'. Most likely, some of them were in that very restaurant. Gemma, Grey *decided*, undoubtedly felt humiliated being seated at the same table with him. She *must have known* that her kind was laughing at her. She also must have known that they would laugh about this episode all the way home in their car. They would tell everyone how far The Honorable Gemma had fallen. Knowing that Gemma *must have felt* this way angered him. How Gemma really felt didn't really matter. It's what Grey *thought* she felt that did. Gemma would pay for it.

What had begun as consensual had suddenly become violent and terrifying. He wanted to hurt and humiliate her. The American wanted to traumatize her. And he did just that.

'Please. Stop. It hurts. You're hurting me!' cried Gemma.

He ignored her pleas. He owned her. He owned this woman. This living being was his property to do with whatever he wished. She was his slave. She had no choice.

She felt lost, completely lost. Time seemed to stand still. Eventually— finally—he stopped, and she fell to one side. She was sobbing. She was torn and bleeding. She could feel it.

The American was breathing heavily. He looked down at her slim body. She was one of the spoils of war. Grey felt like a Roman god.

Gemma sobbed quietly on the bed; however, it wasn't over yet. Everything kept getting worse. Gemma's torment continued. It was torture, truly.

Gemma didn't know how long it had gone on; it continued as flashes of pain, darkness, then shadows, then violent movements. He was extremely rough with her. Gemma cried the entire time. Gemma tried to resist, but she couldn't. He was too strong for the diminutive Gemma.

Her entire face was wet with tears. She could hear herself crying, but it seemed to be disconnected from her, as if it were someone else crying out and she was only listening from a distance. Gemma's mind folded in on itself and went dark. Gemma was awake but her mind was somewhere else. She had never experienced anything like it. She was confused. She could feel jabs of pain and hear screams. What was happening? Gemma really didn't know.

More than once, Gemma had begged him to stop. She told him repeatedly that he was hurting her. He continued. Afterwards he lay back against the headboard; her head against his stomach.

'Will you marry me?' he asked quietly.

Gemma--her mind swirling with numbing and confusing patterns and chaotic thoughts--responded mechanically. 'Yes,' she said in barely a whisper. Then she blacked out.

**The next morning** the slender American woke up. He was lying on his side in bed. Two pillows, one behind his head and the other against his back, propped him up. The high thread count white sheets had blood stains on them.

Gemma lay across from him naked. She was on her stomach. The sheet only covered her upper back and shoulders. Her long glossy brown hair lay off to one side. Her body was beautiful. Her skin was supple and unblemished—he was somehow completely oblivious to the fresh bruises on her body.

The American lay next to her and gazed at her in silence. She was perfect. Gemma, at 40, had the body of a much younger woman. Grey watched her breathe while she slept next to him: inhale; exhale; inhale.

Gemma's legs were slightly spread apart. Gemma's entire body was not covered entirely by the sheet. He looked at her carefully. Then he noticed the blood. Dried blood had run down between her legs. The American had done that to her. He suddenly felt deeply ashamed. It was like a source of heat had suddenly risen up inside him.

Gemma was a good-hearted person. Sure, she only wanted him for his money, but she didn't deserve what he had done to her. Gemma was a cultured, well-educated, and gentle person who had suffered a lot of reversals. He had savaged her to get revenge on the universe. He had healed his psyche and badly damaged hers. He was a bastard. And then a wave of regret swept over him, filled him, and wouldn't leave.

Grey suddenly realized that Gemma would never love him or *even care about him*, **ever**. He had injured, violated, and humiliated her. He would always be the beast that had raped her. No matter what he did to attempt amends or how many years passed, Gemma would only think of him as the animal that had raped her.

He loved her. He really did. And he had hurt her badly. She had not submitted to him; she had endured what he had done to her. She was now left injured.  He hated himself. For the first time in Grey's life, he hated himself.

He wanted to keep her. He would have to buy her love. Not love. Not loyalty. Her services. She had been left a whore. He had turned her into a prostitute. He would marry her. But she would never be his. He had ruined everything. He had destroyed everything. He had destroyed Gemma.

He got out of bed carefully. He didn't want to wake her up. He was ashamed to make eye contact with her. He walked down the hall and into the guest bedroom's bathroom. He took a shower. He stepped out of the shower and looked at himself in the mirror. He looked at his slim and muscular body. No one would love this body. No one would ever love him.

When he came back to the room in a white Egyptian cotton bathrobe, Gemma was still asleep. She was so beautiful. He wished he could go back in time. Go back to last night and not done what he had done. Grey felt wave after wave of panic surging through him.

Gemma stirred. She opened her eyes and looked sleepily at him. Then her face twisted a bit. She was in pain. She tried to hide her discomfort. The American had noticed.

'Going to work?' She smiled gently. Everything Gemma did was gentle.

'Yeah. I have a meeting at eleven today,' he lied. He just wanted to get out of there. 'Gemma. I am going to deposit some pocket money in your bank account today. I also want you to move in with me. You will have the bedroom down the hall as you own room. I want you to have your own space. Buy some new clothes today. Anything you want. Visit a spa. The money will be in your account in an hour. What is your account number?'

'That's alright. I don't need any money,' she replied, and Gemma smiled.

The American ached. He felt sick to his stomach. He felt flush. His knees grew weak.

'Are you alright? You are as white as a ghost,' asked Gemma.

'I'm fine.' The American was too ashamed to even look at her.

'I think I'll just stay here today. Would that be ok?'

'Of course, Gemma. You're my girlfriend, my fiancée' now. Do whatever you like. The maid arrives at 10am. She is Portuguese. You'll like her. She is really nice.'

Gemma stared at him for a few seconds. 'Girlfriend? Fiancée?' thought Gemma. 'You hurt me last night, and now you call me your fiancée?'

Gemma only thought this, but the American could read her face. He looked out the window. 'Primrose Hill is a beautiful area. You should explore it.'

'I grew up just a mile away from here. I know the area well,' replied Gemma.

Gemma spoke with a posh accent. Gemma *was posh*. She had been a Sloane Ranger in her youth. Her style, her walk, they way she spoke, even the way she ate and drank, revealed her posh background to even the most casual of observers. This is what had really attracted him to Gemma.

## MODERN LONDON

Gemma was beautiful, but so were a lot of girls in London. Grey had had stunning girls; some of them had just been teenagers, mostly from Eastern Europe. Grey never paid for sex. He didn't like what that would have made him. When you are rich, the girls are always free. The girls are auditioning to be your wife. But Grey knew what kind of girls they were. He knew exactly. He had had quite a few, but the relationships never lasted. He didn't want to marry a girl who had been with some of his associates and clients. He also didn't want a girl like that on his arm or for one of them to be the mother of his children. He knew better.

The butcher, the baker, and the candle stick maker married used up gold diggers and felt lucky to have bagged one. He wasn't one of them.

No, this middle-class American wanted an aristocratic woman. He wanted a girl from Burke's Peerage. He wanted a blue blood to be his wife and have his children. And from the day he decided to seek out one of these women, he had wanted to know how it felt to have the daughter of a baron or a countess as a wife. Yeah, he wanted to break through the phalanx and storm into the gilded world that had rejected him.

He wasn't really rich by London standards.

The house in London was worth about 3.5 million dollars. For that area, the house was modest. It was Edwardian: 'a modest dwelling' they had said at the estate agency. The house had a 'back garden', whatever that meant. It didn't have a garage. No biggie. He didn't want to drive in Britain anyway. He was content to hail a black cab or even take The Underground. His office was only a fifteen-minute walk. Grey could also summon a driver whenever he needed one.

Truth be told, he had gotten the house in trade from a Ukrainian oligarch for a Dadaist painting by a noted (and rather notorious) German painter. The house had been purchased for a son to attend university in London. At the last minute, the son decided to attend school in France. The old man had just wanted to unload it, even if it wasn't quite an even trade. The old man liked Grey, so it was practically a gift.

The house had been completely renovated and decorated by one of London's best interior designers. It was also the American's ticket into posh London.

Grey owned millions in London real estate. Grey owned three houses in London (one in Primrose Hill, the other two in Greenwich), a building in Primrose Hill that he used as an office (and storage facility), and a former factory that he had converted into apartments in Notting Hill. These properties alone provided Grey a healthy income.

In addition to residential properties, he owned an art gallery in Central London. The art gallery was run by an extremely intelligent and well-educated young woman named Imogen. She was one of Grey's chief protégés, and as Grey would tell those closest to him, one of *his greatest creations*. It was art that had brought Grey to the attention of the London elites. Grey, with Imogen's help, had turned a derelict building into one of London's most exclusive art galleries. The art world had opened doors for Grey that no other business ever could.

He only had about ten million dollars in cash and gold. That was loose change for the foreign billionaires, oligarchs, and the other assorted rich lowlifes which now dominated London society. Well, at least their segment of it.

He was debt-free. He was healthy. He looked good for his age. He was still in good shape. That was enough.

He was involved in everything: art, real estate, classic cars, luxury watches,

Fabergé objects, and antique furniture. He had connections in Ukraine and Croatia. He had enemies in Russia and Serbia. These connections fed him a steady stream of Czarist and Hapsburg artifacts. It was a good living.

He had also learned something else living in London: **always look much wealthier than you really are.** This was paramount in the shallowness of modern London. Wear an expensive watch. Wear expensive clothes. Drive an expensive car. Dine at the best restaurants. Join certain clubs. *Only he hadn't done any of that.*

He didn't like expensive clothes. He liked nice clothing, but he thought the suits and shoes the elites wore were just overpriced. He didn't like tailored clothing. He was from North Carolina. He was comfortable in blue blazers and striped ties. J Crew, if he could get it. No, you take the boy out of the Carolinas, but you can't take the Carolinas out of the boy.

The London elites were left unimpressed with Grey. He was just 'a country boy'. It didn't matter that he had come from a good family. It didn't matter that his grandfather had been a senator. The family, once wealthy and powerful, had become middle class by the time Grey had arrived. The family's prestige had eroded away. This bothered Grey immensely.

He didn't like gourmet food. He hated mustard. He hated the condiments the Brits put on food. He didn't drink. He didn't smoke. He didn't take drugs, even when a Russian girl had sprinkled it on her breasts and invited him to snort cocaine off of her.

He did manage to appear much, much wealthier than he really was. He had a certain level of poshness all his own. It was enough to attract the low-hanging fruit.

## THE ART GALLERY
Violet, 'an Honourable', had purchased a Vorticist painting from him. It was fairly expensive. She paid cash. The posh, stylish, and rather attractive blonde-haired Violet was chatty. She wanted to know all about him.

'Not married? How did you manage that? You haven't met the right woman. I know someone I think you would like,' said The Honourable Violet.

'No', he answered. 'I don't have time for a relationship right now.'

'This girl is different. She studied with me at Oxford. She is a fashion editor. She's really stunning. You would love her,' said Violet while she was walking around the white walled art gallery in central London.

Grey walked beside her and thought about what she had said. The American figured this chick was probably some fat hag her friend was trying to foist on him.

'She is staying with a mutual friend in London right now.'

Violet knew how badly off Gemma was. Poor girl. She had made seemingly good choices in life only to end up discarded. This American wasn't much, but Gemma's reputation had been blackened—no—ruined, by her scandalous divorce, house foreclosure, and her horrid father. No one in their 'set' would even invite her to tea now. Gemma was at the end of her tether. What would become of her? This American was a lifeline.

'She is a daughter of the landed nobility. You can look her up in Burke's if you like,' said Violet casually. She then stopped to look at a painting on one of the white walls of the gallery.

Burke's Peerage? That was enough for him. 'Alright. Sure. I'd like to meet her.'

PRIMROSE HILL

Now Gemma lay naked in his bed. The American couldn't stand it any longer. After all that Gemma had been through, Gemma had been horribly abused *by him,* too. He nodded and then headed for his wardrobe. He dressed quickly and headed downstairs.

Gemma lay in bed until she heard the door shut and the electronic security system engage. She was in pain. She was injured.

'What have you done to me?' Gemma said as she slowly got out of bed.

She limped to the bathroom. She stood naked in front of the mirror. She

11

noticed bruises on her stomach, right shoulder, arms, thighs, and neck. Gemma was horrified. She turned slowly and noticed several more bruises on her back. 'Oh, no,' said Gemma as she examined her reflection in the mirror.

She looked behind the mirror and found a new toothbrush and toothpaste. She brushed her teeth. She leaned against the sink while she did this to avoid putting too much weight on her feet. She really hurt.

Gemma looked down between her legs and saw the blood. She was too humiliated, too defeated to really react. 'I hope he didn't do any serious damage,' she thought.

Gemma climbed into the shower and gently sprayed her body with warm water. The blood washed down between her legs. She gently cleaned herself. She shampooed her hair three times. She must have been in the shower for at least an hour.

She got out of the shower and examined herself in the mirror again. There were black and blue bruises on her hips, back, shoulder, abdomen, legs and arms. 'What have you done to me?' said Gemma out loud as she continued to look at her reflection in the bathroom mirror.

She would have to cover up. She would also have to see a doctor. But who? She couldn't see any of the really good ones; they knew all of her friends. What if they talked?

She walked out and lay down on the bed. She had found an arrangement, but it wasn't perfect. **It was a disaster.** What could she do? She had no good options left.

COVENT GARDEN

Gemma went to her friend's house in Covent Garden to pick up her things that afternoon.

Her friend, Poppy, was still at work, and would not be home until about 6pm. Gemma packed the same two suitcases she had left with from her house three years earlier. Her life still fit into two suitcases.

Gemma wrote out a letter to Poppy in her beautiful florid handwriting thanking her for her incredible kindness and generosity, and Gemma told her of her sincere wish to repay it all someday. She was terribly sorry for the inconvenience she had caused her.

She felt ashamed and embarrassed to have been such a burden to her former classmate. Gemma was a good house guest, but her classmate had a long-term boyfriend, and with Gemma there, he couldn't sleep over. (At least he was gentlemanly enough to realize how ungentlemanly it would have been to do so.)

Gemma still worried that she had damaged their friendship. She didn't want that to be the case. She told herself that as soon as Grey, her American fiancé, deposited money in her nearly empty account, she would buy Poppy something really nice. That is, of course, if Grey was generous, which she hoped he would be.

After putting the letter in an envelope, she placed it on the kitchen table. Gemma then walked out to her white Peugeot hatchback and drove away to what she hoped would be her new life with Grey. Not that she looked forward to it—she didn't. But as one of her friends had told her, 'Just find a man to take care of you.'

PRIMROSE HILL
She arrived at the front door of her Primrose Hill house an hour later. Gemma, wearing faded denim blue jeans and a light blue cashmere top, was about to open the front door when Maria, the Portuguese maid, dressed in a simple black uniform, opened it for her.

'Senhora! Let me help you with your luggage. Are there any more suitcases in the car?'

'No,' said Gemma, a little embarrassed. After all, what kind of posh woman can fit everything she owns into two suitcases?

Maria was very kind, and if she did think it odd, she gave no hint of it.

Maria was younger than Gemma. Gemma guessed she was in her early 30s.

Maria spoke English well. She had graduated from university with a chemistry degree, but the Portuguese economy, already shaky at the turn of the century, collapsed in 2008. She moved to the UK and had spent the last ten years working as a barista, a house cleaner, and finally a house maid. Grey was generous, and he was nice.

Maria didn't ask Gemma any questions at all. Gemma wondered if Maria was just disinterested or a clever girl who had already figured everything out.

Maria was quite attractive. She was slim and had light brown hair and blue eyes. Gemma wondered if she had a boyfriend, but Gemma didn't want to ask too many questions on her first day.

'Can I help you unpack, Senhora?'

'No, thank you,' replied Gemma politely, and she smiled. 'I don't have much to unpack.'

Gemma looked around the house. It was really nice. Not really small. It was a normal house. But in today's London, people either lived in shoe boxes or palaces. This house was in between. It was very comfortable and the interior decorator had done wonders. The hardwood floors shined beautifully and the Persian rugs were of the highest quality. Everything about the house was beautiful, tasteful, opulent, and luxurious.

Gemma hadn't lived in a place like this since her childhood. Her house in Notting Hill had been nice, but it was not opulent. Gemma's ex-husband had spent most of his salary on high living, expensive clothing, automobiles, and unbeknownst to her, a young daughter. Whatever money he had left, he gambled away. He hadn't always been like that, but slowly, oh so slowly, his life had degenerated.

She didn't realize how bad things were until the bailiffs showed up trying to collect almost a million pounds in unpaid debts three and half years ago.

Gemma had purchased some really beautiful silver candlesticks, a silver Georgian tea pot, and set of expensive silverware once owned by a Prussian noble family—their coat of arms adorned every utensil. All of that was taken by the bailiffs to be auctioned off to pay her husband's debts.

The neighbors all watched as the bailiffs removed everything of value from her home. Her husband, unbeknownst to her at the time, had had advance notice of the coming raid and had *taken all of his valuables* out of the house.

The Circassian walnut chairs had also been taken, along with her mother's jewelry box and jewelry.

There was a beautiful, yet relatively modest, tiara that had belonged to her maternal great grandmother. It was silver and set with small diamonds and tangerine garnets. It was unusual, and not only that, it had been passed down from mother to daughter for four generations. It was Gemma's. It fit her perfectly.

There was also a matching silver bracelet set with small diamonds and tangerine garnets. It had been made for Gemma's great grandmother by Asprey at the turn of the 20th century; it had been made to be a companion piece to the tiara.

Neither piece of jewelry was particularly valuable—not by tiara standards. Gemma had worn the bracelet almost every day since her mother's death. The bailiffs had ordered her to remove it from her wrist. She begged them to let her keep it. She tried to explain how important it was to her. They wouldn't listen. They had a writ.

The jewelry should have gone some ways towards paying off the debts, but the auction drew low bids.

She lost virtually all of the family heirlooms her mother had given her, including her great grandfather's army medals, which included a DSO he had been awarded in 1915.

The next time Gemma saw her husband was in court at the divorce proceedings. He never looked at her once. He never tried to explain or even offer an apology. He had ruined her life, her finances, and her reputation, and he walked away debt free.

Gemma did not consider Grey's house in Primrose Hill to be hers. It was a hotel—a temporary lodging. The house had the feel of a five-star hotel: everything perfect and beautiful. But it didn't feel like a home.

## VIOLET

She had met Grey at Violet's house in the West End of London. (Grey at Violet's…) She had known Violet since they were five years old. Violet was good-hearted, but she had never known struggle. She had married her husband, the son of a wealthy baron, and a member of the House of Lords, just after graduating from Oxford. She had majored in Art History, but had zero intention of ever getting a job.

Violet was attractive in a way. She was slim, had a brilliant complexion, and blue eyes. She was also a natural blonde. She knew how to select the proper eyewear to enhance her slightly above average looks. She was also extremely stylish and had healthy, shiny, glossy hair which she was smart enough to keep at least shoulder length into her 40s.

Violet's real strength lay in her manner. She was always extremely attentive to her man. 'Are you comfortable, darling? Can I get you another drink, darling?' She always adjusted her man's collar and made sure he never forgot his umbrella.

Her husband was 10 years older. 'Vava' at 21, had married a man of means. To be fair, Violet loved Hughie. Gemma knew that. And Hughie truly loved Vava.

'Why marry a young pauper?' she had told Gemma on her wedding day. Her new husband, the son of a baron, was also extremely kind to her.

## MEETING GREY

Grey entered the drawing room of Vava's house in Marylebone on an overcast rainy day in September. He was wearing a white dress shirt, blue blazer and dark khaki trousers. A red and purple striped tie completed Grey's look. He was slim and relatively short, about 5'7". He had light brown hair. He had nice teeth. His face was alright, but the visage that appeared before Gemma was steely. Gemma could also detect a certain coldness in his blue eyes. It was difficult for Gemma to really read Grey.

Grey looked like a Roman soldier. Gemma was disappointed, but she didn't let it show.

Grey's opinion of Gemma on the other hand was easy to read: He thought Gemma was stunning. Yes. Gemma was unlike any girl Grey had ever seen. Gemma was so beautiful that Grey couldn't help but stare.

Gemma was used to men undressing her with their eyes, but this was different; Grey was probably going to be sleeping with her in the near future, and it made her feel like a slave on auction. Gemma hated being in the desperate situation she was in. Grey was unaware of how dire her situation really was, but Gemma still felt terribly vulnerable. She was at his mercy.

Grey seemed nice. He was just so American. He was a bit of a braggart, but he wasn't arrogant. He was intelligent, and the conversation was interesting. If only he hadn't stared at Gemma's chest the whole time...

PRIMROSE HILL

Gemma lay down on the bed upstairs in her new bedroom. The closet held her blue Burberry coat, a little black dress from Chanel, and a pair of leather Dior boots that the bailiffs had missed, a pair of inexpensive high heels from Zara, and a pair of Puma trainers she only wore to the gym.

Gemma was still wearing the pair of brown leather shoes she now wore almost daily. The dresser held a couple of white blouses, some white t-shirts, several pairs of panties and bras, two pairs of faded denim blue jeans, two pairs of wool trousers, three skirts, and a pair of navy blue Adidas track pants (with three white stripes down each pant leg) that she liked to wear around the house. She also had a couple pairs of flannel pyjama bottoms. Gemma was wearing the rest of her wardrobe.

Well, not exactly the rest. Gemma had the rest of her wardrobe scattered across England. She still had a few things at Poppy's house in London. She also had some country tweeds, boots, and a beautiful fur hood at Poppy's country house. Vava might have a few things too. Gemma really couldn't remember for sure.

She stared at the white ceiling. She was in a lot of pain. She would have to find a doctor tomorrow. She dreaded having to have sex with Grey again that night. She decided that she would tell him she was too ill to do it if he asked and retreat to her own bedroom.

## LONDON—ACCORDING TO GREY

Grey had lived in London for more than twenty years. He had acquired a British passport, and yet, he remained as much an outsider as he had been when he first arrived. Grey was obviously American (even though he no longer held an American passport), his mild Southern accent gave him away quickly. The locals often told him he 'dressed like an American'. Grey really didn't care what the locals thought of him. Grey had never wanted to be 'British'. The idea had never entered his calculus. The British passport was just another means to an end.

Grey felt the British to be rather strange. Their empire had collapsed a long time ago, and the British seemed to be living vicariously off of faded imperial glory. A lot of British institutions like universities still included 'imperial' in their names. Orders and decorations awarded by the Queen did so as well. Grey didn't understand why they bothered to keep up such pretenses. But, to be honest, he really didn't care that they did.

The British class system was something Grey found amusing. He had met so many Londoners who had tried to pass themselves off as upper-class people. They thought Grey wouldn't notice their middle-class accents or mannerisms. He did. Many middle-class Brits tried to pass themselves off as upper class, but their poor vocabulary and lack of education (even among university graduates) always gave them away. Grey thought it was pathetic.

In North Carolina, if you were a good guy, you were a good guy. While many in North Carolina were proud of their family background (Grey included), one's family background really wasn't that important.

Grey didn't have that much contact with the native white British population. Foreigners made up 90% of London's citizenry. Officially, London was 60% immigrant and 40% British. However, there were the British, and then there were the 'British'. Most of the population in London classified as 'British' was made of 2nd and 3rd generation people from places as far flung as Pakistan, Nigeria, Hong Kong, and The Sudan. Not to mention all of the people from Eastern Europe that had flooded into the city since the 1990s.

London was a bizarre mishmash of disparate peoples—a toppled Tower of Babel with people living amongst the ruins. Grey figured the native white British population only numbered around 10%, at best.

More than two decades had passed since he had settled in the city, and London had only grown more and more alien and bewildering to Grey. London had become a very strange place indeed.

A large number of Grey's clients were from Eastern Europe. That suited him just fine. He knew where he stood with them. Most of them viewed him with begrudging respect. Grey was American. America still held people in its thrall the way England never had. And Americans were looked upon as being more open and accepting of people than the British. Grey used all of this to his advantage.

Grey also had another advantage over the native British population: he was an outsider. Foreigners living in the city felt more comfortable dealing with him than with a local.

SANGRE AZUL

Grey had had British girlfriends in the past, but Gemma was different. For starters, she was a blue blood. Gemma was descended from a long line of English nobility. Gemma was part of a noted bloodline. Women like Gemma were part of a virtually unattainable group of women. She never described herself as 'British'; **Gemma was English**. She seemed to be extremely proud of that. Grey found that aspect of Gemma's character rather appealing. Gemma was also extremely beautiful. She was perfect. Gemma was also genuine. She was sweet and good-hearted. And Grey had decided that he loved her.

She deserved better than life had given her. He had Googled her after getting her full name from Violet. There her whole sordid life was laid out online—all the humiliating details. Poor Gemma.

Grey remembered that when he first met her in Violet's drawing room, he thought she should have gone into porn or become a stripper. She could have made a lot of money. Now Grey hated himself for even thinking that.

Gemma was way out of his league, but life had gone against her, and now she was all his. And he had wrecked everything. He wanted to cry. Gemma deserved better than him. He didn't deserve someone as good as Gemma. *How could he win forgiveness for the unforgivable?*

Occasionally Grey's phone would ring, but since caller ID didn't show Gemma calling, he didn't answer. Gemma occupied all of his thoughts. He wanted to apologize for what he had done, but how? Jesus.

He sat at his polished desk and looked out over the park across the street. Beautiful children were playing and walking around with their beautiful and posh mothers. Had he not humiliated and injured Gemma last night, he could have spent a happy day visualizing Gemma and their child playing together in the park in Primrose Hill. He wanted a happy, loving marriage and family with Gemma more than anything he had ever wanted in his life. He had blown it. He had only himself to blame.

He was afraid to go home. He didn't want to face Gemma, but at the same time, he wanted to spend every moment of the rest of his life with her. The sun was going down. He contemplated sleeping on the couch in the office, but decided it would be better to spend the night in his own bed.

He looked at the paper bags on his desk. One was a purple Asprey's bag, the top decorated with a purple ribbon. He had purchased a bracelet for Gemma for almost £ 9000. He also bought her a sterling silver keychain for her key to the house. Another bag was from Chanel. He had purchased her some sunglasses. The kind Audrey Hepburn would have worn. He thought they would look good on her. And he knew this would all be interpreted for what it was: a fucked-up apology.

Grey had spent a miserable day at the office. He had finally bagged the girl of his dreams, and he had already messed it up.

He left the bags on his desk. He left the office after nightfall. He hoped he wouldn't be attacked and robbed on the walk home even though he lived on one of the most expensive streets in London.

PRIMROSE HILL

Grey took his time walking home. He needed time to think. Well, more time to think. It was a cold night. Grey liked the cold.

He walked by the rows and rows of what the British call 'semi-detached' and 'terraced' houses. Many of the houses were dark and looked unoccupied; probably because they were.

Half the expensive homes in London were owned by people who lived abroad. The Russians and the Saudis bought them as a hedge against turmoil back home. If the homeland was turned upside down, or the government turned against these people, they could escape to London, sell one of their houses for few million pounds, and live luxuriously in exile. Or they could use the money to plot revenge.

The Chinese bought houses for the same reason. Well, there were other reasons too. Real estate was a great way to launder money.

The UK was once a great industrial power. It wasn't anymore. The UK was largely de-industrialized. The City, the British version of Wall Street, still brought in money, but most of it was dirty. England's economy seemed to be kept afloat by money laundering of one kind or the other. Foreign investment was flooding into real estate and the financial system was bloated with cash. There was a lot of talk of cracking down, but everyone just laughed when they heard that. What would the British government do for revenue?

Grey felt that modern England was nothing but a twisted simulacrum, a shadow of its former self. A country that continued to try and live off past glories, but was fraying everywhere; England was coming apart at the seams. De facto open borders had left an overcrowded country ready to burst open and sink beneath the waves. Grey could see that England was deep into a breakdown crisis.

The immigrants hated each other. Violence was constant. A low-level war raged on virtually every city block. The police were useless. The mayor was worse than useless. The city was in a downward spiral, and everyone knew it. It really wasn't safe for the average person to walk the streets day or night.

However, people like Grey thrived in such chaos. Grey was able to operate undetected. He had done so for years.

Grey finally reached the front door of his house. The glossy black door gleamed in the glow of the street lamp. He glanced around quickly to make sure he hadn't been followed, and then he moved forward and opened the door. He entered and quickly shut the door behind him. The security system surged to life, and Grey breathed a sigh of relief.

Maria was still there, later than usual, as per Grey's instructions. He didn't want Gemma home alone that first day.

'Boa noite, Senhor'.

'Boa noite, Maria. How is Gemma?'

'Good, Senhor. She moved in this afternoon. She is upstairs. I made dinner for you. It's on the stove. It's still warm. Would you like me to stay and serve dinner?'

'No. That's alright. I'll call you a taxi. I don't want you walking to the subway station alone at night.'

'Thank you, Senhor.'

Maria went back into the kitchen leaving Grey alone at the base of the stairs. His stomach was in knots. Gemma appeared at the top of the stairs a minute later. She looked down at Grey. She didn't smile. She just stared.

'How are you?' Grey asked. He felt like he would pass out. The effect this woman had on him was beyond belief.

'I'm fine. How are you? Long day at the office?'

'It was a busy one. I have a lot of clients right now.'

Grey wanted to break down crying. He had fucked up everything. He was shaking now. His whole body trembled. He could feel Gemma slipping further away from him. Grey was fighting to control himself.

Gemma walked slowly down the stairs, her slippered feet treading softly over the Persian rug running down the steps. She was wearing navy blue Adidas track pants (with three white stripes down each pant leg) and a new light grey hoodie she had purchased online that day. It had been delivered to her front door in less than 90 minutes.

'Do you like it?' Gemma finally smiled as she modeled the light grey hooded top. Some of the weight lifted off of Grey's shoulders at the moment. Maybe all wasn't lost. Maybe not. Maybe not.

'It looks nice on you.'

'It's almost winter. I'll need this to work in the garden.'

'You garden?'

'Yes. Surprised?'

'Ah, no. Well, maybe, yes. No.'

Gemma smiled gently. 'Alright, let's have dinner. I'm famished.'

'Famished'. Interesting choice of words,' thought Grey. 'I would have said 'starving', but I'm not posh,' Grey thought to himself and smiled.

Gemma walked in front of him into the kitchen. Grey noticed how fit she appeared in her dark blue track pants as she walked. It was hard to believe that Gemma was 40. She had the body of a teenager.

The kitchen was filled with the aroma of delicious food. Maria had already set the table. Nothing too formal, just white porcelain plates and inexpensive silverware. There were glasses and cloth napkins.

Maria soon departed, and they were alone.

Gemma turned on the overhead lamp; no romantic lighting tonight. Gemma went over to the stove top. There were several covered plates. She started placing them on the table.

Grey was suddenly filled with regret; a burning feeling that felt like it would burn right through him. He felt a wave of panic sweep over him. Gemma would never be his. Never. It was all his fault.

If Gemma noticed anything, she didn't acknowledge it.

After she uncovered the plates, she turned to Grey and said, 'Please have a seat.' Gemma then smiled slightly, gently. 'Gently,' that word again. If there was one thing Grey was not was gentle. He was a violent beast. A thug. An animal. He had so much he wanted to say to her, but he couldn't speak.

'Please, have a seat. Or do you prefer to have dinner standing?'

'Oh, sorry.' Grey pulled out the chair and sat down.

Gemma remained standing and *like* a good wife, served Grey dinner as expertly as a member of the waitstaff at a five star hotel. The way Gemma did the smallest things impressed Grey. She did everything with grace, elegance, and style, even when wearing track pants, a hoodie, and slippers. Gemma was beautiful.

The light from the overhead lighting failed to reveal any flaws. Gemma had taken good care of herself, **perhaps because no one in her life had even tried to protect her,** including Grey. Yes, Grey had damaged her too.

Grey was living in his own private hell. And his was hotter than most.

Gemma ate her food slowly and in silence. Grey hadn't eaten anything all day, but he wasn't hungry at all. His stomach was still in knots. He wanted to scream. He held his fork and looked at the food that Gemma had served him. Gemma continued to eat and said nothing.

What was she thinking? Gemma was a mystery. He knew she hated him. It hurt him more than anything he had ever experienced in his life. And Grey had experienced a lot.

Grey was deep in thought (or was it just agony?) when he noticed Gemma had stopped eating and was staring at him.

'Not hungry?'

'Gemma. I'm sorry.'

Gemma's eyes closed and when they opened, they were filled with tears. Her shoulders slumped, and she looked off to the right. The sight of Gemma crying sliced into Grey like a knife. It was killing him. He felt his body burning. Gemma said nothing.

'Gemma, please talk to me.' Grey then lost his voice. He couldn't speak.

Gemma stood and left the kitchen crying. It was all too much. Not just Grey, but everything. What had she done to deserve all of this?

Gemma started to walk up the stairs, stopped halfway, and then sat down and continued to cry. Grey followed her out into the hall and stood at the base of the stairs.

Gemma finally spoke. She spoke very softly. Gemma was grieving her lost happiness. 'Why did you do that to me? I asked you to stop. You hurt me. You humiliated me. So many bad things have happened to me, and you do that? What do you want me to say? Why is it my responsibility to speak? Am I supposed to fix everything for you? Am I supposed to make *you* feel better?' Gemma broke down in sobs.

Grey slumped down to his knees at the base of the stairs. He was gazing ahead as if in a trance. *This was all his fault.*

'I'm exhausted. The last two days have been terrible. The last three and half years have been terrible. They last three decades have been terrible,' sobbed Gemma.

Gemma got up and stumbled up the stairs. It felt as if all the blood was rushing into her head. She stumbled down the hall to her room. Grey followed her up the stairs and down the hall. Gemma entered her room and closed the door. She locked it behind her.

Grey stopped. He stood there in the quiet hallway before Gemma's door. The sound of a car driving down the street distracted him for a moment. His attention turned back to her door. Gemma was crying. Grey turned and went down the hall to his room.

He had ruined both their lives. Grey deserved to suffer, not Gemma. This was a road with only one direction. Grey knew that now without a doubt. But still, he loved Gemma. He didn't want to lose her. Even though he already had.

## 2 MY FRIEND GREY

### Gemma—London—My friend Grey

WINTER

Grey had few real friends. He had associates, contacts, and clients, but none of them were people he would ever call friends. Grey had lost his faith in humanity a long time ago. However, he did have one friend he thought of as a brother: Winter.

Grey had met Winter in the Balkans during the tumultuous 90s. They were only six months apart in age, Grey being the older. At first Grey had intimidated Winter, then it was love. They were brothers. A bond was forged. **Unbreakable.**

Winter, for his part, considered Grey the brother he had never had. He loved him and looked up to him. And this is where it got dangerous: Winter had developed a blind spot for Grey. And *Grey knew it.*

Grey always protected Winter. And people feared Grey.

Many people had warned Winter to be wary of Grey. Some had even begged him to cut ties, but Winter wouldn't hear of it. Even when Grey had exploded in rages, had really hurt people, Winter had remained loyal. Winter, known for his chivalrous nature, became a kind of enigma to the others. How could Winter be so oblivious to what was actually happening?

Now, decades later, Grey had only one confidant: Winter.

Grey turned on his encrypted cell phone and dialed a number he knew by heart.

'Hello?' a sleepy voice answered. 'What's wrong, Grey?'

'I need you to come to London tomorrow.'

'Okay.' The line went dead. No questions.

Grey went to sleep.

PRIMROSE HILL

The next day Grey was in his office when someone rang the buzzer. Grey looked at the CCTV screen in his office. It was Winter. Winter was wearing faded blue jeans, a white undershirt, a white button-down Oxford dress shirt, and a blue blazer. Grey smiled. An ally. An unquestioning one. Grey pushed a button under the edge of his desk and the bulletproof front door clicked open.

Winter entered the office. Grey, wearing grey wool trousers, a white undershirt, and a light blue dress shirt, rose to greet him. The men embraced. They were brothers.

'How are you?' Winter smiled. He was happy just to be back in Grey's presence.

'I met a girl.'

'Fantastic. Sounds like this one is special.'

'She is.' But Grey didn't smile. He looked pained.

'Okay. So, what's going on?'

'I fucked up.'

'Oh.'

Winter had *never* heard Grey say that before. Grey never acknowledged his failures or excesses. He always blamed others. Nothing was ever Grey's fault. This should be interesting…

'Things are going badly. I don't know what to do. I'm at a loss,' said Grey.

'What exactly have you done, Grey?' Winter wanted to add that it couldn't have been that bad, but knowing Grey, *things could easily have been that bad.*

Grey didn't answer. He sighed. 'Why don't you meet her today? I'll take you by right now. She's at home.'

Grey telephoned Gemma and asked if it would be okay if he brought a friend by the house for lunch. Winter's eyes narrowed. He had never heard Grey talk like this. This must be quite the girl. Winter wanted to joke that a box of chocolates and flowers might be enough to smooth things over with his new girlfriend, but he knew this couldn't be that type of situation.

## THE HOUSE IN PRIMROSE HILL

Gemma changed out of her dark blue track pants (with three white stripes) and put on an orange wool tartan skirt and a white blouse. She fixed her hair in the mirror and then put on her Japanese house slippers. She paused. London wasn't Japan. It wasn't really appropriate to meet someone wearing these. She changed into a pair of inexpensive high heels from Zara. She looked at herself in the full-length mirror next to the door of her room. All better.

Grey opened the front door of his house, but not before scanning around the street. Winter closed the door behind them and the security system engaged again.

Grey turned to Winter and said, 'I'll go make some tea. This is the maid's day off. Go have a seat in the drawing room, Winter.'

Winter walked through the large open entrance to the drawing room. And then lightning struck. Standing in the whitewalled room was Gemma. *She was beautiful.* She looked to be in her early 30s. She was perfect: perfect hair, perfect skin, perfect body, perfect attire, and perfect blue eyes—and Winter rarely ever noticed someone's eye color. Gemma wasn't very tall, but that was alright. Winter was only 5'7", the same height as Grey. *Grey.* Oh, yeah. *Him.*

'Hello. You must be Grey's friend. My name is Gemma.'

Winter stood and stared at her, but said nothing.

'May I ask you your name?' asked Gemma.

"Winter. My name is Winter.'

'Are you American?'

'Yes. I'm from North Carolina.'

'Winter? Doesn't anyone in North Carolina have names like Henry, Charles, James, or *Cuthbert*?'

Winter smiled and then burst out laughing. 'And you have a good sense of humor too.'

'Too?'

'Beautiful and a good sense of humor.' Winter smiled innocently.

Winter *was* innocent. Gemma could read Winter's face easily. He wasn't enigmatic like Grey. In other ways they were similar in terms of height and perhaps age. Winter looked to be in his late thirties or early 40s. He was also noticeably thinner and less muscular than Grey. Winter was rather average looking. Not the kind of person anyone would ever notice. And Gemma could immediately detect something else about Winter: he was truly good hearted.

'Please, have a seat,' said Gemma.

'Thank you.'

'How did you meet Grey, Winter?'

(Winter, Grey…Grey, Winter?) What kind of names were these?

'Winter was part of a gang that broke me out of jail, weren't you, bad boy?' said Grey.

Grey was standing in the doorway smiling. Normally very observant, he failed to notice the spell that Gemma had cast over his friend.

'Oh, please. Must you always make me look bad? I'm not the dangerous one here,' replied Winter, and Winter smiled.

Gemma agreed with that.

'Winter isn't my friend. **He's my brother.**' Grey smiled. He finally had Winter back with him.

'I'll go make some tea. You arrived earlier than I expected,' said Gemma.

'I've already made it,' said Grey.

'Where is it?' asked Gemma.

'In the kitchen,' replied Grey.

'I'll get it,' said Gemma.

'No, wait, I'll get it,' said Grey in his Southern drawl, starting to turn, towards the kitchen.

'Please, let me play the hostess,' she said, and Gemma *glided* past them both. Gemma disappeared into the entry hall in the direction of the kitchen.

'Wow. Just. Wow,' said Winter.

Grey was suddenly catapulted back into the reality of the situation. It was jarring. Grey's smile disappeared. Winter could see something was going on, but what? Winter sat quietly and said nothing.

A minute later Gemma entered the room. She placed the sterling silver tray on the polished drawing room table. She served the tea the way a well born

31

woman should. Winter noticed her every movement and gesture. *How did Grey ever land a woman like her?*

There were two sofas in the living room. Gemma sat down next to Winter, not Grey. Grey noticed, but said nothing.

'So, Winter, how do you like London?' asked Gemma.

'I've visited many times, but only for a few days each time. I really haven't seen much of it. Well, really, none of it,' said Winter.

'I'll take you around. I know a lot of nice places. What are you interested in?' asked Gemma.

'Plays. The theater,' responded Winter.

'London is perfect for that,' said Gemma, and Gemma smiled.

I prefer small theaters, not the West End. I like to watch young and hungry actors perform. They do it for the joy of acting. There is a special energy in their performances.'

'I understand, and I agree. I know several theaters like that. I'll take you.'

'Thank you. I would like that,' replied Winter.

'Sounds good,' said Grey. 'Gemma, put all the tickets on your account. I deposited a little in there for you this morning. Take Winter to a nice restaurant. But not too nice. Winter has terrible table manners. I swear, he's an embarrassment to the State of North Carolina.'

Winter smiled and then laughed. He was happy to be back with Grey. And—*dangerously*—to have met Gemma.

THE BANK IN PRIMROSE HILL

That afternoon Gemma walked to the bank. She entered and headed for the ATM inside the lobby. Gemma never used ATMs outside. London was too dangerous for that now.

The bank branch in Primrose Hill was a restored Art Deco structure from the 1930s when the bank had operated under a different name. She had had an account at this bank since she was a teenager. She hadn't been back to this particular branch since the late 1990s, and the memories poured over her as she entered.

The vaulted ceiling had once had a map of the British Empire inlaid in it in tile. Now the empire was gone, and the tile had been painted over, but Gemma knew the map was still there.

Gemma entered her PIN and the screen flashed in front of her. Fifty thousand pounds had been deposited in her account. Fifty thousand. Grey was generous. A week ago, this money would have meant something different. But now, after what had happened, it felt like a payoff. Well, it was, wasn't it?

Gemma already had a mental list of everything she was going to do that day. Buy a gift for her former Oxford classmate Poppy. Also, one for Violet. Oh, and she had a doctor's appointment with a specialist. Yes, they had people who specialized in that. Thank you, Google.

POPPY
Poppy welcomed Gemma with a warm hug and a smile. She loved the gift, but she said it wasn't necessary and that Gemma had been no trouble to her. Poppy's boyfriend Brian was also there. He was as gentlemanly as ever. There were still a few left in London.

'It's nice to see you smiling again, Gemma,' Poppy gushed. Gemma's smile didn't falter. Gemma was happy to see Poppy, but not about her engagement to Grey. *Engaged to Grey. Jesus.*

VIOLET
Gemma then drove to Violet's House in Marylebone. Violet detected Gemma's true mood immediately. 'What happened? What's wrong? I knew I shouldn't have set you up with an American. What did he do to you, Gemmy?' Violet was her friend. A true friend. But how could Gemma tell her what had happened? Gemma didn't want to discuss it. Gemma grew pale.

Violet sighed. 'You don't have to tell me. I'm sorry. I think I've put you in a bad situation. I'm really sorry, Gemma.'

'Don't worry. We got off to a rocky start, but things are better now,' Gemma lied.

Violet knew Gemma was holding back, but it was because she wasn't ready to share what had happened. What actually did happen bothered Gemma a lot. Poor Gemma. Violet promised herself she would smash Grey in the face with a hard object the next time she saw him.

THE DOCTOR'S OFFICE
The doctor, a woman (Thank God), was really conscientious and kind. Gemma didn't explain exactly what had happened. She told the doctor what was necessary, and the doctor was experienced and decent enough not to ask for any further information. The doctor talked about the recommended course of treatment with her, and Gemma agreed to it.

PRIMROSE HILL
Gemma parked her white Peugeot hatchback in front of the house. Winter, wearing faded blue jeans, a white undershirt, a white button-down Oxford dress shirt, and a Richmond Grey half zip pullover, crossed the street and approached her car as she was getting out.

'Good afternoon, Gemma,' Winter said happily.

'Hello, Winter. How are you?'

'I'm good. Grey had to leave London for a few days. He wanted me to apologize for leaving without telling you. He tried calling you, but you didn't answer. He figured your phone must have been turned off.'

Gemma had seen Grey's calls on her caller ID, but ignored them.

'Where did he go?'

'Croatia,' responded Winter.

'What is so interesting about Croatia?'

'Memories. And money,' replied Winter.

Gemma walked to the front door. Maria opened the door for her and Gemma and Winter entered. The security system engaged after they door was closed behind them.

'Would you like me to serve tea, Senhora?'

'Yes, thank you, Maria. We'll have it in the drawing room.'

Gemma sat opposite Winter. He was relatively short—about the same height as Grey, only thinner. He was alright looking. Nothing special. Nothing a girl would glance at twice. Not the kind of person that anyone would take notice of. He dressed simply; nothing he wore was expensive. He looked like he had stepped out of the 90s. Still youthful. How old was Winter?

'May I ask why your parents named you Winter?'

'It's actually a nickname. It's a long story.'

'So, may I ask what your real name is?' asked Gemma.

'Cuthbert.'

Gemma burst out laughing. She hadn't laughed like that in years. It felt good.

'You asked,' said Winter.

Gemma liked Winter. Or Cuthbert. Or whatever his true name was. He had made her laugh.

'I bought three tickets to see a play tonight. It's at a small theater in a rather dodgy part of London. I know one of the actresses. She's the daughter of a former co-worker. Maybe we could see her after the performance. That would be nice,' said Gemma.

'Thank you, Gemma. I really appreciate this. What time does the play start?' asked Winter.

'Eight. It's only 90 minutes. We can go to dinner afterwards,' replied Gemma.

'Where are you staying?' she asked.

'Here. Didn't Grey tell you?' answered Winter nervously.

'No.'

'He didn't want you to be home alone. If you feel uncomfortable with that, I can check into a hotel. I'm sorry. I thought Grey had cleared it with you.'

'It's ok. I don't mind.'

THE PLAY
The play was about an Austro-Hungarian noble family that had lost everything after the collapse of the Hapsburg Empire. A German family stranded in a new country that had emerged from the wreckage of the empire.

The father, an elderly major, had survived the war. His son had not. The daughter worked in a rundown factory to support them both. The German girl, now considered a foreigner in her hometown, was badly mistreated by the neighbors. The end of the play saw her walking alone down a muddy road to Austria.

Gemma watched the play intently. This was a story she could sympathize with. By the end of it, she was crying.

Winter hadn't really watched the play. Winter, clad in a blue blazer and white button down Oxford dress shirt, had spent the entire time surreptitiously glancing at Gemma and her reactions.

What did Gemma see in Grey? It was a mystery to Winter. Winter could sense that Gemma was a good person. He liked her. Now Winter started to wonder, 'What had Grey done to her?'

After the play, Gemma and Winter waited in the small lobby of the theater. The theater had been a furniture factory in the 1950s, but had practically fallen down after the factory went bust in the late 1970s. The theater group purchased it for a song in the early 90s.

Gemma had sent a note back stage letting Avril, her friend's daughter, know she had attended. Avril sent word back to please wait. She wanted to see Gemma.

Gemma and Winter sat in chairs near the entrance. Soon the crowd dispersed, and with the exception of two young staff chatting on the stairway to the theater, they were alone.

'What are you thinking about?' asked Gemma.

'Nothing.'

'Of course, you must be thinking about something. I can see the smoke positively pouring out of your ears.'

'Just thinking about the play,' replied Winter. Not that that was true. He was actually wondering what had gone on between Gemma and Grey.

'Did you like it?' asked Gemma.

'Yes.'

'What did you like most about it?' asked Gemma.

Winter hadn't actually watched most of the play. He had spent the entire time looking at Gemma. He was momentarily at a loss for words.

'What did *you* like most about it?' asked Winter. (Think fast, Winter. Think fast.)

'The end. When she was walking down the road alone,' replied Gemma.

'I thought that the end was rather sad. I noticed you were tearing up during that scene. The girl has lost her family, her home, and her country,' said Winter.

'True. But. She hadn't given up. She refused to lay down and die. Her story wasn't over,' said Gemma.

'Yes. You are right. If you don't give up, there is hope. *Dum spiro spero.* 'While I breathe, I hope,' said Winter.

'Latin. You studied Latin?' asked Gemma happily.

'No. It was the *unofficial motto* of my college. I *would have* told you that I had studied it, but I suspect you actually have and would have tried conversing with me in it,' responded Winter.

Gemma laughed. 'Is that what you do with other girls?'

Winter smiled. Gemma was different. She was well-educated, cultured, and genuinely sweet. Winter couldn't help but wonder what Gemma saw in Grey. Gemma's relationship with Grey was as much a mystery to him as Winter's relationship to Grey was to her.

## 3 GEMMA'S SCHOOL DAYS

**Gemma—London—All Saints**

### COVENT GARDEN

August 2018

Gemma checked her bank balance at the ATM inside the lobby of the bank: ninety-two pounds. Gemma breathed in slowly and then exhaled. What would she do?

Gemma had no family.

Her brother, long brutalized by their father, had cut off contact with the family after their mother had passed away. He was almost ten years older than Gemma. The last thing he told her was that she would never see him again. He left penniless for Hong Kong the day after their mother's funeral.

Her father, the 8th Baron, had accepted the news of his wife's death with complete indifference; they had separated years earlier because of his womanizing, heavy drinking, gambling, and cruelty. He hadn't even bothered to attend the funeral.

The multimillion-pound estate left her father by the 7th Baron had been lost. The family home, over 150 years old, was auctioned off to pay debts.

Gemma was alone in the world. She had no family left to turn to now.

SUSSEX
All Saints Boarding School
1991-1996

Gemma had always envied her classmates at school who had had 'normal families.' Her father had refused to spend any money on her education. It was her maternal grandparents who had paid for Gemma to attend All Saints.

She shared a room at school with three other girls: Violet, Poppy, and Külli. All three would later attend Oxford with her. Violet and Poppy were still very much in her life. The blonde-haired Violet was the daughter of a viscount, making her an 'Honourable.' Poppy and Gemma were the daughters of barons, making both of them 'Honorables' as well. Külli, on the other hand, was a commoner. The three English 'Hons' would go on to be Sloane Rangers and lifelong friends. Külli would not.

Külli's family were ethnic Estonians who had immigrated to England in the late 1940s. Her father had made a small fortune selling expensive leather footwear. When Külli was very young, her father had leather riding boots made for her, thus earning her the name 'little boots', or in Latin, 'Caligula.' That was her father's dreadful pet name for her. Külli arrived at school with the unlikely nickname of 'Gula.' Only the girls in the second floor alcove called her by her nickname, or variations of it.

The four girls became an inseparable happy gang. The girls shared whatever care packages they received from home. They tutored each other in the subjects they excelled in and offered a shoulder to cry on when school rivalries or school girl crushes proved to be too overwhelming.

A small number of the girls in school had special relationships with choice classmates. While not spoken about openly, it was, for the most part, accepted. It was considered 'a phase' that some girls went through. **But just a phase.**

Poppy had a crush on Alexa; Violet had a crush on Tallulah, and Gula had a crush on Isabel. School girl crushes—by their very nature fleeting—come and went like gentle breezes.

The two girl rooms at school—known strangely enough as 'singles'—were favorite spots for trysts. The four student rooms were known as 'alcoves.' Girls would occasionally make deals with their classmates to use their single rooms for romantic rendezvous. Some lucky couples were roommates. That is, lucky until they broke up.

Among the alcove gang, only Gemma remained unaffected by the cloistered circumstances of an all-girl boarding school filled with exploding hormones.

School girl crushes came and went, leaving behind a trail of broken hearts and bad poetry. The worst school girl poets would eventually go on to become left wing journalists and write for The Guardian.

It was bewildering to Gemma. Gemma could only dream of one day being a wife and mother. Gemma's own family, so dysfunctional, had made her yearn for a family of her own. Barely a day went by when she didn't dream about cooking meals for her future husband and their twin daughters—no doubt, both future Sloanes themselves. She had already chosen names for them. Only one dilemma remained: which of her friends would be the Godmothers? Perhaps she could give birth to triplets?

Gemma was easily one of the most attractive girls in school. She was the object of sighs, longing glances, and tears for the entire five years she attended.

One day Gemma found a note under her pillow:

*Dearest Gem,*

*I have loved you since the moment I met you. I apologize if you find this distressing, but I couldn't live a day longer unless I told you so today. If you have any feelings for me at all, please relieve my suffering and tell me.*

*Love,*

*G*

'Not only do I have a chemistry test tomorrow, I shall also have to explain why I find it impossible to be in love with another girl,' Gemma sighed.

Külli was one of her dearest friends. She would have to let her down as gently as possible.

Gemma did not see Külli again that day until they gathered in the dining hall for dinner. Wearing the red, blue, and purple tartan skirts of All Saints, the teenage girls all said grace together while standing in front of one of the myriad of square tables which were covered with white tablecloths, expensive porcelain, and gleaming silverware.

Gemma enjoyed eating in the Edwardian dining hall, especially on special occasions when everything was illuminated by candle light. This was one such night. 'How romantic,' groaned Gemma.

The girls from the second floor alcove sat together at a table near one of the large windows. Külli took the seat directly across from Gemma. Gula was beautiful; perhaps the second most beautiful girl in school after Gemma. Gula was at least four inches taller than most of the other girls in her class. She had also been blessed with perfect facial symmetry and long glossy brown hair.

Külli sat ramrod straight and avoided eye contact with her potential paramour seated directly across from her.

'This lasagna is *marvellous*!' said Violet in her posh Sloane accent (which meant she pronounced the word with only two syllables: 'marvlous').

'As well it should be, Vava, considering the tuition,' replied Poppy. 'It's been *yonks* since they served us lasagna.'

Gemma, Violet, and Poppy were all Sloane Rangers and peppered much of what they said with posh Sloane terms such as *yonks* and *yah*, and all of it was pronounced with the unusual posh Sloane intonation (often joining consonants to vowels). Being a Sloane Ranger was more than just how one spoke or what words one chose to use. It was an attitude, a way of life. For Gemma, Violet, and Poppy, it was only natural for *Hons* to adopt it.

Külli, though born in Surrey, was the daughter of Estonian refugees—a commoner. Though Külli's family had become wealthy, she remained an outsider. The world of the Sloane Ranger remained an **almost impenetrable mystery** to her. Külli had picked up a few Sloane phrases and was as well-spoken as any of the *Hons* she boarded with, but she really had no interest in becoming one. Külli's oft utterence of Sloane terms and Sloaney intonation delighted her alcove roommates. The girls wanted Külli to be one of them.

Gemma, Violet, and Poppy chatted happily about the day's events. Külli sat and ate in silence.

'Is something wrong, Gula? Or are you just trying to be *a bore* tonight?' asked Violet.

Külli glanced at Violet and replied cheerfully, 'No. I'm just *terribly* tired.'

Külli finally directed her gaze at Gemma. Gemma smiled, and Külli's face lit up.

'Gemma? How was your day?' asked Külli.

Gemma was bathed in the soft glow of candle light. Gula had never seen, nor would she *ever see*, anyone as beautiful as Gemma was on that night in December.

'Good,' replied Gemma. 'And how has your day been, G?'

'Getting better, I think,' Külli replied.

'Is this some sort of secret code?' asked Violet. 'Don't pretend there isn't something going on between the two of you.'

'*Was* there something going on between them?' wondered Külli. Gemma

ˈsmiled. How on Earth would she handle this?


### Gemma—London—Gula
MARBLE ARCH
October 2018


Külli sat in her office looking through photos of the previous days shoot. She had to select the pictures for the online catalog and the paper one that would be mailed out to her client base. Her father's line of leather riding boots had expanded into equestrian and later hunting outfits, bits and kit.

After a short and highly successful career in modeling, Külli had returned to London to work at the family firm. She had learned everything she could about the business. It was Külli's decision to expand into clothing. Now her company produced beautiful red, blue, black, and tweed riding outfits and tweed hunt coats. Everything the firm produced was of the highest quality; leather riding crops, jodhpurs, hunt caps and hats, leather saddles, spurs, hunting whips, and leather shotgun shell pouches included. Her clients expected it. Bespoke kit was common among her moneyed clientele. Külli had been extremely successful.

Külli, now 40, had stayed fit through swimming, horseback riding, proper skincare, and a strict diet. Her skin was flawless and her hair was shiny, glossy, and healthy. Külli stood nearly six feet tall. Men seemed to be afraid of her. Girls were entranced.

Külli had never had any trouble picking up girls in clubs, or coffee shops, or church, for that matter. 'What's on the menu for today,' Külli would think as she entered chapel each morning back in school. 'It's a grievous sin, Gula,' Violet would whisper in her ear as Külli's eyes roved the church in search of prey. Violet would then smile and then begin to recite The Lord's Prayer aloud with the other Anglican school girls—sinners all.

She enjoyed going on hunts. She always met the best kind of girls there. Külli had no interest in hunting animals. She privately felt a tremendous amount of pity for the foxes and birds her clients hunted. Külli secretly attended hunts to meet *hunt* women. Well, young women. Gula, towering over most of the men in her blue or black hunt coat, beige jodhpurs, and leather riding boots always drew all the attention. She always carried a hunting whip. She loved that whip. So did the girls. But Gula was always gentle. 'I'll keep my boots and spurs on for this one,' she would sometimes quip to herself. The memories of those particularly eventful trysts always brought a smile to Külli's face.

Sexual trysts among the girls were not uncommon back at school in Sussex. Külli's teenage years had been filled with amorous adventures with deliciously beautiful classmates. Külli couldn't believe her luck; she was beautiful, desirable, and surrounded by more of the same.

For most of the girls at All Saints, this was just a phase. Young girls, isolated in an all-girl environment, away from home, lonely and stressed, needed affection. Girls are girls after all. Naturally (or perhaps unnaturally), they turned to each other. Yes, 'just a phase,' the girls would say.

'I'll miss this,' said one of Külli's girlfriends as she was putting her school uniform back on. 'Boys really don't know how to please me. I need a girl to do that. But next year I'll be at *uni* and I'll have a boyfriend,' she sighed as she adjusted the school's red, blue, and purple tartan skirt.

Külli would be at Oxford next year, and she would definitely not have a boyfriend. You see, Külli, was not going through a phase. She was gay. A lesbian. Her parents would kill her if they ever found out. Külli didn't feel ashamed of it. Why should she? This was as natural as breathing. But Külli wanted *love*. And for Külli, there was to be only one love: Gemma. A love so unshakeable that it consumed her thoughts. A love that pure. A love that Gula *needed*.

Poppy, the cute one, had only experimented really. Violet, only slightly attractive, but never attractive to Külli, had *sexual* relationships with a number of girls.

Gemma had never had any interest in it. Gemma didn't appear to have any sexual interest in other girls at all, only boys. Well, to be more specific, 'the one' as Gemma called her future husband. *Husband.*

Poppy was a natural blonde. Poppy wasn't just cute; she was really cute. Gemma had always called her 'dangerously cute.' One morning while getting dressed, Poppy started to cry.

'What's wrong, Poppy?' asked Gemma. Gemma came over and put her arm around Poppy.

'Alexa has broken it off. She told me last night that she has a boyfriend now and that she wanted to be loyal to him. I understand, but I love Alexa.' Poppy started to cry again.

'Ahh, a broken heart,' said Gemma gently. 'Wipe away your tears,' said Gemma in a soothing tone. 'I love you, Poppy. I always will.'

Gemma picked up a soft white hand towel and gently, very gently, dabbed the tears from Poppy's face. 'You can always practice kissing with me,' said Gemma and she smiled. And with that she leaned forward and kissed Poppy gently on the lips. Poppy melted. Külli, watching this from just a few feet away, melted down.

Külli had never lusted after Gemma. It had been *love* at first sight. Külli had had sex, lustful, intense sex with other girls. Gemma was altogether different. Külli was deeply in love with her. She had pined away for Gemma for years. Gemma *did love* Külli; she even told her so and hugged her tightly. Gemma's scent, like a spring breeze, sent Külli reeling. 'Be calm, Gula,' she told herself every time she had found herself in Gemma's presence. But the love Gemma felt for Gula was not the love she really wanted.

And now, at 18, Gemma's first kiss was with Poppy. Poppy! Why Poppy?! Poppy was the luckiest girl in the universe and she didn't even know it. Külli was privately dying inside. She was seething with jealousy one second and dying the next. She wanted Gemma so badly it physically hurt.

46

Violet rolled her eyes. 'Gemma has just become the biggest tease in the world.'

Poppy smiled and said, 'More of that please, Gemma,' and she laughed. 'I feel better already.' Poppy knew there would never be any more kisses (like that), but Gemma, with a few kind words and gentle physical contact had mended her broken heart.

Gula's heart had remained broken.

## Gemma—London—The Gang at Oxford

OXFORD UNIVERSITY
Michaelmas Term 1996
Gemma, Poppy, Gula, and Violet were fortunate enough to be accepted into Oxford University. Gemma, Poppy, and Gula had entered on merit; Violet was fortunate to have entered on the merit of her father's status as the 5th Viscount and an alumnus of Christ Church, Oxford.

Gemma, Poppy, and Violet entered Somerville; Gula entered St Hilda (at the time, one of the last remaining women's colleges at Oxford). Gemma and Poppy roomed together in a room off the grass quad. Violet roomed with a shy Japanese girl that could only smile politely at all of Violet's wild antics, and Külli arranged to share rooms with an attractive girl whose hair was so blonde she had acquired the nickname 'Flax.'

Külli's room in St Hilda's was on the top floor and had a *glorious* view of Oxford.

She was disappointed that she had been unable to room with Gemma, but Gemma had always had her heart set on Somerville. She missed not having her sleeping across from her.

Back in school in Sussex, whenever Külli woke up in the middle of the night, she never failed to look across the room and rest her eyes upon Gemma. Gemma's bed was positioned in such a manner as to catch the moonlight which flooded in through the leaded glass windows. And it was at those fleeting moments that Külli could observe Gemma without anyone noticing.

Külli would roll onto her stomach and rest her chin on her pillow. Sometimes Külli stared at Gemma for 10 minutes and then when back to sleep. Some nights Külli would stare longingly at her for *hours*. Sometimes Külli would watch Gemma until the first orange rays of dawn broke the horizon and illuminated Gemma's face and glossy brown hair. These were happy moments for Külli. It was at night when everyone was asleep that Külli could stare at Gemma without fear of being caught. Külli, adrift in her hopes and dreams of a life with Gemma, was at her happiest—and saddest.

Gula, at 18, was finally 'free'; that is, away from the supervision of her parents and teachers. She was now completely free to pursue anything she wanted. And she wanted Gemma.

Külli's immigrant parents were extremely proud of their only child being accepted into Oxford. Külli was intelligent, academically-gifted, *and beautiful*.

Külli's parents were both relatively short and often wondered where Külli had gotten her height from.

Külli's father was raking in money at the time. He deposited twenty thousand pounds in Külli's bank account, and gave her a company credit card with a thirty-thousand-pound credit line. What could possibly go wrong?

## Gemma—London— Michaelmas term

OXFORD
Gemma, Poppy, Gula, and Violet resumed their friendship as the Inseparable Gang of Happy Girls after they were reunited at Oxford.

Gemma loved everything at Oxford. She loved her classes, her dons, her classmates, the books in the library, and her newfound access to male undergraduates.

Gemma was now determined to find the man of her dreams. So many nice looking young men wandered around in their striped jackets and ties. She loved the Harrovians and Old Etonians the most. They *tried so hard* to be charming. No one wanted to be known as a *bore*. And the boys usually dressed so well.

And all the young men of Oxford had *noticed* Gemma.

Gemma had zero experience with boys and was extremely nervous about dating. She was also extremely selective. She refused to sleep around. The virginal Gemma would be a prize.

While Violet and Poppy plunged headlong into the dating and party scene at Oxford, Gemma held back. She would spend the term observing what was available and then make her selection *known.*

On Friday nights, the girls would gather at an Oxford pub and happily chat about their new lives at uni. They always tried to sit at a certain corner table with just enough room for four. Poppy and Violet would talk about all of their disastrous dates and everyone would laugh until they cried.

Gemma was not dating anyone, much to the immense relief of Külli. Gemma was fully aware of Külli's feelings for her. At school when Külli had professed her love, Gemma had held her hands and told her she loved her. But not in that way.

'I'm sorry, Gula. Please understand me,' said Gemma in a pained voice. 'I don't want to lose you, Gula. You are one of my dearest friends.' Gemma's blue eyes became moist, and then tears started to roll down her cheeks.

Seeing Gemma suffer in any way was too much for Külli to bear. 'Gemma. I understand. I don't want to lose you, either. You are my life.' And then the pair embraced in the alcove and Gemma cried softly in Külli's arms. Külli cried softly too. Gula had finally revealed herself; she had gambled all and lost.

It was beyond terrible for Külli. She really *didn't understand* why Gemma found it impossible to fall in love with her. Everyone else had. No girl had ever refused Gula. The irony was not lost on her.

The athletic and beautiful Külli was the object of considerable male attention at Oxford too. However, Gula found the idea of sex with a man to be abhorrent, *even unnatural.*

Gemma had seemingly been lost to her, so Külli turned her attentions to other girls. And there were lots. Flax was stunning. Her long straight blonde hair, blue eyes, and supple body competed for best attribute. Flax had been a welcome diversion, at least for a while. Külli would usually invite other undergraduates to her rooms in St Hilda on weekends. The encounters were pleasurable, intensely so, but they were just a poor substitute for what Gula really wanted: Gemma.

'Why can't I escape this girl?' thought Külli. 'What spell has she cast on me?' And then Külli's thought process would always inevitably lead her to two questions:

1 How do I get over Gemma?

2 Do I want to get over Gemma?

The answer to the latter was invariably 'no.' **Gula was a swan that had found her mate.**

That Gemma was apparently out of her reach did not anger Külli. It saddened her. It tormented her. After Külli's declaration of love had failed, Külli had become deeply depressed. Any fantasies she had happily harbored had evaporated. Gemma was never to be hers. This was all too much for Külli. Külli felt like she was going mad.

Sometimes she would wake up and start crying. Flax, sleeping next to her, would sometimes wake up and ask what was wrong, but Külli would never answer. The devoted Flax would embrace and stroke her hair until she fell back asleep. That Flax, beautiful, sweet, and intelligent, loved her really meant nothing to Külli. (Though she would never admit it, Külli didn't want to hurt anyone like she had been hurt.)

Towards the end of their first term at Oxford, the flaxen haired Violet, wearing faded blue jeans and wrapped in a navy blue quilted jacket from Holland and Holland and a lilac and purple striped wool scarf she had taken from Poppy's wardrobe, knocked on Külli's door.

'Oh, Lord. Who could that be?' thought Külli as she stirred awake. Again, another light knock on the door. 'Who would come around at *this hour* of the day?' thought Külli. Külli took her platinum watch off of her night stand and looked at it: 1:07 pm. 'Oh,' said Külli outloud.

Külli climbed over the naked Flax and another nude girl, just as tall as her. She got out of bed without a stitch of clothing, walked to her door, and opened it. It was Violet. Seeing Külli standing completely naked in the doorway made her smile and then laugh.

'My, we are at home here at St Hilda's,' laughed Violet.

'Come in,' said Külli as she tugged Violet into her room and closed the door. Violet noticed the two naked girls in Külli 's bed.

'Two girls? Really, Gula?' whispered Violet.

'I wanted intimacy last night,' said Külli and Külli smiled.

'Okay, Flax is on the right, but who is that girl on the left?' asked Violet.

'She's Dutch. Her name is Lotte, or Sophie. I can't remember. It's nice to meet a girl that is as tall as me,' replied Külli, and Külli smiled.

Violet stared at both sleeping girls and said, 'Yes, I do miss it.' Violet smiled. 'Well, aren't you going to ask me to join you?'

'No.'

'Really, Gula. Sharing was never one of your strong points.'

'I'm happy to see you, Violet, but what brings you here?'

'My father is hosting a fox hunt this weekend at his country house. I'm inviting everyone. Well, the four of us. It's been *yonks* since I was on a fox hunt. Gemma, too. Poppy has never been on one. How did a *Hon* manage that?'

'I don't have the clothes for it, Violet.'

'I know. I'm here to take you to an outfitter right now. Gemma and Poppy are already there. I think you'll look nice in riding kit,' answered Violet.

Külli, still naked, stood quietly and stared at Violet for a moment. This would be a chance to spend the weekend with Gemma. 'Okay. I'd love to go.'

Külli had never been on a fox hunt. Her father supplied hunting and riding boots to all the best clubs in England, and Külli could ride well. She had, however, never been on a hunt. Gula had no interest in hunting, but she did want to see Gemma again.

Külli's trip to the equestrian outfitters was extremely enjoyable. She loved the riding gear, jodhpurs, and leather riding boots (She bought a pair that had been made by her father's company). She also purchased an expensive hunting whip. 'For Lotte,' Külli quipped to Violet, and Violet emitted a sly knowing smile.

'You see. You're expanding your horizons at Oxford,' answered Violet.


### Gemma—London—Off to the Country

THE ENGLISH COUNTRYSIDE
Late November 1996
Gemma, Poppy, and Violet travelled to the countryside in Violet's white Volkswagen Golf GTI. Külli, wanting to drive her own vehicle, declined the invitation to ride with them.

Friday afternoon, and the traffic leaving Oxford was terrible.

Gemma was happy to sit alone in the back seat. She could watch the scenery or go to sleep. Poppy sat in the front passenger seat, which meant she would have to spend the entire journey looking at the map and trying to spot exit ramps, turns, roads, roundabouts, and landmarks.

Violet was actually quite a good driver. She didn't speed along the road like Külli. Külli loved speed.

Külli's father had given her a blue Bristol 603S motorcar the month before the hunt. It had been built in 1977. Her father had purchased it in 1985. He had recently paid the Bristol Car Company to have it totally restored and upgraded for Külli. This included modern seat belts, air conditioning, and a new black leather interior. Her father had loved that car, but now, he wanted Külli to have it: a classic British car for a 'new' British family. Külli loved the car too. It was ugly to some, but beautiful to her. It also had a new V-8 engine.

The girls wouldn't arrive at Vava's country house until after 9pm, so they had all decided to have dinner at a local pub in order to avoid bothering the staff at the house. And besides, local pubs could be a lot of fun. This pub was one of Violet's favourites. She knew the owners; they served excellent food. They were also open late on hunt weekends.

When Violet pulled into the parking lot, Külli was waiting for them outside.

 Külli had arrived after dark an hour earlier and had been wondering around the small village. There were a lot of people out in spite of the cold weather. People were still arriving in the village from London. Some were there for the hunt; most were just staying at their weekend homes. Gula found the village to be very pleasant. The locals were friendly.

Külli, wearing denim blue jeans, a white cotton blouse, a grey wool jacket with white piping, and the red, blue, and purple All Saints scarf, was standing next to her car when suddenly she was illuminated in Violet's car headlights.

'Good to see you!' said Külli as the girls were exiting the GTI. Külli was genuinely happy to see everyone.

She hadn't seen Gemma or Poppy in almost two weeks. Everyone had been busy at school. Well, everyone but Violet. Academics weren't something she really excelled at. Gemma and Külli were first rate students. Both were considering careers in academia. Poppy worked hard at her studies, but was still undecided about what she wanted to do in the future. Violet was putting most of her efforts into finding a wealthy husband. Surely Oxford was just the place for that.

Gemma had fallen asleep in the backseat of the car. She was a little groggy when they arrived. Külli opened the door for her and helped her get out of the GTI. 'Come on, my sleepy little angel,' cooed Gula. Gemma smiled and hugged Külli. Everything seemed normal. There was no tension.

'Come on, everyone. I'll show you my new car,' said Gula. The girls gathered around the Bristol 603. It gleamed beautifully with its fresh coat of glossy blue paint under the light from the sole street light next to the pub.

'It's beautiful,'said Poppy. Poppy was sporting faded denim blue jeans, dark brown leather shoes, and a light grey v-neck cashmere sweater with slate grey stripes running the length of both sleeves, the cashmere top contrasted nicely with Poppy's shoulder length glossy blonde hair. 'I love these classic cars. They are so British,' said Poppy as she walked around the dark blue motorcar.

Violet, still wearing Poppy's lilac and purple striped wool scarf, stood in front of the Bristol and examined the car as she buttoned up her navy blue quilted jacket. 'It looks brand new.'

'Father had it totally restored by Bristol,' replied Gula happily.

'It's really beautiful. I *rather* like it, *yah*,' said Gemma and Gemma smiled.

Külli looked at Gemma. Gemma was standing next to the Bristol 603 illuminated by the street lamp in a pair of stone washed blue jeans, a white opened collared cotton blouse and dark blue wool coat with silver buttons that glinted in the light. She looked beautiful. And then Külli remembered how much sadness Gemma brought her.

'Come on, I'm famished,' said Poppy. The four teenage undergraduates then made their way into the pub. There was a big crowd that night, but they owners had reserved a corner table for Violet and her set. The girls, exhausted and hungry from a day of driving in heavy traffic, sat down to eat.

'I'll have everything on the menu,' said Gemma smiling.

'If you get fat, Gemma, no one will ever marry you,' teased Violet.

'I'm sure a few extra pounds won't deter everyone,' replied Gemma and she laughed.

Külli sat in silence next to Gemma. 'I would still love you, Gemma,' Külli thought to herself. 'No matter what.'

The food was served. The cold weather outside and general feelings of hunger made the excellent food taste even more delicious. Everyone ate and chatted happily. Even Külli forgot about her sadness and had a nice time.

Towards the end of the meal Külli accidentally brushed Gemma's hand. 'Sorry,' whispered Külli. Külli didn't want Gemma to believe she had done it on purpose. Gemma smiled and held her hand. 'No need to apologize, G,' whispered Gemma, and Gemma smiled.

Külli felt a warmth move through her body. Gemma's small, soft, and warm hand filled her with love. Memories of sunny school days and happy times in the dining hall came flooding back. Külli hadn't been this happy since that fateful day she had left the letter for Gemma under her pillow. After that day, Külli's life had been *crushed*. Gemma had never told anyone about Gula's letter. Gem was like that. Gemma protected her friends. Gula would have died if the others had found out about the letter.

'Come on, let's get to the house,' said Violet. The girls walked out to the parking lot.

'Gem, why not ride with me?' asked Külli.

'Sure, G.'

Gemma opened the passenger side door and slid into the car. The car's interior smelled of leather and the burlwood dashed gleamed under the street light.

'This is *fantastic*, G,' said Gemma, and Gemma smiled. She ran her manicured fingers over the leather and wood. 'They did a great job restoring the car, Gula.'

Külli started the car and pulled out of the parking lot. She knew the way to Violet's country house; it was just a few miles away. The road to it crossed thousands of acres of land owned by the 5th Viscount.

After they cleared the village, Külli pressed the accelerator and the 603S bolted forward. Külli loved speed. And now, in her metal shell, with the love of her life seated next to her, Külli was exhilarated. It was late; there weren't any other cars on the road ahead.

It was extremely cold. Külli turned on the heater. 'Thanks, G. I was freezing,' said Gemma. Gemma leaned back in the leather seat with the shoulder belt across her.

Gemma kept her glossy brown hair shoulder length. Külli loved the smell of Gemma's hair. Külli was now firmly back in her pre-letter mode. The future was filled with possibilities again. Külli was happy, really happy. Not since the letter had she felt this way. And Külli had hope again. Why? She didn't know. She didn't ask herself that question. She had recovered hope and her happiness.

'This car can really move,' said Gemma.

 Külli signalled and switched lanes. Then she slowed, signalled, and turned onto another road. This road led to the house and went through a heavily wooded part of the estate.

Ahead Gemma and Külli could see the family pile. There were lights on and several SUVs and sedans were parked in the gravel area in front of the large stone two storey house.

Külli pulled into the main driveway and parked under a large tree near the large open stone gates. 'Let's wait for the others to arrive in the car. It's warm in here,' said Külli.

'Good idea,' agreed Gemma, and she leaned back into the seat. 'We used to have a house like this. We lost it to the bailiffs last year.'

'Last year?' replied Külli. 'You didn't say a word.'

'I was too upset. I didn't want to discuss it. I didn't want anyone to know.'

'I'm sorry. That must have been horrible,' replied Külli, and she reached over and took Gemma's hand.

'My father has never been good with money,' explained Gemma.

They both became quiet. Outside it was freezing. The car windows had fogged up. Now Gemma and Külli were in their own private world.

'Gem.'

'*Yah*,' replied Gemma sleepily.

'What was your first impression of me? I mean, what did you think of me when you first met me?'

'Why are you asking?' asked Gemma.

'Just curious,' answered Külli.

'I noticed your height first. Then your smile. You have such a beautiful smile, like a movie star. I immediately noticed how beautiful you are. And you have an exotic and sophisticated look. I said to myself, "Surely this girl is a foreigner."'

Külli laughed and smiled. 'I'm Estonian, not Japanese.'

'Are all Estonians as beautiful as you?' asked Gemma.

'No. I'm extraordinarily beautiful.'

'And modest,' teased Gemma, and she smiled. Gemma had a beautiful smile with perfect healthy white teeth like Külli. Gemma and Gula were both known for their smiles.

Külli sat happily with Gemma in her warm metal shell. She was floating through space with Gemma.

Lights suddenly illuminated the car. Violet had arrived. Car doors slammed. 'Let's go inside,' Gemma said sleepily. 'I need some sleep. I'm exhausted'.

The girls walked up the stone steps to the large glossy black double doors. Violet took out a key and unlocked them. The house was beautiful. The house really wasn't that big. It was a Palladian structure. The interiors seemed to be trapped in the 1920s—not a bad thing. They made their way up the main staircase and walked quietly to the end of the hall.

'We have two rooms allotted to us. Who wants to stay with whom?' asked Violet.

Poppy was about to speak when Külli seized the opportunity. 'Come on Gemma, we will sleep in here. Good night,' said Külli and she led the sleepy Gemma into the bedroom and shut the door behind them. A small lamp on the night stand bathed the room in a dim glow.

One bed. Külli smiled. Tonight, she would sleep next to Gemma.

Both girls started to undress. Külli had seen Gemma undress a million times, but this time was different. Külli stripped down to her bra and panties. Gemma did the same. The nineteen-year-old Gemma had *really filled out* in the seven months since they had graduated from All Saints. Gemma, oblivious to Gula's stare, crawled into bed and fell asleep almost immediately.

Külli got in on her side of the bed. The room was warm. Külli didn't need any additional sources of warmth, but she wanted to hold Gemma next to her. She moved closer, eventually snuggling up against Gemma. She was soft and warm. Külli was in heaven. She fell asleep quickly.

## Gemma—London—Vava's Country House

THE HOUSE

The next morning was cold and foggy. Külli woke up alone in bed. She raised her head and looked around. Gemma wasn't there. Had Gemma awoken in her embrace and bolted? Külli felt a sense of panic starting to rise in her. Just then the door to the bathroom opened and Gemma entered the room in a white bathrobe.

'Good morning, G!' Gemma beamed. 'I feel fantastic. A warm meal and warm bed were exactly what I needed. Oh, last night was bliss,' gushed Gemma. 'It's amazing what a good night's sleep can do for someone.'

Külli was confused. Was Gemma including their snuggling together in her morning declaration, or was she really just referring to a good night's sleep? Külli suddenly decided it didn't really matter; she had spent a heavenly night with Gemma, and Gemma hadn't balked.

'What time is it, Gem?'

Gemma picked up her silver wristwatch and looked, 'It's almost 8:30. I hope it's not too late for breakfast.'

Their conversation was interrupted by a knock. Violet opened the door and said, 'Good morning. How do you feel?'

'*Fantastic,* Vava! What a beautiful morning. Is it too late for breakfast?' asked Gemma.

'Of course, not. Breakfast is being served downstairs. Or, if you prefer, the staff can bring breakfast to your room.'

Gemma and Külli looked at each other and smiled. 'Breakfast in bed, please, Vava!' said Külli.

'Thank you so much, Vava. It will be *rather* nice to idle away in my bathrobe for just a little while longer,' said Gemma.

Violet smiled. 'You are positively glowing this morning, Gemma. A good night's rest has done wonders for you.' Violet, still wearing her white Turkish bathrobe and slippers, turned and exited.

Külli got out of bed, took off her bra and panties, and walked into the bathroom. 'Did you save any warm water for me, Gem?'

'*Yah.* Plenty,' replied Gemma happily.

Gemma's hair was still wrapped in a white towel. She sat on the edge of the bed and looked out the window. The view was spectacular: The house was surrounded by trees, grassy fields, and fog. No manmade structures could be seen. There was a knock at the door.

'Come in,' said Gemma.

The door opened and a young blonde housemaid in a black uniform entered pushing a rolling cart ahead of her. 'Good morning, ma'am. I was told that you both would like to be served breakfast in your room.'

'Yes. Thank you,' replied Gemma.

The house maid rolled the silver cart into the middle of the room and stopped at a small polished wooden table. She was about to start placing the covered porcelain plates on the table when Gemma said, 'That's alright. We can do that. Thank you.'

'Will that be all, ma'am?'

'Yes'.

The maid left the bedroom.

Gemma got up and walked over to the silver cart. She picked up the morning edition of The Daily Telegraph and starting reading the front page.

'Anything interesting?' asked Külli. Külli had just walked into the room with only a towel wrapped around her. Her wet hair was also wrapped up in a towel.

'Not sure, G. I'm famished. Let's see what's being served this morning.'

Gemma lifted one of the sterling silver cloches to see. Gemma was not disappointed. The large plate held scrambled eggs (Gemma's favorite), toast, bacon, sausage, baked beans, grilled tomatoes, and fried Portobello mushrooms. The aroma was intoxicating. Gemma inhaled it all in deeply.

'It's fantastic, G!' said Gemma, and she smiled.

'I'm going to eat my food in bed like a Baltic peasant,' said Külli. She then walked over to the tray, picked up her covered dish, carried it over to the king-sized bed, and sat down.

Still wrapped in a large white towel, Külli sat on the white high thread count sheets, surrounded by a number of large white pillows. She lifted the lid. '*Marvellous,*' cooed Külli imitating a Sloane perfectly.

Gemma smiled. 'We'll make a Sloane Ranger out of you yet, G,' said Gemma happily.

Gemma brought her tray over and placed it on her side of the bed, close to Külli. They both started to eat in a rather unlady like fashion. 'I could eat a horse,' said Gemma. 'I could eat you,' replied Külli. Gemma smiled, and they both continued to eat heartily.

'This is one of life's pleasures,' said Gemma. 'Spending time with your friends and enjoying a sumptuous, if unhealthy, meal.'

The food *was* really good.

'This is the best breakfast I have ever had and being with you makes it even better, G', said Gemma, and Gemma smiled once more.

At that moment Külli knew what it would be like to spend the rest of her life with Gemma. This every morning: Gemma's happy smile and warm embrace. Külli smiled at Gemma while this imaginary scenario floated through her mind. Külli *knew* that she could make Gemma happy, if Gemma would only let her.

After finishing breakfast, Gemma picked up her dish and returned it to the tray. 'Would you like some more orange juice, G?'

'Yes, please,' answered Külli. Külli watched as Gemma filled both of their glasses. Külli looked at Gemma longingly. Gemma was innocent. It wasn't fair to push her in a direction she didn't want to go, but how could Külli survive without Gemma?

Gemma sipped her orange juice. Külli drained her glass. 'That was refreshing,' said Külli.

Külli then lay back on the bed. 'Gemma, come lay down next to me,' said Külli. Gemma complied. 'Gemma, I'm glad I met you.'

'I'm glad I met you too, G,' replied Gemma.

They both looked up at the white plaster work which adorned the ceiling. Külli had *never* been happier.

There was a knock at the door. Külli wanted whomever it was to go away and have the whole world leave them both alone forever.

'Come in,' said Gemma.

'Ah, you two, you're still not dressed? You'll miss the hunt at this rate.'

It was Poppy. She was already dressed for the hunt. Her blue hunt coat and beige jodhpurs contrasted sharply with the white walls and soft white bedding as she crossed the room.

Poppy was tiny (even shorter than Gemma), but the blonde-haired and blue-eyed Poppy, the *bantam* daughter of a baron, was always full of energy and fun. She was also a fiercely loyal friend. Külli appreciated Poppy's character. Poppy was a cute little thing, 'dangerously cute' as Gemma would say.

Poppy's family still had their relatively small baronial home in the Lake District. The family was no longer really wealthy, but they still collected rents from a few tenant farmers; careful budgeting and frugality allowed the family to keep their home and status. Her father, the 12th Baron, was a moderately successful banker. Poppy's father also didn't have any bankrupting vices and was a kind and loving father. Poppy's mother was also kind. She always greeted Gemma with a hug. Poppy's older brother had already graduated from Oxford and was now working in The City, but at a different bank than his father. More than anything else, Gemma envied Poppy for having such a family.

Külli loved Poppy. She had always been kind, accepting, and generous.

'If it had been anyone but you, Poppy, I would have stabbed them,' replied Külli.

Poppy smiled. 'Come on, Gula. Get dressed. I want to see what you look like in your new outfit.'

'Ask her to show you her hunting whip,' said Violet as she entered the room.

Violet was also dressed in her hunting outfit; Vava actually looked quite dashing in her blue coat, white hunt shirt, white stock tie, and beige twill cavalry hunting breeches.

Külli had always been impressed with Violet's ability to enhance her looks through clothing, eyeglasses, and her posh mannerisms. Violet was also more Sloane than anyone Külli had ever met.

'You look really nice, Vava,' said Külli.

Violet was pleasantly surprised. Gula had never really complemented her on her looks before. Violet smiled, 'Thank you, Külli. That means a lot coming from you.'

'I've always been impressed with your style, Vava.'

'Really?' asked Violet.

'Yes,' replied Külli.

'If you weren't practically naked, I would hug you, G,' said Violet.

'Oh, please, that never stopped you before,' retorted Külli, and she smiled.

### Gemma—London—The Hunt

THE STABLES
Gemma, Poppy, Külli, and Violet walked to the stables to select their mounts. All the girls were wearing their newly purchased riding outfits. They were a wave of blue coats, blue velvet hunt caps, beige jodhpurs, black leather riding boots, and silver spurs moving through the fog. All of the girls wore beige wool hunting gloves and carried an assortment of hunting whips.

There was a chill in the air. Beyond the stone stables, the hounds could be heard and horsemen seen riding about. There were several Range Rovers and Land Rovers parked along the road.

The girls were the last to arrive at the stables that day.

'Come on, girls! You'll miss the start!' said Violet's mother, the Viscountess.

Violet's attractive and stylish mother was dressed in a blue hunt coat, blue velvet hunting cap, beige jodhpurs, long black boots, and silver Prince of Wales spurs. She stood at the entrance holding a hunting whip in one of her beige wool gloved hands. There were two stable hands with her.

'Sorry, Mummy,' said Violet. The girls hurried into the stables. The girls mounted their horses with ease. They were all experienced riders. They slowly rode out and headed for the large open green beyond.

There were dozens of riders and seemingly hundreds of hounds. Horns started to blare. The 5th Viscount, wearing a scarlet hunt coat, beige breeches, and tall black boots, gave a brief sort of speech to the assembled riders, and then they released the hounds. The hunt was on.

The girls rode off in pursuit of the fox. No one could really say it was a beautiful day; it was grey, overcast, and cold. Being able to ride through the country was particularly exciting for Gula. She hadn't had a chance to ride since the summer.

The hunt wound through a small valley, through bare trees, and over fog shrouded and damp hills covered in dark and waxen dead leaves. The hunt progressed nicely. The cold damp air was filled with the sounds of fox hunting horns, hounds, and occasional shouts.

Three hours after the start of the hunt, the fox was cornered and its life ended. Külli sat on her horse as she watched the pack of hounds rip the poor hapless animal to shreds. Violet and Poppy looked on with excitement. The hunt had been successful. Gemma was nowhere to be seen.

Külli rode back to the stables. She found Gemma walking down the road towards the house. 'What's wrong, Gemma?' asked Külli.

'I have to be honest with you, G. I have always felt sorry for the fox. I saw one being torn to pieces when I was 15 and I cried all day. I enjoy the camaraderie of the hunt. I just don't like what it leads to,' said Gemma staring up at Külli, who at nearly six feet tall and mounted on a horse was a literal giant compared to the diminutive Gemma.

'Would you mind waiting a moment for me, Gemma? I'll take the horse back to the stables and then we can walk back to the main house together.'

'Sure,' said Gemma.

Külli trotted back to the stables and quickly dismounted. She talked briefly with one of the stable hands and then walked down the road to the waiting Gemma.

'Gula,' said Gemma, 'Please don't tell anyone I dislike blood sports. I don't want to alienate anyone.'

'I won't.'

The girls walked back to the house together. Their boots and outfits were splattered with mud. They were both tired and sore. It was time for a bath, and then a delicious dinner.

'I wonder what's for dinner tonight?' asked Gemma. 'I hope they serve steak. I haven't had a good steak in *yonks.*'

Külli was hungry as well.

'Gem, to be honest, I don't like hunting either. The sight of the fox being killed today was heart rending. I don't understand why some people enjoy it so much.'

'I'm glad you feel that way, G,' replied Gemma. 'I don't understand how Poppy and Violet could enjoy hunting so much.'

The girls walked along the road until they reached the main house. 'This house is beautiful, Gem. My parents own a stone cottage in the Cotswolds, but it's only four rooms. It's in a beautiful location, but it's nothing compared to this.'

'My father now lives in a four-bedroom cottage in Sussex, two of which are bedrooms,' said Gemma and she sighed. 'He lives there alone surrounded by old photographs and some furniture he managed to retrieve from our house before the auction. I telephoned him last year, but he just asked me why I was calling him, and then he hung up.'

'That's terrible, Gem,' said Külli. 'Where do you stay when you are away from school?'

'My grandparents. My maternal grandparents. They pay for school and help me as much as they can. Grandfather is a retired army colonel. At least I have kind grandparents. When they pass away, I'll be alone in the world.'

'You'll never be alone, Gemma. You'll always have me,' said Külli. 'I mean that, Gem. I'll never abandon you, no matter what.'

'Thank you, G,' replied Gemma. 'That means a lot to me. You're a true friend.'

'What about your brother, Gemma. Doesn't he contact you?'

'Never. Father mistreated him so much, he will never return to England. He told me that England is nothing but a collection of bad memories for him. He lives in Hong Kong now. One of his former classmates from Eton told me he was working in finance. I wonder if he is happy there. I don't know. I've never seen my brother happy. I hope he can find happiness somewhere one day.'

'Do you miss him?' asked Külli.

'Yes. But I understand him. He's a good person, but he is damaged,' said Gemma wistfully. 'It would be nice to have a brother again.'

'Gem, I'm so sorry you have had to go through all of this.'

'I could say that one gets used to it, but that wouldn't be true,' replied

Gemma in barely a whisper.

Külli put her arm around Gemma and said, 'Gem, never forget that I love you. I will always be here for you.'

At these words, Gemma started to cry. 'You promise?' asked Gemma through tears.

'Yes,' replied Külli.

Gemma looked *up* into Külli's eyes and whispered, 'Thank you, G. I love you. I would be lost without you.'

Külli held Gemma's hand tightly and said, 'Come on, Gem. Let's take a bath and then get something to eat. A snack before dinner is in order.'

Gemma wiped her eyes and followed Külli into the house. They removed their boots and left them in the entry for the servants to clean. They headed up the stairs and down the hall to their room.

They took off their riding outfits and hung them up carefully in the wardrobe. 'Gem, you go first. I can wait,' said Külli sitting on the edge of the bed.

'Are you sure?' asked Gemma.

'Yes.'

'Thank you, G.'

After they had both taken a bath, they got dressed. Gemma put on a pair of rum-colored wool trousers and a white open collared blouse. Külli buttoned herself into a pair of khaki narrow leg trousers and a dark blue high neck cashmere jumper. She pinned up her long brown hair and, then they headed downstairs to the kitchen.

'Could we have a little something to take back to our room, please?' asked

Külli as she towered over one of the kitchen staff.

'What would you like, ma'am?'

'Do you have any cheese?'

'Yes, what kind would you like?'

'Any.'

'Would you like bread with that?'

'Yes, please. Thank you.'

The girls took the basket they were given and headed back upstairs. Once in their room they changed into their white bathrobes and laid the contents of the basket out on the small round table in the bedroom.

The staff had given them several wedges of cheese and slices of several different types of bread. The basket also had two silver knives and a spoon rolled up in three white cloth napkins. An octagonal glass jar of raspberry jam with a sterling silver lid rounded out the selection.

'It's been *yonks* since I've had raspberry jam,' said Gemma. Gemma took one slice of freshly baked white bread and spread some raspberry jam on it with one of the sterling silver knives.

'Pure heaven,' said Gemma after finishing her first bite.

Külli took a piece of cheese and placed it between two pieces of whole wheat bread. 'Mmmmm,' said Külli as she chewed the sandwich. The girls sat happily on the bed and enjoyed their afternoon treat *together*.

Afterwards, Gemma crawled into bed and went to sleep. Külli went over to the bookshelf and pulled out a book; she opened the copy of 'Brideshead Revisted' and looked down on the page. One of the characters in the novel expressed a notion that being in love with another human being is the root of all wisdom. Külli could not agree more.

'Yes,' said Külli to herself. 'Please, God, bring Gemma to me,' she said in silent prayer. 'Just this one thing.' Külli looked over to the sleeping Gemma. 'Everything I have ever wanted or *needed* is sleeping just a few feet away from me.' Gula felt tears starting to well up in her eyes. 'Please,' she prayed.

Külli sat down in the chair next to the window and started to read the book. She had read the book half a dozen times. It was Gemma's favorite book. She had probably read it a hundred times. At some passages in the book, Külli laughed out loud.

Gemma finally stirred awake. 'What are you reading, G?' she asked.

'Brideshead Revisited,' replied Külli with a smile.

'That's my *fave*, G,' said Gemma and she smiled. She looked out the window, the sun was going down. Dinner would soon be served.

'I'm hungry,' said Külli as she lounged in the chair.

'Me, too,' replied Gemma sleepily. 'I suppose we should get dressed for dinner.'

There was a light knock.

'Come in,' said Gemma and Külli simultaneously.

'Where did you both disappear to this afternoon?' said Violet. She had already put on her evening dress. Violet's glossy blonde hair contrasted nicely with the pale blue dress she was wearing. 'We had quite the gathering outside under the tent after the hunt. Everyone wondered where you had both gone off to,' said Violet.

'Sorry, Vava,' said Gemma. 'I was exhausted after the hunt and went back to the house. The kitchen staff was kind enough to give us some *rather* delightful cheese, bread, and jam.'

'The afternoon was *marvellous*,' replied Violet. 'But I think you had a pleasant afternoon here. I'm glad. I wanted this to be a relaxing weekend for us.'

'Thank you for inviting us,' said Gemma,

'Yes. Thank you, Vava. This has been one of the happiest weekends of my entire life,' said Külli.

'Really?' she asked and Violet smiled. 'Then we shall have to do this more often.'

Poppy entered the bedroom wearing a dark blue dress. 'What have you been doing here all day? The gathering outside under the tent was *splendid*, *yah*. I met so many nice people today.'

'That sounds nice, Poppy,' replied Gemma happily. 'I'm sorry. I was just really tired.'

'That's okay, Gemmy. As long as you had a nice day,' said Poppy.

'Hurry up, girls. Get dressed or you will miss dinner, too,' said Violet.

Poppy went over to the basket on the desk and picked up a slice of cheese. 'This is really good. You didn't save me any bread,' said Poppy. 'Mmmmm. This cheese is really good.'

'Poppy,' sighed Violet wearily, 'you'll ruin your appetite. Tonight, they are serving Gemma's favorite: steak. I asked Mummy to serve it just for her.'

Gemma's face lit up. 'I love you, Vava,' said Gemma, and Gemma smiled in the most innocent way one could.

Violet returned the smile and then said, 'Come on, Gem. It's time for dinner.'

## Gemma—London—Michaelmas Ends

OXFORD UNIVERSITY

The girls returned to Oxford after the hunt weekend. Everyone was in high spirits. Violet was thrilled that her friends had had a fantastic time at her family's country house. Poppy had enjoyed the hunt and made a lot of new friends. Gemma had repaired and cemented her friendship with Gula, and Gula had regained her happiness and hopes for a romantic relationship with Gemma.

Of the four, two had badly deluded themselves.

The end of 1996 found the four girls studying hard for their exams. The last couple of weeks were devoid of any activities other than preparing for finals. Gemma, Poppy, and Violet spent a lot of time together studying in their rooms at Somerville. Black coffee kept them all awake into the early hours.

Külli, lost in her studies, did not see any of the girls at all. Her peace of mind fully restored, Külli didn't have a care in the world. Külli had regained her focus and did extremely well. Gemma had also done well. Poppy studied really hard, but did only moderately well. Violet, never much of a student, ended up on academic probation.

Everyone was exhausted at the end of the Michaelmas term. They just wanted to go home. After her last exam, Gemma telephoned Külli in her room at St Hilda's.

'Hello.'

'Hi Gula. It's Gemma. Have you completed all of your exams?'

'Yes. I took my last one this morning. I'm glad this term has come to an end. Have you?' asked Külli.

'*Yah.* Could you come over to Somerville in a couple of hours? We are going to have lunch in our rooms and would like you to join us,' Gemma said sleepily.

'Thank you. I would like that, Gem,' answered Külli happily.

'Everyone is going home afterwards. We didn't want to leave without seeing you,' said Gemma.

'Yes. It will be good to see everyone before the holidays,' said Külli.

'*Fantastic*, G. Lunch is at 2pm. Oh, we are ordering pizza,' Gemma laughed. 'Not exactly the feast Sebastian offered Charles at their first luncheon,' Gemma mused while referring to part of the story from her favorite novel.

'I like pizza much more than plover's eggs, Gemma.'

'Me, too!' Gemma replied happily.

'We are ordering three pizzas. Do you still like ham and pineapple?'

'Yes.'

'Alright. So, that will be one ham and pineapple, one pepperoni, and one cheese pizza with broccoli.'

'They make pizza with broccoli?' asked Külli.

'*Yah*, well, they do now,' replied Gemma happily. 'Oh, and Violet's Japanese roommate will be joining us. Akiko is really sweet, and we feel *rather* sorry for her. It can't be easy living with Violet.'

Külli laughed, 'Yes. I can imagine that poor girl has suffered quite a series of shocks.' Gemma laughed too.

'See you, G'.

'See you, Gem.'

The girls had an extremely pleasant lunch of pizza and pasta. Külli ate like a Baltic peasant, and thoroughly enjoyed herself. She was completely relaxed. She was back with her friends.

Akiko spoke English perfectly; she had started to pick up a posh accent from Violet and she had even added numerous Sloane words to her English vocabulary—'*Okay, yah!*' Gula liked the petite young undergrad from Nippon.

The girls ate everything. They were exhausted and starving after completing their exams. This lunch of take-away pizza and pasta was just what they needed.

Poppy, Gemma, Violet, and Akiko took the train back to London for the holidays. Violet had invited Akiko to spend Christmas with her and her family in Mayfair. Poppy and Gemma were to spend Christmas with their families.

Külli drove to the Cotswolds to spend Christmas with her parents and the family cat. Külli hadn't seen much of her family during her first term at Oxford. She had really missed them. And the cat.


**Gemma—London—George**

CHRIST CHURCH

Trinity Term 1997

Gemma's life at Oxford in the spring continued to be idyllic. The spring had brought warm weather, sunshine, and, for Gemma, the first stirrings of love.

Gemma had first spotted the young blonde man of epicene beauty on the grass quad at Christ Church. He was wearing a white boating blazer and tie as he walked across the lush green lawn. Gemma had never seen anyone like him. He was so beautiful that she couldn't help but stare.

'Gemma?! Are you listening?' asked Poppy.

'What?' Gemma had suddenly been shaken out of her trance.

'What are you looking at? Oh. He is quite nice, isn't he?'

Gemma turned her head quickly at stared *ferociously* at Poppy. 'I saw him first, Poppy.'

Poppy smiled. 'Gemma! At last! Someone has stolen *your* heart.'

'No one has stolen anything, Poppy. I don't even know his name…yet.'

'George Howard,' replied Poppy.

'George? *How do know his name?*' Gemma responded in an almost alarmed tone.

'Simple. He went to Eton with my cousin Harold. I met him last year when he visited us in the Lake District. He's really *rather* sweet.'

'Poppy! Why didn't you tell me about him?'

'Tell you what? I meet nice young men all the time at the house. Besides, Gemmy, I don't even know what type of man you are attracted to.'

'I'm attracted to him. Please, introduce me. Immediately.'

Gemma's gaze then returned to the quad, but he was gone. 'Oh, no, look! You distracted me, and now he is gone.'

'Don't worry, Gem. I know where he lives,' said Poppy, and Poppy smiled.

'Introduce me today.'

Poppy was a little taken aback. She had never seen Gemma behave so aggressively about *anything*. Poppy adjusted her blue blazer and thought for a moment.

'Let me call Harold. I'll have them come over to our rooms at Somerville this evening. '

'Don't tell Harold I want to meet George. Ask in a roundabout way, Poppy.'

'Don't worry, Gemmy. I know what I'm doing.'

'Poppy.'

'Yes.'

'Why haven't you pursued George?'

'I don't like to date men that are cuter than me.'

SOMERVILLE
Gemma looked in the mirror. Her glossy brown hair was as glossy as ever, but still, something wasn't quite right. 'Poppy? Does my hair look alright?'

'*Yah*. You look nice. You're the most beautiful girl I have ever seen, Gem.'

Gemma smiled briefly, and then she suddenly looked panicked. 'What if George doesn't like me?'

Poppy could only stare wordlessly at Gemma for a minute. What was going on with her? Was this how Gemma acted when besotted? Really, who would have ever guessed Gemma could ever be such a wreck?

'Gemma. Don't worry. I'm sure George will like you.'

'How do you know? He might only date girls that are much taller than me,' replied Gemma.

'Then I'll direct him in Gula's direction. And when she's done with him, he will be so traumatized he won't ever date a girl over 5'3" again,' replied

Poppy.

'Don't say that, Poppy. Gula might steal him from me,' replied Gemma in a worried tone.

'Gula? Gemma! Gula doesn't have any interest in any man. Have you been sleep walking the whole time?'

'Poppy? Are you going to torment me the entire night?' asked Gemma.

Poppy's patience was nearing the end of its tether.

'Gem. Please. Stop this. George will either like you, or he won't. Besides, who's to say you will like him? You might find him a *terrible bore.*'

'Impossible!' replied Gemma.

And then there was a knock on the door. 'Merciful God! He has answered my prayers!' said Poppy.

Poppy looked at Gemma. She was staring intensely at the door. Another knock. 'Poppy! Answer the door!'

Poppy walked over and opened it. Harold appeared first. He bore a surprisingly strong resemblance to his cousin Poppy, except that his hair was brown.

He smiled and greeted Poppy, 'Pop! It's good to see you!' His gaze drifted past her and rested on Gemma. Harold looked a bit startled. Gemma *was* as beautiful as Poppy had told him. 'Hello. You must be Gemma.'

'*Yah.* It's nice to meet you, Harold.' And Gemma flashed a smile that scorched all the upholstery in the room.

Harold was smitten.

George then entered the room. He was wearing a blue blazer and his Eton tie. He wasn't handsome; George was pretty. He was slightly below average height and slim. His blond hair was the same color as the hair of Gula's roommate Flax. And he had a smile that could match Gemma's. George then caught his first glimpse of Gemma, and that was it. George had met his future bride.

## Gemma—London—Rupture

ST HILDA
The spring of 1997 in Oxford was beautiful. The domes and spires of the city glowed in the twilight. Nightfall fell on the city later and later with each passing day. The days were warm, but the nights remained cool, sometimes even cold.

Külli was at her desk wrapped in a thick buffalo hide that her father had purchased during one of his many trips to the United States. She had found it useful and had spent the winter wrapped in it as she studied at her desk or lay in bed.

Tonight, Gula was enjoying a hot cup of tea while she studied Carthaginian history. 'Hannibal Barca,' Külli said outloud. 'Barca should have been my nickname,' Gula said. 'Not Caligula.'

There was a knock at the door. Külli sighed, and wondered who that could be.

'Gula, it's me,' said Violet.

'Just a minute,' said Külli. Külli, clad in a pair of faded denim blue jeans and a white cotton blouse with a wide collar, adjusted the clasp on her platinum wrist watch as she walked to the door.

Külli opened the door and there was Violet. Vava was wearing a retro Mod poly knit dress that clung to every one of her curves. It was made up of horizontial white, surf blue and bright red stripes. The dress looked good on Violet. She could pull off almost anything. And this Mod dress was really working for her. Vava smiled.

'Gula, no one has seen you in *yonks*. We have all been wondering what you have been up to.'

'Research. I'm working on a paper right now. Flax is at the library. She studies even harder than me these days. I'm *terribly* sorry. The last couple of weeks have been busy ones. Well, come in, Vava. It's good to see you.'

Violet entered. She was a shapely girl. Attractive in her own way, Violet liked to wear eyeglasses to enhance her looks. She owned several pairs. She was wearing a pair of transparent frames when she entered Külli's room. Violet's eye sight, however, was perfect. The glasses were just another tool in Violet's arsenal of tricks she had developed to draw attention away from her imperfections and highlight her positives, such as her slim figure. Violet always came across as attractive and stylish. Even Külli granted her that much.

The flaxen haired Violet sat down on the old leather chair in the corner of Külli's bedroom. She stretched and laid back in it. 'Gula, have you met Gemma's boyfriend yet?'

'What?'

'Gemma's boyfriend. George. You haven't heard? They met almost three weeks ago and have been almost inseparable ever since. He spends as much time in Gemma's rooms in Somerville as his own rooms in Christ Church. Gemma is a frequent guest there now. She makes quite a splash every time she passes through the gates. Gemma is positively glowing these days. She has never looked more beautiful.'

Külli looked at Violet, but said nothing. Her visage was stony and inscrutable. Inside, Külli was experiencing a wave of panic that was moving through her that she had never known. Külli was using every bit of energy she had to stay calm.

'I can't believe Gemma hasn't introduced you. Well, then again, she's been off in her own little world ever since she met him. She is truly, madly,

79

deeply in love with him. *I've never met anyone that was this deeply in love with someone,*' reflected Violet while she gazed out the window at the night sky.

Violet had spent years with someone who had felt exactly that way without ever realizing it. Külli had felt that way about Gemma from the first moment they had met. How could the other girls be so blind to it?

Every syllable of every word Violet said was like a knife stabbing Külli in the heart. Külli was unable to speak, unable to even ask for Violet to stop talking, even though it was killing her. Külli felt as if she was bleeding out.

'Gemma wants to get married as soon as possible. Well, fortunately, they both have agreed to wait until they graduate. George is planning a career in banking, and Gemma plans to have children and write news articles or cook books. Something like that. I don't know. It's so dreadful dull to me. I can only imagine Gemma in the morning serving breakfast to her brood of children; such a gruesome spectacle that will be. What a waste of Gemma's intellect.'

Külli looked out the window into the night sky. The lights were dim enough in Oxford that one could still observe the stars at night, if one only took the time to do it. Külli finally managed to speak. 'Where is Gemma now?'

'She is in her room at Somerville. George is dining with the rowing club tonight. Gemma couldn't go, so she is studying in her room.'

'Where's Poppy?'

'Poppy? Oh, yes, she took the train to London. Her parents are having a dinner party for her brother and his fiancée. They are getting married in June. It seems everyone is planning a wedding but us.'

'I'm sorry, Violet. I have to go. I have to meet someone in 15 minutes.'

'That's alright, G. I understand. It was good to see you, Gula.'

SOMERVILLE

Gemma was lying on top of her bed in a pair of grey cotton track pants and a red hoodie. She loved relaxing in bed while she studied, or leaned up against a mountain of pillows while she ate mushroom soup from her favorite pub, or just lay in bed and listened to the rain against her bedroom window. Gemma liked solitude; sometimes she needed it.

These days, Gemma was in love. Finally. But all had not been unbridled happiness. There remained a very real problem: Gula. How would she break the news to her? Gemma was aware of how impossible situation she was in. Yes. The situation *was impossible*. Gemma had spent as much time thinking about Gula as she had George. With no solution in sight, Gemma had chosen to evade, delay, and pretend. That stance was about to come to an abrupt end.

There was a knock on her door. And Gemma knew exactly who it was.

'Just a minute,' called Gemma. Don't panic. She is your friend. She will understand. You just have to explain things to her and be kind. Everything will be alright.

Gemma opened the door. Külli was standing there. She was crying. Gemma felt a wave of remorse wash over her. Why had she not told Külli immediately?

'Please come in, Gula,' said Gemma softly.

Külli entered. Gemma walked through the small sitting room and into her bedroom. She sat down on her bed and motioned for Külli to sit next to her. Külli slowly followed her. She was crying, almost sobbing. Külli could no longer contain her emotions. She was devastated. Külli sat down next to Gemma and looked straight ahead at the leaded glass windows which lined the bedroom wall.

Gemma's room was only dimly lit by a small reading light on the nightstand.

'I'm sorry, Gula. I know I should have told you. I was wrong. But I didn't know how I would tell you. I'm sorry.'

'I'm the last person to know.'

'I'm sorry.'

'I had to hear it from Violet.'

Gemma closed her eyes and sighed.

'I can't believe you didn't tell me. You've hurt me, Gem.' Külli's face was wet with tears. Gemma had never seen Külli like that. It was almost shocking to see someone Gemma had always considered strong, almost steely, look so vulnerable.

Gemma struggled to find the words to comfort her friend, and most importantly, repair the damage her decision had inflicted on Gula. Gemma lightly bit her lip, but said nothing.

'I love you, Gem. You know that. And you know exactly how I feel about you. You've known that since last year. I know you know how much I love you. I tried to find someone to replace you, but there is no one. It's not your fault. I don't blame you. I don't. I understand everything. I know your heart, Gemmy. I know you don't want to hurt me. I know you would do anything to avoid hurting me,' said Külli softly.

Gemma started crying. She knew where this would ultimately lead.

'I can't bear this, Gemmy. It's too much for me. I knew this day would come. So did you. I think we both felt that some miracle would occur and we would both be spared.'

Gemma could only stare straight ahead, the same direction as Külli, and cry. She was unable to speak. What could she say?

'I *can't* ever see you again,' said Külli.

Those words struck Gemma hard, and suddenly, instantly, panic engulfed her. Gemma grabbed one of Külli's hands tightly. Gemma finally spoke.

'Gula, please don't do this. I need you. I need you more than anyone else. More than even Poppy. You have always been my closest friend. You understand me more than anyone else in the world. I have told you things that I have never told anyone else. You know my secrets. All of them.'

Gemma continued to speak while she was sobbing. Gemma felt as if she were fighting for her life.

Külli pulled her hand away. 'I can't do this anymore, Gemma. You have no idea what this has done to me already. *I am so damaged,*' Külli said in a whisper. 'You can never love me the way I want you to. I know that. But you have found love. I will never know anyone but you. You are moving forward, and I have been left behind. You don't need me anymore. You will be a wife and mother; you will have a family. You have talked about this ever since the first day I met you. It's not fair for me to ask you to give this up.'

Külli sighed. This was harder than Külli thought it would be. 'Gemma, for my own mental health, we have to part. I can't just be friends with you. It's not possible. I know you don't understand. *I don't understand why I can't get over you.* The spell you have over me. The affect you have on me. **I wish I had never met you.'**

*Those words cut deeper into Gemma than any words her own father had ever said to her.*

Gemma didn't have the words to respond. She was at a loss. This, the most crucial moment of her life, and she was at a loss. 'Please, God, help me,' prayed Gemma silently.

Gemma turned to her and took one of Külli's hands in both of hers and held it tightly. 'I love you, G. I know it's not what you want or need, but I do love you, more than anyone else in this world. Even more than George. I mean that,' she said and Gemma started to cry again.

Gemma had never cried harder in her life. Not even at her mother's funeral. Gemma felt a connection to Gula that she had never had with anyone else. But how could Gemma explain it to her in a way Gula would understand?

Both young women were exhausted, emotionally drained, numb.

Külli, always the stronger of the two, (or was she?) decided she would have to bring things to a final end. 'Good bye, Gem. I hope you find happiness. I really do. I never wanted to hurt you either.'

Külli pulled her hand away from Gemma.

Külli then stood up and wiped the tears from her face. She walked towards the bedroom door, and as she was about to cross the threshold, she turned around and said, 'Please. Don't ever contact me again. If you see me in Oxford, please don't say anything to me. I know you won't ever tell anyone why we parted, not the real reason. I know you will protect me. Thank you for that. You are not vengeful. I know that, too. Please tell the girls that I don't want to see any of them again, either. Just say that we had a bad fight, and that I said terrible things to you. Blame me. I deserve it. This is my fault. I'm sorry. **I'm not strong, Gemmy.** I was always the weakest one in the group. I have always known that.'

Külli looked at Gemma sitting on the edge of her bed. Gemma was still crying. Gemma looked smaller, more fragile, than Külli had ever seen anyone look.

Külli turned to leave, and then Gemma began to speak; her voice breaking with emotion as she spoke. Gemma was choking back tears.

'Please, G. Please don't go. Please stay with me,' Gemma said in a strained inconsolable voice.

Gemma bolted up and off the edge of her bed and moved quickly to embrace her. Gemma was sobbing. Külli towered over the tiny young woman that had wrapped her arms around her so tightly. Külli lifted her arms and broke the hold. Gemma grabbed one of her hands, and Külli snapped hers back.

'Enough.'

And with that final word, Gula exited Gemma's rooms in Somerville, and her life.

## 4 PRIMROSE HILL

**Gemma—London—Dinner at Grey's house**

PRIMROSE HILL
October 2018
Winter and Gemma left the theatre and caught a black cab back to Primrose Hill. They arrived home just after 10:30pm. They had planned to have dinner at a restaurant, but both agreed that they would rather just go back to Primrose Hill and have dinner at the house.

Winter paid the cabbie and then led Gemma to the front door. As they walked down the pavement towards the house, Winter scanned the area with his eyes. Gemma noticed, but said nothing. Who were Winter and Grey looking for?

Winter reached the front door and unlocked it. He motioned for Gemma to enter first, and after looking behind him once more, he entered the house and locked the door behind him. He activated the security system and it engaged with an electrical whirling sound. The door's extra locks clicked as the system sprang to life.

Gemma had only been in the house for a few days, but she had quickly noticed the CCTV system, the motion detectors, the reinforced doors, and bulletproof windows. Somewhere in the house, there must be a control room, but where was it?

'Can you cook, Winter?' asked Gemma.

'Not really.'

'You're lucky I can,' Gemma said cheerfully.

She was glad Winter was staying with her. She really didn't want to be alone in this house. Gemma had quickly realized that Grey was more than just an art dealer. But what exactly was he involved in? How bad could it be if Winter was involved in it?

'I'm going to shower and change. I'll be back down in 20 minutes. What would you like to have?' asked Gemma.

'What would you like, Gemma?'

'How about steak? I noticed Grey has several in the freezer.'

'Sounds good,' replied Winter.

Gemma headed up the stairs and down the hall to her room. She turned on the lights and closed the door.

Winter decided to shower too. He was exhausted. He would have preferred to skip dinner and go straight to bed, but he didn't want to miss an opportunity to talk with Gemma. Gemma was a real mystery to him.

How did Grey manage to bag these girls? Every girl Grey had introduced to him in the 90s had been a stunner. And more than that, each one had been special in their own way.

There was Ana, a Croatian girl who could speak four languages. She had also been a champion volleyball player while a student at Zagreb University.

Then there was Lotte, the blonde girl from Denmark. Her hair was so blonde it was practically white. She had a fantastic white smile to go with it.

Of all the girls Grey had dated, the only one Winter had really liked was Cosima. Cosima was the product of an American father and an English mother. She had attended posh boarding schools and had aspired to be a musical actress. She had been the most beautiful of the group (until Gemma had arrived on the scene). Cosima was the only one of Grey's girlfriends that Winter had befriended. She took him to musicals and plays and introduced him to her friends, all of whom were involved in some aspect of theatre. Cosima was really sweet and considerate.

When Winter returned from The North Caucasus in the spring of 2000, Grey told him that Cosima had left him for another man. Grey was really upset about it, so Winter didn't press him for details.

Winter missed Cosima and had tried calling her back in 2000, but both her cell phone and home phone had been disconnected. Cosima had started a new life and had wanted a clean break. Winter could understand that, but still, he felt that he had really connected with her. He had wanted to stay friends.

All of Grey's girlfriends had left him. Winter hadn't been present for any of the breakups, so he wasn't really sure what had gone on. All Winter knew was that Grey couldn't seem to hang onto anyone for very long.

Since Cosima's departure, almost twenty years ago, Grey had had an assortment of shallow, vapid, and self-absorbed (albeit beautiful) girlfriends. Winter hadn't bothered to get to know any of them. He hadn't even noticed they were out of Grey's life until a new girl had shown up. Winter couldn't even remember the name of a single one of Grey's girlfriends since Cosima. Winter highly doubted Grey could either.

Gemma had already started cooking dinner when Winter entered the kitchen. He was wearing faded denim blue jeans, a white undershirt, and a white Oxford dress shirt.

'What do you do, Winter?'

'You mean for a living?'

'Yes.'

'I do a little of everything. I've been working in real estate development and property management in the Carolinas for the last few years. What do you do?'

'I was a fashion editor.'

'Sounds interesting.'

'It was until the management decided I was too old and disconnected from urban culture to continue working there,' replied Gemma gloomily.

'I'm sorry to hear that.'

'How did you meet?' they both started to ask simultaneously. They both smiled.

'You first,' said Winter.

'My friend Violet introduced me. She bought a painting from him.'

'And you clicked?' asked Winter.

'Not exactly,' replied Gemma. How could Gemma tell Winter that financial desperation had driven her towards Grey?

'Okay. Your turn. How did you meet Grey?'

'We met in Croatia in 1992.' Winter volunteered nothing else.

'What were you doing there during the war?'

'It's a long story. It would probably be better if Grey told you.'

So, Winter didn't want to talk about it. I guess Grey gets to tell the official version. Still, Winter probably felt he had to tread lightly with his friend's new girlfriend. Gemma was more curious than ever now.

There was an awkward silence lasting several minutes. Grey might as well have been standing in the room. Grey seemed to control Winter from a far, like some form of remote control. Winter was either loyal to Grey, or afraid of him.

Gemma made dinner. Winter, wanting to be helpful, helped prepare ingredients. He was an enthusiastic and cheerful assistant. When they had finished making dinner, Gemma, clad in a navy blue hoodie and faded denim blue jeans, sat down to have dinner with Winter.

Grey seemed to have total faith in Winter. How many men would leave a girlfriend alone with one of their friends, even their best friend?

'This is really good, Gemma. Thank you.'

'I'm glad you like it. Cooking is one thing I'm good at.'

'I'm sure you're good at a lot of things.'

'I wish I were,' she replied and Gemma sighed.


## Gemma—London—Winter

ZAGREB TO LONDON
Grey slept through most of the Croatian Airlines flight back to London from Zagreb. The deal had gone well. Grey had gotten the deal he had wanted and the client was happy.

He had also secured a Croatian passport. Well, to be more specific, two Croatian passports: one in his legal name and the other with an alias. Either could come in handy.

He wondered how Winter and Gemma had gotten on while he had been away. He wanted them to be friends. That was important. Grey, Winter, and Gemma were to be a set. Similar to the way it had been with Cosima.

Well, Gemma was far better than Cosima. Gemma was special. Grey knew he couldn't mess this up. Gemma was special—unique.

## PRIMROSE HILL

Gemma slowly opened her eyes. She was lying flat on her back in bed above the covers. She stared at the white ceiling and listened to the rainfall hitting the bedroom window of the house in Primrose Hill. What time was it?

Grey would be back sometime today. *Grey.* The mere thought of Grey filled her with apprehension.

Winter was nice, but he seemed to be completely under Grey's thumb. Gemma didn't want to live like that.

Gemma needed financial stability to survive, but Grey seemed to offer only uncertainty. A strange sense of foreboding filled her. Grey was definitely involved in something nefarious. Grey's background was growing murkier by the day. And even more upsetting, Grey seemed to be struggling within himself. Gemma had already experienced at least part of Grey's deviant streak; she worried what else might be in store for her.

Winter didn't seem to be hiding anything; he seemed completely *oblivious* to whatever was going on.

Gemma rolled over onto her stomach. She dreaded having sex with Grey again. The first experience had been horrifying. If only Grey hadn't done *that* to her, it might have been possible to stay with him. Men who do things like that never change. Grey was remorseful, but how long before he reverted to type? Gemma had never found Grey attractive. His deviancy had turned her off completely.

Gemma then suddenly made up her mind. She would leave Grey and move back in with Poppy. Poppy would welcome her back. Poppy was her friend. She hated to impose on her again, but Gemma *knew* that Poppy would understand and help her.

'Thank God I can't get pregnant,' Gemma said to herself. The idea of carrying Grey's baby made her shudder. She would never have been rid of him if that had been the case.

Gemma's heartbreak at discovering her sterility still haunted her. George had been doubly disappointed. George had wanted children just as much as Gemma. The discovery during the first year of marriage had been a devastating blow to both of them. Gemma had cried for a week when the doctors informed her.

It was only after the divorce that she had discovered George had fathered a daughter with one of his co-workers in the City. The little girl was now ten years old. And what of George? He was in a *new* relationship with a woman 15 years younger than him. Gemma wondered if she had had a baby with him too. She hadn't heard anything from or about her ex-husband in almost three years. George had bankrupted her, humiliated her, and walked away. Had fate kept her alive for all this?

SPINNING

Gemma had been spinning out of control like a badly damaged satellite wildly orbiting the Earth since the day the bailiffs had arrived to seize goods three years earlier. She had to get her bearings again. The brief interlude with Grey, as truly terrible as it had been, had also been a traumatic jolt to her system that had brought with it a degree of clarity. Gemma suddenly felt a new found surge of confidence pulse through her. She would survive all of this. She *was* a survivor.

'Okay, now how do I tell Grey I'm leaving him?' Gemma wondered.

He would be terribly hurt. He would feel that Gemma had only used him. Well, that was true. She had used him, but not in the way she had intended. She had agreed to marriage with Grey to survive what she had believed at the time to be an unsurvivable situation. Instead, what she had discovered was that she had no choice but to find a way to survive on her own.

Dependency is even more terrifying than being alone. Dependency means helplessness, defencelessness, vulnerability. It was better to strike out on her own than be dependent on Grey.

Why this moment of clarity now? Why couldn't she have had this revelation three weeks ago when she had first met Grey at Violet's house? Then all of this could have been avoided.

Gemma breathed a sigh of relief. She felt good. This had been a really terrible experience, but she had learned something important about herself from it. She had rediscovered her inner strength. And then Gemma smiled.


## Gemma—London—Grey Returns

POPPY
Gemma left the house in Primrose Hill in her white Peugeot hatchback and headed over to Poppy's place in Covent Garden. The traffic was heavy, but Gemma was so happy that she didn't mind being stuck in traffic. It gave Gemma a chance to organize her thoughts and plan out her future. Yes! Gemma had a bright future after all.

Gemma's bright smile contrasted with the grey overcast day and the rain which pelted her old white Peugeot hatchback.

Gemma had rediscovered her happiness after years of misery. She felt reborn. There wasn't any obstacle that could not be overcome. Gemma now had purpose. She would find happiness on her own. Gemma would get a new job, she would find a flat, and she would find a new man to share her life with.

Why had she not seen the possibilities before that morning? This mystery was becoming less and less important as she slowly approached Poppy's flat in Covent Garden. She wanted to see her dear friend Poppy and share the joyous news with her.

Gemma dialed her number on her smartphone and Poppy answered.

'Poppy!' Gemma said excitedly. 'How are you?'

'I'm good. How are you, Gem?' replied Poppy who was standing in her front room.

'Poppy. I'm sorry to ask you this, but can I move back in with you for a while?'

'Sure, but what's wrong?'

'I'm leaving Grey. It was an awful mistake. I can't stay with Grey another minute.'

'What happened?'

'It's in the past. The important thing is that I have rediscovered my happiness. I have direction again, Poppy!'

'Gemma!' Poppy responded happily, 'Where are you?'

'I'm just a few blocks away. I'm stuck in traffic. I'll be there soon,' Gemma answered while slowly manoeuvring her car through the heavy London traffic.

'I'm coming to meet you, Gemma. I'll be there in five minutes, Gemma. I want to hear about this right now!' Poppy gushed happily. Poppy hadn't heard Gemma talk like this since she was at Oxford. Poppy thought her heart would burst.

Poppy put on her beige raincoat, grabbed her umbrella, and ran out the door of her flat. She walked quickly through the rain and down the pavement until she spotted Gemma's white hatchback slowly inching along in traffic.

She walked briskly through the rain and then knocked on Gemma's car window. Gemma reached over and unlocked the car door. Poppy closed her black umbrella and climbed in. Gemma smiled brightly—Gemma's boarding school smile, not seen in nearly two decades—reappeared. Poppy burst out crying and hugged Gemma.

'Gemma! It's so good to see you smiling again!'

Gemma held Poppy tightly; Gemma could feel tears rolling down her face.

'I love you, Poppy. Thank you for always being there for me. You never abandoned me. Thank you,' Gemma said through tears.

'Tell me, Gemmy, what happened?'

'Things went wrong with Grey. He isn't what I thought he was, or would be. I don't think I even knew what to expect. I just know that he is not my future.'

'Did he do something to you?'

Gemma sighed. 'It's over now. Poppy. I woke up this morning, and I had an epiphany. I have to make my own way in life. I can do it. I have ability. I work hard. Someone will see that and give me a job. I can do so many things. Maybe I could teach kindergarten. I love children, and this would be a chance for me to be around them.'

'You would be good at that, Gemmy. You would be good at anything you tried. I'm sure.'

The car behind them honked.

'Oh! We are almost home,' said Gemma, and Gemma smiled.

'Yes! Home! You are always welcome to stay with me, Gemmy! I love you, and I will always be here for you,' Poppy said happily. Poppy could feel the nuclear levels of energy radiating from Gemma, and she felt 18 again.

## Gemma—London—She tells Grey

COVENT GARDEN

Gemma parked her car in front of Poppy's house. They got out of the car and huddling under Poppy's black umbrella, walked together to the front door of Poppy's small semi-detached Edwardian house. Poppy unlocked the door and they walked inside. Poppy closed the door behind her. Gemma was expecting an electronic security system to engage behind them just like at Grey's. One didn't, and Gemma felt almost disappointed.

Gemma and Poppy took off their rain coats and hung them up in the entry hall. Poppy walked into the kitchen.

'I'll make us some tea, Gemmy.'

'I'll help,' replied Gemma. She wanted to talk with Poppy *right now*.

The two stood in Poppy's tiny kitchen. Poppy put the kettle on, and Gemma looked at her smartphone. It was Grey. He was texting her. *Oh, no.*

'It's Grey. He just arrived at home,' said Gemma.

'Are you going to tell me what happened, Gem? I'm worried about you.'

Gemma sighed and shook her head. 'I want to move forward, Poppy. So many bad things have happened to me. I feel like I have finally turned the corner. I don't want to look back.'

'I understand, but still. I worry, Gemmy.'

Gemma smiled. 'I'm alright. Now I am.'

Gemma put her cell phone down on the counter. 'I'll have to break the news to Grey today. I know he'll be upset.'

'Does his possible reaction worry you, Gem?'

'No. I'm sure he'll deal with it. He has had a lot of women in his life.'

'Really?'

'Yes. Winter told me.'

'Who's Winter?' asked Poppy.

'Grey's friend. Probably his only friend. He's American too.'

'Would you like me to go with you, Gemma? I could say I'm driving you because you're having car trouble.'

'No. Grey would see right through that.'

PRIMROSE HILL

Gemma took the Underground back to Grey's house. It would be faster. She didn't need to bring her car; she only had two small bags to pack.

When Gemma emerged from the tube station, it was still raining. She walked briskly along the pavement. It was a little cold today; she adjusted her raincoat. She should have worn a sweater, but she had been so excited when she exited the house in Primrose Hill earlier that morning that she hadn't even thought about it.

Gemma unlocked the door and entered. She activated the security system, and once again, it surged to life behind her. The electronic locks clicked behind her.

Gemma placed her long black umbrella in the stand next to the front door. Gemma unbuttoned her honey-colored Burberry raincoat, but she kept it on.

'Grey? Are you home?' Gemma called up the stairs.

'Gemma!' replied Grey happily. The slim and somewhat muscular Grey emerged from the kitchen on the first floor. He was wearing a pair of dark gray wool trousers, a white button-down Oxford dress shirt, a white undershirt, and an Omega watch. 'I missed you. How was the play? Are you settling in? Where's Winter?'

'So many questions,' replied Gemma quietly. 'I don't know where Winter is. He has been in and out all week. I think he's trying to buy a house in Portugal. He has been on the phone to a local estate agent all week. Maria has been helping him. I think he is at the estate agency now. How was Croatia?'

'Great.'

Grey walked back into the kitchen, 'Wait right there, Gemma. I have something for you.'

Gemma felt a tinge of apprehension. Grey re-emerged from the kitchen holding something in his hand.

'Gemma, I want to make this official.' Grey opened the small red leather Cartier box to reveal a platinum and diamond engagement ring. Gemma felt her heart sink.

'Grey, let's go into the drawing room.'

Grey looked surprised. 'Okay.' Grey followed her into the white walled drawing room and sat down on the sofa. Gemma sat opposite him.

'Grey. This won't work,' Gemma said softly.

Grey didn't have to ask why. *He knew*. He had destroyed everything all by himself. Why would Gemma want to stay with someone like him? Still, Grey felt like the ground had given way under his feet.

'Gemma. I know I can't make up for what I did. I don't know why I did what I did. No, that's not true. I know what and why I did it. It's inexcusable. I'm sorry.'

Grey sunk down into the sofa. He looked completely defeated. And then, to Gemma's dismay, tears started to roll down Grey's face. Gemma had expected a tantrum, even rage, but not this.

Gemma didn't feel badly for Grey. How could she? **He had raped her.** Okay. She had finally admitted it to herself. Grey had raped her. A wave of devastation seemed to sweep over her, and she started to cry.

Grey looked at Gemma, not intensely, not with the least bit of surprise, but instead with remorse and guilt. Grey found it difficult to speak.

'I have to go, Grey.'

Grey simply nodded. Gemma stood up and walked out of the living room and headed upstairs. Grey did nothing but stare straight ahead.

THE UNDERGROUND
Gemma packed quickly. She didn't want any further discussion with Grey. She felt as if she were escaping a high security prison. Well, wasn't she? She practically ran down the stairs, with her two leather box suitcases (which contained all of her worldly belongings) and opened the door. The security system activated and an alarm went off. Gemma quickly punched in the security code and the alarm deactivated. She exited the house and closed the door behind her. She never looked back.

It wasn't until Gemma took her seat on the subway that she breathed a sigh of relief. She had broken with Grey. It was over.


**Gemma—London—Grey stirs**

PRIMROSE HILL
Grey was sitting in the living room when he heard the front door alarm system being deactivated and the door open. The door closed and then the security system engaged again.

Winter appeared in the entryway facing the open entrance to the drawing room. Winter kept his hair cut like a British army officer. He was clean shaven. Winter was wearing faded blue jeans, a pair of brown leather shoes, a white Oxford button down dress shirt over a white undershirt, and a navy blue half-zip pullover.

'Hey,' said Winter. Grey did not respond. His mind seemed to be elsewhere.

Grey was sitting on the edge of the sofa and was working on something that was sitting on the coffee table. Winter entered the living room and tried to see what Grey was up to. Grey had a book open in front of him. There were piles of paper on either side of the book that looked like loose piles of paper dolls. There was also a semi-automatic pistol lying on the table next to the book. Grey was using a box cutter to cut some sort of pattern out of the open page.

'What are you doing?' asked Winter.

'I'm making a book safe. I'm going to conceal this Yugoslav pistol inside of this dictionary. This way I can carry it in my brief case or even hold it while I'm walking down the street and no one will know I'm actually concealing a gun,' said Grey matter-of-factly.

'Grey. How many people actually use paper dictionaries these days? If the police spot you carrying a paper dictionary, they're going to be suspicious,' Winter said laughingly.

Grey seemed to reflect on Winter's statement for a moment, and then went back to cutting the pistol pattern out of the book's pages.

Winter looked around the living room. Everything felt somehow different.

'Where's Gemma?'

Grey stopped cutting with the box cutter and looked up at Winter. 'She left me. She walked out of here a few hours ago. Did you buy a house in Portugal?'

Winter stood in stunned silence for a moment, and then answered. 'Grey. May I ask what happened?'

'Sure. Gemma left me.'

'Okay. Are you going to tell me why?'

Grey looked blankly ahead. His demeanour gave nothing away. He seemed to be either deep in thought or his mind had just gone blank. It was impossible to tell.

'It's my fault. I finally found someone and I ruined everything. I don't know why I always do things like this. I just can't seem to get things right with women. We have both survived the impossible, Winter, yet something supposedly as easy as getting married has proven elusive to both of us. We are both alone, Winter.'

Winter didn't know quite how to respond. Grey had had other girls walk out on him in the past, but it never really seemed to have bothered him that much. The vibe was palpably different this time. Winter really didn't know what to make of it all.

Grey went back to cutting away at the book. Winter stared at him for a few minutes and then turned around and went upstairs to his room.

**Gemma—London—Külli remembers**

MARBLE ARCH
October 2018
Külli was upstairs in her office. She knew those invoices had to be somewhere in there. She searched through the old metal filing cabinet that her father had used when he was still running the business. She finally made her way to the bottom drawer and pulled it open. Inside were several files and at the very back a slim cardboard box.

'What is this?' thought Külli. She pulled the box out and placed it on her

101

desk. It was an old carboard box from the Royal Mail. On it were several postage stamps with the Queen's image. She looked at the post mark: May 3, 1994. The box had been sent from her old boarding school in Sussex. The sender: Gemma. 'Oh, yes. I remember this,' said Külli to herself.

She opened the box and looked inside. An envelope from a photo lab, a video cassette, and a DVD case (obviously from a much later period). On the DVD case there was a white label which read Sussex 1994. Yes, now she remembered. She had had the VCR cassette transferred to DVD in 2005. However, she had never watched it. Placed in the cabinet, it had been forgotten.

Külli then opened the envelope and took out the photos. The very young teenage faces of her classmates and roommates peered out at her. Photos filled with young smiling girls in All Saints school uniforms and blue cotton tracksuits(with three white stripes). She found several of herself. There was Poppy looking 'dangerously cute.' This one was of Violet, looking posh and imperious in the blue, red, and purple All Saints tartan skirt and white cotton blouse. Another photo showed Külli playing volleyball (she had been really good at it).

And then she found a photo of Gemma. Gemma must have been around 16 at the time. She was so tiny and fragile looking; just like the last time she saw her sitting on her bed that night in Oxford. Külli felt a tinge of sadness as she looked at the photo.

Gemma was sitting on her bed in her school uniform. Spread out in front of her were pictures that Gemma had cut out from magazines of brides in wedding dresses and young children in French baby clothes. Gemma had always said she would dress her children like the French. Gemma also promised to teach all of her children to speak French, and that they would spend their summer holidays at her (hoped for) country house in France.

Fate had not been kind to Gemma.

Then another photo appeared. It was Külli and Gemma together outside. They were standing in the snow. Both wore their navy blue school duffle coats and were bundled up in the blue, red, and purple wool All Saints scarves. Külli towered over Gemma. Both were smiling. And then Külli noticed a small detail: they were holding hands.

Külli couldn't help but think back to the night she had pulled her hand away from Gemma at Oxford and said, 'Enough.' That had been the last thing she had ever said to Gemma, her dearest and closest friend? Gemma, truly, the one being she loved more than any other. And that was the last thing she had ever said to her?

Külli turned the photo over and written in Gemma's florid 18th century style handwriting was:

*I will never forget how happy I was on this day, Gula.*

*Love, Gemma.*

Külli started to cry.

She missed Gemma so much. Not a day had passed that she didn't think of Gemma. Always kind. Always gentle. Always smiling. Always except for the last time she had spoken to her that night in Oxford. Külli—'Gula'—had left Gemma sobbing at the edge of her bed in her rooms in Sommerville.

Gula broke down and cried. She walked over and laid down on the sofa at one end of her office. She literally cried herself to sleep.

DARKNESS
'Madam?' a voice called out from behind the door. There was a gentle knock. 'Are you there?'

Külli opened her eyes and sat up. It was dark. What time was it? She moved through the darkness illuminated by the street lighting outside her Marble Arch house. She turned on the desk lamp.

'Yes. I'm fine,' replied Külli. She looked at her platinum watch: 7:30pm. She had been asleep all day.

'Madam,' replied the voice in accented English, 'Would you like to have dinner in your office tonight? Would you like me to bring it up to the office?'

'Yes. That would be nice, Ivika,' said Külli as she walked over and opened the door.

Standing in the hallway was her black-uniformed housemaid, a diminutive young Estonian immigrant named Ivika that Gula had hired earlier in the year. She was hardworking and trustworthy. She was also very sweet and polite, plus Gula could practice her Estonian language skills with her.

Ivika's blonde hair reminded her of her Oxford classmate, Flax. Flax was now married to the CEO of a chemical conglomerate and had two blonde daughters. Gula and Flax occasionally met for lunch, and occasional romps. Gula smiled.

Ivika soon returned up the stairs with a covered silver tray. She placed it on the desk.

'What would you like to drink, Madam?'

'I have a special container of juice in the refrigerator marked with an 'M'. Please bring that up to me with a large glass. Thank you, Ivika.'

Gula was soon seated at her desk and enjoying her steak dinner. Steak had always been Gemma's favorite. Of course Ivika would have to choose tonight to serve it. Of course.

Gula then opened the DVD case. She hadn't watched the video since 1994. What was on it? She couldn't even remember. Okay, into the laptop. Gula opened the laptop on her desk and continued to eat while she waited for the DVD to load.

The DVD consisted of a montage of home movies that the girls had made on Violet's camcorder in the mid-90s back at their boarding school in

Sussex.

There was Violet practicing her lines for the school play; she was Cleopatra. She was chosen for her inherent regalness and posh demeanor. Her performance had been a brilliant success.

Then Gula appeared playing volleyball. Gemma, Violet, and Poppy could be heard cheering her on—to yet another victory over a rival school. The team had gone undefeated that year, thanks mostly to Gula's athletic ability.

Then a montage of images from outside the school. The girls were running around in the autumn leaves. Violet was sporting her new leather riding boots while stomping around in the fallen leaves. 'Your father makes the most *marvellous* boots, Gula!' gushed Violet.

There was Poppy wrapped in a white bed sheet like a Roman senator reciting Mark Anthony's speech to the Roman crowd: 'Friends, Romans, countrymen, lend me your ears...' Poppy was so cute. Gula melted at the site of the young Poppy earnestly repeating the famous speech.

The scene switched again and there was Gula in her blue cotton track suit (with three white stripes down the sides) and a white T-shirt emblazoned with the school crest on the shirt pocket. Gula could hear Gemma's voice ask, 'Gula, what are you thinking about?'

'Nothing.'

'Oh, come on, G, you must be thinking about something?'

'It's a secret, Gemma.' And then Gula looked directly into the camera and said, 'I am trying to imagine my life after this place. After uni. It's not easy.'

'You are only 16, Gula. I don't think most girls our age have their lives mapped out.'

'You have your life mapped out, Gemmy. You want a husband and a hundred children,' said Gula and she smiled.

'Not that many, G. Maybe 90,' and Gemma could be heard laughing happily.

Gula looked into the camera and smiled.

'Gemma. Let me hold the camera and ask you questions.'

'Okay.'

The video showed a sudden blur and then the camera focused again, only this time Gemma was in the picture. Gemma's young and intensely beautiful face seemed to almost sway on the screen. Her glossy brown bangs partially covered her eyes and Gemma used her soft hand to brush them away.

'Gemma,' Gula's voice could be heard asking,' What will you remember most about our school days in Sussex?'

'My friends. Poppy, Violet, and you; most of all, you.' Gemma then stared pensively into the camera. 'I will miss being able to live in this alcove with my three best friends in the world.' Gemma looked one direction, then another. She stared back into the camera. Gemma's face became serene, and she said very gently, 'I love you, Gula. Please don't ever forget that.'

Gula's voice could then be heard breaking with emotion. 'I love you, too, Gemma. More than you realize.'

Gemma then smiled happily into the camera.

The video switched once more and it showed a group of Sussex school girls, arms interlocked, loudly and happily singing the school song. The video ended.

Gula had been so transfixed by the alcove images on the video she hadn't realized she had started crying while watching it.

## Gemma—London—The Honourable Violet

THE WEST END

November 2018

Violet usually slept until noon. Today was no exception. Sleeping comfortably under layers of white high thread count sheets and a white duvet, Violet was awakened by the gentle ring tone of her smartphone.

'Hello,' answered Violet sleepily.

'Hi Vava! It's Gemma! Awake yet?' asked Gemma who then dissolved into laughter.

'Gemmy. Will you ever change? Just a little?' replied Violet. Violet sat up in bed. 'Why are you calling me so *terribly* early?'

'It's noon, Vava. Poppy and I would like you to have lunch with us. It's been *yonks* since we have had lunch together.'

'It will take me at least an hour to be ready, Gem. Wait for me?'

'Sure.'

Violet spent the next hour bathing and applying expensive skin creams. Violet's strict regimen of diet, exercise, and skincare had kept her looking at least a decade younger than she actually was. Her daily routine also consisted of staring at herself naked in the full-length mirror she had had installed in her bathroom. She was still slim and toned. Violet smiled.

BRIGHT FUTURE

The restaurant was still relatively crowded when the girls arrived at 1:15 in the afternoon. The restaurant was one of Poppy's favorites. Its specialty was Hungarian cuisine. The decor: Hungarian hussar.

The owner, the grandson of a former Hungarian hussar (of the Austro-Hungarian Empire), had always liked the blonde bantam daughter of the 12th Baron. She was outgoing and good-hearted, and she had managed to maintain her 'dangerous cuteness' even at 40. Poppy, a mid level investment banker, had lunch there at least once a week.

Poppy liked the decor, which consisted of red walls adorned with framed 19th century hussar Attila style coats, cavalry swords, paintings, old photographs, and a few hussar caps. And there were always a few Hungarian migrants noisily enjoying their meals.

The restaurant was not expensive by London standards. The owner's father had purchased the small building in the 1940s when the property was dirt cheap. Its location on the edge of London's financial district assured it an eclectic clientele of bankers, hedge fund managers, Hungarian workmen, and the occasional tourists.

The sight of suited and booted British bankers sitting in close proximity to London's shabbily dressed migrant builders always made Poppy laugh and smile.

The food was good, too.

'Oh, Poppy. Why must we have lunch here?' asked Violet. 'It's so…foreign…'

'Come on, Vava. The food is good, and it will be a nice change for you,' replied Poppy.

The waiter seated the girls in the back of the main dining room next to a large window which looked out onto a small garden which featured cafe seating. Gemma sat near the window, Poppy sat next to her, and Violet sat next to Poppy. The white table cloth was set with recently purchased silverware.

The waiter returned with menus and then left them to make their selections.

'Is this menu entirely in Hungarian?' asked Violet. 'Doesn't anyone speak English in London anymore?'

'Not many, Vava,' teased Gemma, and Gemma smiled.

'Is this, well, some kind of meat dish?' asked Violet.

'Yes, Vava,' replied Poppy. 'It's very good. They kill the cow with a large axe out back, so the meat is always fresh.'

'How revolting. You would think the Food Standards Agency would inspect the place and shut them down.'

'It's settled then,' said Gemma. 'I'm having steak.'

'Don't you ever get tired of steak, Gemmy?' asked Violet.

'No.'

'Do Magyars eat steak?' asked a bemused Violet.

'Of course. They just usually eat them raw,' replied Poppy.

'Bloody Huns,' said Violet.

'Oh, come on, Vava. Have steak with us. It's a special occasion,' said Gemma.

'Alright. I'll have a steak too. Medium rare. Happy, Gemmy?' asked Violet and Violet smiled.

The food was excellent. Even Vava agreed. It was also fun for the three of them to sit and chat together in a restaurant after not doing so for years (not since before Gemma's bankruptcy and ruin three years earlier).

The restaurant had largely emptied out by the time their food had been served. Towards the end of the meal, only two of the waiting staff occupied the main room.

Every time the front door opened and closed a cold breeze would blow in.

'So, Gem, what are you going to do next?' asked Violet.

'I'm going to teach kindergarten. I love children; this would be a chance to be around them,' she answered and Gemma smiled.

'Does that pay well?' asked Violet.

'It pays enough,' Gemma replied and she smiled.

'Really, Gemmy. You must think carefully of your future.'

'I know, Vava. But I want to be happy.'

You can't pay the rent with happiness. The real world is what it is.'

'Oh, come on, Vava,' said Poppy. 'Let Gemma be happy. And besides, I believe in Gemmy. I know she will be successful at whatever she does. After all, who wouldn't want someone like Gemma to take care of their children?'

FREYA
Violet sighed. Her own turn at motherhood had been a disaster. Her only child, a daughter named Freya, had grown up to be a rebellious teenager. She was currently in her final year of the same Sussex boarding school that the girls had attended, but was doing poorly academically. Freya had also had a lot of school discipline issues. She had failed to enter Oxford and had instead been accepted by a third-tier university in the Midlands. Freya didn't even like fox hunting. The horror of it all.

Freya modeled part-time and had even appeared on the cover of **Tatler.** Freya's ambition: to become a flight attendant. *Really, Freya?* The granddaughter of barons twice over, and she wanted to serve coffee on airplanes.

Violet had the feeling that Freya had grown up liking the nanny more than her. The Croat nanny, Karmen, had even taught Freya to speak her language. That's how they communicated, in Croatian.

'I wish Freya would speak English when she was with the nanny. I always get the distinct feeling they are talking about me,' she told her husband. 'I'm sure they are,' he replied.

At least Freya was attractive. She could marry a man of means and stop being such a burden to her parents.

Violet had done one thing right in her life in regards to Gemma: she had made her Freya's godmother. Gemma was deeply touched by the gesture. It was especially surprising considering it came from someone as self-absorbed as Violet. Violet had a good heart under all of the posh indifference. It was just hard for even Violet to find it sometimes. Gemma showered her goddaughter with gifts and affection; the affection that Violet seemed incapable of.

Violet's pregnancy had been difficult. She had hated every moment of it. She resented her husband and future off spring for having to endure morning sickness. Her slim figured had been (temporarily) deformed by pregnancy, and she suffered a terrible bout of postpartum depression. Gemma had been there for her and the baby.

Gemma quickly befriended the Croatian nanny and arrived after work almost every day to help care for the infant Freya.

Violet was usually on some form of medication and had refused to breastfeed Freya. Gemma had bottle fed her, bathed her, and had put her to bed. She often sat next to her crib, sang her lullabies, and watched her while she slept. Gemma's affection had earned her Freya's unconditional love. Gemma was more of a mother than Violet ever would (or could) be.

Gemma never forgot Freya's birthday.

Every year she would attend her birthday party. That is, until three years ago, after Gemma's scandalous divorce.

DOWNFALL

The tabloids had had a field day reporting on George Howard's fall from grace. George was the scion of an ancient aristocratic English family. A baron, an Old Etonian, and an Oxford graduate, George was the kind of person the tabloids loved to destroy. And George had given them more than enough ammunition to do it with.

*Old Etonian's Secret Daughter*
*5th Baron Declared Bankrupt*
*Bailiffs Raid Notting Hill Home of Lord*
*Baron's Staggering Gambling Debts Revealed*
*Baron Investigated for Embezzlement of Bank Funds*
*What did the Wife Really Know?*
*Scotland Yard Now Investigating Baroness's Finances*

You see, Gemma had once been a baroness. She had gone from being The Honourable, to Her Ladyship, and now back to The Honourable. However, she was now a dishonoured 'Hon', and most of the other 'Hons' would have nothing to do with her.

Poppy and her family never abandoned Gemma and refused to listen to anyone who told them otherwise.

Gemma's father, a baron, was already an outcast. Her brother was living in self-imposed exile in Hong Kong. He must have been aware of the scandal engulfing his younger sister, but he had remained silent as had their father.

Violet remained loyal as well. Her husband and his family, especially Violet's father-in-law, the 4th Baron, rallied to Gemma's side. Violet, however, being Violet, was concerned about the family reputation and the potential impact it could have on Freya. Freya, after all, was Gemma's goddaughter.

Freya herself refused to endure anyone attacking the good name of her godmother. She had been in several arguments at All Saints in Sussex defending Gemma's honor, including two fist fights (which she had won). It was only through the 4th Baron's intervention that Freya had not been permanently expelled (instead of just suffering a brief suspension) from school.

Freya, slim and blonde like her mother, was as academically deficient as her mother had been. However, she was tough like her grandfather, loved Gemma, and knew she was innocent. Gemma had been George's victim. Her reputation had been ruined unfairly. Freya would never allow anyone to smear her godmother again.

When the trial ended, George was convicted and given a suspended sentence (much to the outrage of the public).

Gemma had been cleared of all wrongdoing. The case against her had been so badly mishandled that the judge felt it necessary to publically state her innocence and apologize to Gemma on behalf of the Crown. The judge also publically derided the moral cowardice of George for attempting to deflect guilt from himself and onto his wife.

None of the newspapers had reported any of that. Why would they? Innocence doesn't sell newspapers; guilt does.

However, for many in London society, 'Not guilty' did not equate with 'Innocent.' Gemma's reputation had not yet recovered, if it ever would.

## A COLD NIGHT
It was shortly after the trial had ended, and on Freya's 15th birthday, that Gemma learned of Freya's true regard for her.

It was on that freezing night in January that Gemma had approached the baron's house in London through a light snow. Gemma was wrapped in a dark blue cashmere jacket (that the bailiffs had also missed) and a fur hat. She looked like a Russian Czarina. Gemma knocked on the kitchen door at the back of the house. Like a servant making a delivery.

'Yes, who is it?' asked the housemaid.

'Hello, Elizabeth. It's me. Gemma. Please give this gift to Freya for me.'

'What? Why not come in from the cold and give it to her yourself, ma'am? Freya is just in the other room.' Then the housemaid, revaluating the situation said, 'Why don't you come into the kitchen and wait. I'll go and tell Freya you are here.'

Gemma smiled, 'Thank you, Elizabeth. I would like that.'

Elizabeth invited Gemma inside and seated her at the kitchen table. 'Tea, ma'am?'

'Yes, thank you. You're very kind, Elizabeth.'

Elizabeth was in her mid-40s and had been with the family since she was a teenager. She had been married, and then divorced. Now she was alone. She understood the plight of a divorcée. But what Elizabeth would also admit to herself was that she had no idea what it would be like to stand falsely accused of serious crimes and be forced to live with the stigma as Gemma had.

Gemma took off her hat and quietly and patiently drank her tea.

'Elizabeth? Are you there?' said the slim brunette in a white beaded dress and wearing a diamond tiara as she entered the kitchen. She turned and froze as soon as she saw Gemma sitting at the large kitchen table. The woman, a 'Hon', and a former classmate from boarding school in Sussex, looked at Gemma with disdain.

*'What are you doing here?'*

Gemma looked down. She said nothing.

'Really, Gemma. After all the trouble you have caused Freya and Violet—everyone. You have the nerve to show up here. How *beastly*. And tonight?'

Gemma stared down into her cup, avoiding eye contact. She said nothing. 'Freya was almost expelled from school because of you. You have no shame.' The woman then turned on her high heels and walked out.

Gemma put her head down into her hands and started to cry.

UPSTAIRS

Freya glided down the hall the way only a posh girl knew how. She wore a tiara her grandparents had had made for her at Cartier.

Her grandfather, the 4th Baron, had made his fortune in what was once called Rhodesia. He had supplied Cartier with an envelope filled with Rhodesian diamonds and a single blue Rhodesian sapphire. All had been beautifully set in the platinum tiara with the sapphire as the center piece.

Freya loved it. Not because of its intrinsic value, but because her beloved grandfather had designed it himself and given the jewellers the stones from his personal collection. The tiara meant something to him. And Freya meant much, much more to him than any collection of stones.

Elizabeth approached Freya and spoke to her quietly. Freya smiled. 'Thank you, Elizabeth. Please tell Gemma I'll be right down.'

'Yes, ma'am.' And Elizabeth disappeared down the stairs.

'Gemma?' gasped Violet. 'Oh, no. Why now? Doesn't she understand discretion?'

Freya turned around and faced her mother. Freya raged at her like one of the furies.

'Mummy! Gemma is your friend! How can you speak about her like that?!'

'It's your reputation I'm worried about, Freya,' replied Violet. 'You have no idea how important a woman's reputation is to her. You need only look at Gemma to see what happens when it is damaged.'

'My reputation? *Or yours?*' sneered Freya.

Violet was shocked. She had never really gotten along with her daughter, but she had never faced attack from her either.

'Gemma is innocent,' said Freya furiously.

'But society has found her guilty. I don't make the rules, Freya. London society does.'

'London is bullshit,' retorted Freya.

'Freya! Who taught you to talk like that?'

'Father said just that the other day when I mentioned Gemma.'

'And I suppose the baron agrees?' replied Violet haughtily.

'Yes, he does. Grandfather told me that London was the only city in the world run entirely on bullshit.'

Violet could only stare. 'So that's where you get it from?' replied Violet.

'I'm glad I inherited a backbone from someone, Mummy. Also, grandfather says that loyalty to a friend is more important than any amount of diamonds or gold. He told me he had learned that the hard way while in Rhodesia.'

Violet's shoulders sank. Her daughter was right. Violet slinked away back down the hallway.

## THE KITCHEN

The kitchen door *burst* open; Freya entered. 'My love!' Freya almost shouted as she entered the room. She rushed up to Gemma, who was still seated at the table with her head down. Gemma, startled, looked up. She was still crying.

'Someone said something! Who was it?! I'll knock their teeth out right now!' Freya, at first furious, broke down and started crying. She knelt down and hugged Gemma tightly.

'I'm sorry. I shouldn't have come here tonight. I've caused you so much trouble. I'm sorry,' said Gemma.

'Please never apologize to me again. You've done nothing wrong. I love you, Gemmy. You raised me. I know that. I will never forget that. Karmen said you were the one who bottle fed me and sang me to sleep. You know that means everything to me.' Freya started to sob on Gemma's shoulder. 'It's not fair, Gemmy.'

'Please stay out of trouble at school. I don't want you to get expelled. I was happy there in Sussex. The happiest I have ever been.'

'I can't say I've ever been all that happy there,' said Freya. 'I guess it was different when you and mummy attended. *Maybe people were just different back then.* I don't know.'

'Do you have any good friends there?'

'Yes. One,' answered Freya.

'That's enough then. Even one,' said Gemma.

Freya took a cloth napkin from the large kitchen table and dabbed Gemma's face carefully.

'It's a good thing you're not wearing makeup tonight,' smiled Freya. 'Otherwise, it would be all over the place.'

'I'm sorry. I seem to cry a lot lately.'

117

'Me, too,' replied Freya softly.

'I have caused so many people so much trouble.'

'You haven't caused any trouble, Gemmy. You've just been *blamed* for everything.'

'All my friends tell me that it's not my fault, but if it's not my fault, *then why is everyone always pushing me away?*' Gemma asked through tears.

'I'll never push you away. I'll always be here for you.' With that Freya hugged Gemma as tightly as she could.

Gemma handed Freya a small box wrapped in silver paper. Freya smiled and hugged Gemma once more. She unwrapped and opened it. Inside was a silver bracelet. It was beautiful.

'Do you like it?' asked Gemma.

'Yes. It's beautiful. Thank you.'

'Please come in and join us. I want you here, Gemmy.'

'I don't want to cause you any more trouble.'

At that moment, Gemma and Freya suddenly heard two women in the hallway commenting loudly. 'I can't believe they even allowed Gemma into the kitchen. If I saw her walking down the pavement, I would cross the street and walk on the other side to avoid having to walk by her.'

Freya turned and hugged Gemma once more. 'Don't listen to them. I, we, the family don't care what anyone has to say. I hate most of these people anyway. Mummy invited them. School alumni from a school I hate.'

'I don't hate the school. I loved it. I was so happy there. My life was so simple back then. I never dreamed I would end up like this.' Gemma started crying again.

'Please don't cry, Gemmy. All that matters is that I love you. *You raised me. And you are a good mother.*' At those words, Gemma cried even harder. Now the whole world was conspiring to take Freya away from Gemma, too.

At that moment one of the catering staff entered the kitchen. 'Sorry, ma'am, but I need to get more champagne.'

'That's fine,' said Freya, and she guided the embarrassed young caterer into the next room. The young girl in a black uniform quickly grabbed two bottles from the far counter and exited through another door. When Freya returned to the kitchen, Gemma was gone.

THE STREET
Gemma walked quickly through the dark and down the snow-covered street leading away from the house.

'Gemma! Wait!' A loud masculine voice shouted from behind her. Gemma stopped and turned. It was the elderly 4th Baron. He was in white tie and tails and moving relatively quickly for a man his age.

'Wait!' the baron shouted again. 'Please come back, Gemma,' the white-haired baron said. "You are always welcome in my home. I purchased that pile with my own ill-gotten gains and I decide who can and cannot visit,' the old man said with a kind smile. The baron was a tall man; taller than even Gula. And like Gula, he towered over her as he spoke.

'Don't let them chase you away from those who love you the most. I've known you for 15 years, to this very day. The day Freya came home from the hospital. It was you who carried her into the house wrapped in her pink blanket. Violet was still in hospital. And Violet has never been much of a mother to Freya. You and Karmen raised her. Mostly you. I see everything that goes on under my roof—and you raised Freya.'

The 4th Baron leaned up against a snow-covered car. 'And I love you for it. We all do. Do you think we would abandon you in your hour of need?' The baron smiled. 'You have done no wrong, Gemma. You have been wronged. It grieves me more than you know.'

Gemma had been deeply moved by the baron's words. She approached him and took his hands in hers. 'Thank you so much for your kind words.' Gemma started to cry again.

'Come now,' said the baron. 'Come back to the house. Freya is waiting for you, as are her parents. My son feels the same about you. Violet, well, is what she is. She is a flawed friend, but she is your friend. She feels terrible about tonight. She's crying her eyes out right now. I think she is experiencing shame for the first time in her life.'

'I'm sorry. I just want to go home. I mean, back to Poppy's. I'm staying with her now,' said Gemma, her voice breaking with emotion.

Poppy's a nice girl from a truly noble family, and I don't just mean their pedigree,' said the baron in his clipped Mayfair accent.

'Please tell Freya I said 'Happy Birthday.' I forgot to tell her that. I'm sorry. Please, excuse me.' And with that, Gemma turned and retreated into the darkness.

## THE RESTAURANT
Gemma was unable to have children. Poppy had remained, sadly, unmarried. What a poor hand fate had dealt the girls.

'When I have a baby, Gemma will be her kindergarten teacher,' said Poppy.

'Thank you, Poppy,' replied Gemma and Gemma smiled.

'I have loads of friends with children and grandchildren. Also, Poppy's boyfriend owns a building in North London he said he would let me use rent free for a year.'

Poppy chimed in, 'Yes. Brian wants to help Gemmy get on her feet again. I'm sure it will be a roaring success.'

'Do you have any investors, Gemmy?' asked Violet.

'Not yet,' replied Gemma. 'But I'm sure I'll get a few,' she said, and she smiled.

Gemma was feeling optimistic. Even Vava couldn't bring her down now.

Vava had never had a job. She really had no idea how people made a living; Violet was someone who had always had money, and that was that. Violet had not volunteered to invest anything. No surprise there. Violet was self-centred in a quite unthinking manner. Vava wasn't a bad person; she was just strangely unaware of the struggles of daily life and felt no obligation to extend a helping hand to anyone.

'Well, Gemmy. I hope things work out for you. If they don't, do try marriage again. You are still beautiful.'

'My reputation is in ruins, Vava,' sighed Gemma. 'What man in London would want me?'

'Plenty!' said Poppy. 'You are the kindest and most beautiful girl in the world, Gemmy. There are plenty of men out there. I'm sure you will meet someone.'

'I'm sorry I introduced you to Grey,' said Violet.

Gemma's happy mood had finally been broken.

'It's over now, Vava. I just want to move forward,' replied Gemma.

An awkward silence descended on everyone. Gemma finally broke it. 'Come on. Let's be happy today. I have made plans.'

'Brilliant ones at that,' said Poppy cheerily. 'Oh, and Gemma,' said Poppy, 'I'm going to invest in your school. I have money of my own. I believe in you. It will be enough to get you started.'

Gemma, overwhelmed with emotion, started to tear up. 'Thank you, Poppy. But I can't accept it.'

'Of course, you can,' smiled Poppy. 'It's an investment. I expect a *terribly large return,*' and Poppy flashed the impish smile she had always been known for.

Gemma reached over and held Poppy's hand. 'Thank you, Poppy. I won't disappoint you.'


## Gemma—London—Money Transfer

THE BANK

November 2018

Gemma looked at her account balance on her smartphone: £48,311. She had spent very little of the money Grey had given her five weeks ago. Should she keep it? No, she couldn't. She needed the money desperately, but it was desperation that had gotten Gemma into trouble in the first place.

Poppy had never charged her rent (Poppy owned the house in Covent Garden outright), but Gemma had always split the utilities with her and bought groceries. Gemma was broke, but she wasn't a freeloader. Poppy knew that.

Gemma had difficulty finding work. She was attractive, slim, well educated, well spoken, and posh. It should have been easy to find work at a high-end clothing or jewellery store, even a high-end car dealership, but alas, her reputation always caught up with her. The owners all feared that they would lose clientele because of Gemma's scandalous past. She knew several of the store owners from her days as the Baroness. They were all truly apologetic. Even backroom work could risk their reputations. Gemma was as unemployable as ever.

Then, one day, a phone call.

'Gemma, this is Alexa,' said a posh voice over the phone. 'Poppy gave me your number.'

Alexa had been Poppy's school girl crush; the one who had broken her young heart (the same heart that Gemma had healed).

`Alexa was married to an extremely successful businessman; she had also become successful in her own right. Gemma hadn't heard from Alexa in a long time. Alexa and her husband had made their fortunes in Asia. Singapore based for almost two decades, they had now returned to London to be near their children who would soon be attending universities in England.

'Alexa? It's been a long time. How are you?' asked Gemma in near astonishment. She hadn't heard Alexa's voice for over 20 years. Her voice sounded somewhat different.

'The important question is: How are you, Gemma? Could you meet me today for coffee? I have an office in *The City*. When are you free?'

'I'm always free these days,' replied Gemma.

'How about today? Could you meet me after lunch? I have to meet a client for lunch, but I'll be free after 1pm.'

'Okay,' said Gemma. 'Could you give me your office address?'

'I'll text it to you now. It will be good to see you again, Gemma.'

'Yes. It will be.'

'And Gemma.'

'Yes.'

'I'm your friend.'

'Thank you, Alexa. I don't hear that very often anymore.'

## THE CITY

Gemma emerged from the tube station that afternoon. It was a cold, overcast day, and Gemma was wearing her blue wool Burberry coat and huge grey and white scarf she had purchased from Zara the day before. Gemma thought it made her look like a Taureg.

She looked at the map on her smartphone. The office was located close to the station. Gemma walked through the financial district, soon the skyscraping glassy Gherkin office building was looming up before her. It stood in sharp contrast to the grey and murky sky that seemed to be almost trying to envelop it.

## ALEXA

Alexa had attended the Sussex boarding school with her for the entire five years. They had never been close; their association was through Poppy. When Alexa moved on to boys, she stayed friends with both. Poppy would always be special to Alexa. Gemma had been the object of much longing for Alexa back at school.

Alexa had followed Gemma's downfall in the British newspapers via the Internet while living in Singapore. She knew that the way Gemma had been portrayed in the press during the scandalous trial was completely untrue. She knew Gemma's character; she knew Gemma would never be a party to fraud and embezzlement. She hadn't been in contact with either Poppy or Gemma in almost two decades. Alexa had been busy with her children, husband, and her businesses in Asia. She deeply regretted not reaching out to Gemma three years earlier.

Gemma entered the lobby of the Gherkin office building and scanned the directory. Hmmm. Ahh, here it is: Millennium Investments.

'Gemma?' a voice from behind her said. Gemma turned around. 'Alexa!' Alexa stood before her dressed in a grey blazer, a light grey pencil skirt, and pale blue cotton blouse (the same color preferred by British financiers). She also wore a pair of glossy black patent leather pumps. Alexa had not aged as well as the other girls, but she was still attractive.

'Gemma. It's good to see you,' she said and Alexa hugged her. 'Come up to the office with me. We're on the 10th floor.'

MILLENIUM INVESTMENTS

Alexa swept into the round offices of her investment company. 'Good afternoon, everyone,' said Alexa. A dozen people all stood and nodded; all of them smiled. That was a good sign to Gemma. Her former classmate probably wasn't a tyrant...

Alexa sat behind her desk after seating Gemma. The walls were nothing but glass. The panorama of London didn't so much as stretch out before them as swirl around them. Gemma was impressed.

'Gemma, I want you to work for me. I need a new office manager. The current manager is pregnant and will be leaving permanently in mid-January. I'd like you to replace her.'

Gemma paused for a moment and then answered, 'Thank you, Alexa. And thank you for having faith in me,' replied Gemma. She fought back against her emotions, but Alexa could read her face, and she understood clearly at that moment how terrible the last three years must have been for Gemma. Kind Gemma. Gentle Gemma.

Alexa reached across her desk and held out her hands. 'Gemma. Welcome to Millennium Investments,' said Alexa, and Alexa smiled. 'Gemma, I'm going to give you your yearly bonus up front. It's not a loan. It's a cash advance,' and Alexa handed her a check in an envelope.

'Thank you, Alexa. You have no idea how much all of this means to me.'

Alexa got up and came around her desk. Gemma stood up and the two former classmates embraced.

'Everyone!' said Alexa as she swept back into the main office 'I would like you to all meet Gemma. She will be replacing Susan in January. Please say 'Hello.'

And Gemma smiled.

## THE BANK
Gemma deposited the yearly bonus in her account: £10,000. **Gemma was back on her feet.** There were still a few good people in the world who were not afraid to help her. She was grateful for her friends. 'Please, God. Let this all work out,' Gemma prayed to herself silently.

Gemma then went to the ATM. She transferred the remaining money back to Grey.

## Gemma—London—Nightmares

### WINTER
Winter dreamed a lot. More than most he thought. But the dreams were almost always bad ones—nightmares, horrific nightmares. Barely a night passed that he didn't have a nightmare.

He rarely remembered what the nightmares were about. When he could remember them, they were usually about being back on a battlefield or in a hellish warzone. He was usually alone and lost in no man's land. Or he was wondering down an empty trench. There was rarely anyone else present in the dream. The sky was usually overcast or it was at night. He could hear the sounds of gun fire and incoming artillery. But there were rarely any other people present. Winter would often find himself running down a trench under heavy enemy fire or lost in the dark. He was always terrified. He felt he was being pursued by someone or something.

Winter often woke up breathing hard, exhausted. Sometimes he would wake up swinging his arms trying to fend off someone wielding a knife.

Sometimes he would dream of being stabbed and wake up with sharp pains in his chest. Once he woke up crying, his face was wet from tears. And

126

sometimes he would wake up and he could feel a powerful and invisible hand plunging a knife deep into his chest. He would have trouble breathing and his chest would be physically sore from the attack.

A few times he had awoken and a sinister presence was still there, standing next to his bed looking down on him with a malevolent expression and wielding a knife. The presence was not human, but humanoid. Winter would blink his eyes and the sinister being would be gone.

Grey would often hear Winter having nightmares whenever he stayed with him in London. He never intervened. He felt it was best to let Winter ride it out. After all, Grey wasn't his mother.

Grey never dreamed of the battlefield. He had stopped being curious as to why a long time ago. Grey rarely ever dreamed. If he did, he rarely remembered it.

Grey had only one recurring dream: Cosima. His former girlfriend. They had dated for less than a year. Cosima was beautiful. She was tall; much taller than Grey. She stood almost four inches taller than him. Grey liked that. Grey liked tall women and blondes; Cosima had been both.

In the dream, Cosima would appear in front of him. She was naked and covered in mud. Her hair was a matted mess of muddy knotted blonde hair. She would look at him with a plaintive expression. She was always crying in the dream. Cosima would look at Grey and then open her mouth to speak. At that moment Grey always woke up.

## 5 PAST AND PRESENT COLLIDE

**Gemma—London—Covent Garden**

COVENT GARDEN

Gemma awoke that morning after the most restful night of sleep she had had in more than three years (since before her downfall). She was lying on her back, wearing her light blue pyjama bottoms (with a white drawstring waist) and a white t-shirt. The duvet had proven too warm, so she had taken off her red hoodie during the night. It now lay at the end of the bed.

The day was overcast and Gemma could hear the rain falling outside. Rain drops were striking the window. She felt great. Rested and relaxed. Her life was finally—hopefully—back on track.

There was a light knock at her door. 'Gemma? Are you awake yet?'

'Yes, Poppy. Come in,' replied Gemma.

'Good morning, Gemmy,' said Poppy happily. Poppy was wearing a white cotton waffle pattern bathrobe and white slippers. 'You were asleep when I came home last night. I wanted to ask you about Alexa. She called me while I was on the way to work and asked me for your number. I hope you don't mind me giving it to her. She said she really wanted to speak with you.'

'She offered me a job at her investment company. I accepted. She gave me a cash advance. I'm going to be her new office manager in January.'

'Gemmy! That's fantastic! I can't believe it! I'm so happy for you!' She sat down on the edge of Gemma's bed and hugged her. 'You deserve to be happy, Gemmy. More than anyone. I love you.'

Gemma started to cry. She was overwhelmed with emotion. The day before, Gemma had been stunned, blindsided by the twist that fate had given her. She had been preoccupied with returning Grey's money and finally ending that horrifying, yet pivotal, episode in her life. Now with Poppy she could finally release all of her pent-up emotions. Gemma sobbed on Poppy's shoulder.

'Thank you, Poppy. You took care of me when others wanted nothing to do with me. I would have died without you. I'm sure of it,' said Gemma through tears. 'Thank you so much,' said Gemma softly. 'Poppy. I have more good news,' she said while wiping tears from her eyes. 'Alexa said she would invest in my private kindergarten. She says she knows a good investment when she sees one, and she wants to invest.'

'Will you stay at Millennium Investments?' asked Poppy.

'Yes, for at least a year. Alexa wants me to gain some work experience in finance and build up my savings working for her. She says that I can set up the school, and when it is ready to launch, she will help me. I can pay Brian rent for his building.'

Poppy smiled and said, 'Brian will charge you a cut rate. He loves you, too, and wants you to be successful.'

Gemma became emotional again and said, 'Brian is good-hearted. I'm glad you both found each other.'

'Brian had better ask me to marry him soon. We've been dating for two years now. I have had to suffer through a string of failed relationships to find him,' smiled Poppy.

'I think he will,' replied Gemma happily.

'What are you going to do today, Gemmy?'

'It's Saturday. Why don't we do something together? I'll be moving out as soon as I can find an apartment to rent. We won't be having any more popcorn and movie nights together.'

A profound sadness came over Poppy. 'I was always happy to have you here with me, Gemma. You are not a burden. I love having you here. It was like being back in school in Sussex. I only wish I had invited Violet to come over and spend a few nights with us. We could have camped out in the living room and watched movies and eaten popcorn together like we had in school.'

'We would need Gula to join us to make it like school again,' replied Gemma. The mere thought of Gula made Gemma want to cry. 'I really miss her, Poppy,' said Gemma sadly. Gemma's blue eyes started to fill with tears—again.

'I miss her too. Gemma,' Poppy paused for a moment and then said, 'I have her phone number.'

'What?'

'I have Gula's cell phone number. I got hold of it last year. She has several accounts at my bank. She lives in Marble Arch. I even have her address.'

'Have you tried calling her?'

'No,' replied Poppy. 'Would you like me to? Would you like to?'

'Yes. I would.'

Poppy got up, crossed the hall, and went into her bedroom. She returned with her smartphone, pen, and a post-it note. 'Here,' said Poppy. I have her number in my phone,' said Poppy as she wrote the number down. She handed it to Gemma.

'Why don't you call her right now?' asked Poppy.

Gemma held the small post-it note with Gula's phone number in her small soft hands. Gula was just a phone call away. With one phone call, Gemma could hear Gula's voice again. She wondered if Gula would sound the same. More to the point, Gemma wondered how Gula would react to her phone call. Gemma hesitated.

'I'm afraid to call her. I don't want to upset her,' said Gemma. She looked almost panicked.

'Gemmy. Gula was one of your best friends. I still don't know what happened between you two that night; you have never really told me. And I have never pushed you on it. But could it have really been that bad?'

Gemma sat on the bed in silence for a few moments and then answered, 'It was my fault, Poppy. I disappointed her. I'm truly sorry about that. I think about her every day, every day, Poppy. I wish I could go back and change things, but I can't,' said Gemma as she got up from the bed and started to pace around in her light blue pyjama bottoms, white t-shirt, and bare feet on the cold hard wood floor of the bedroom.

Gemma was suddenly filled with nervous tension. She was reliving those final moments at Oxford University twenty years earlier. Gemma paced around the small bedroom with her panther like movements. 'I miss Gula so much. I have never stopped thinking about her.'

'Me, neither,' said Poppy. Poppy was curious as to what memories could rouse such a response out of Gemma.

'Gemma. Please tell me what exactly happened that night.'

Gemma stopped pacing and stared at Poppy. No. She could never tell anyone what had actually gone on. Gula would be totally humiliated if Gemma ever revealed what had been going on between them. Gula might have broken relations with Gemma, but Gemma would never betray the confidence of a friend.

'I'm sorry, Poppy. I can't. Please understand.'

Poppy sighed, 'Alright, Gemmy. I won't press you. This is why I didn't give you her number last year. You were always so upset about things; I didn't want to make it worse for you.'

Gemma nodded in agreement. She folded up the post-it note and put it in her daily planner. 'Perhaps later,' she thought.

Gemma sat down next to Poppy on the bed and held her hand. 'Do you think Violet would have agreed to stay over with us and watch movies like we used to in Sussex if we had asked her?'

'No,' replied Poppy, and they both laughed.


**Gemma—London—Freya**

WEEKEND VISIT TO LONDON

Freya took the train to London to stay with her parents that weekend and to see Gemma. While on the train, Freya had time to reflect on her years in Sussex at the elite all-girl All Saints boarding school.

Freya was now 18. Soon, she said to herself, she would be 'free'. Free of the confines of boarding school and ~~her parents.~~ No, wait. Her parents had never really exercised any supervision over her. Her mother seemed completely disinterested in her, and her father was always busy pursuing mining interests around the world.

FREYA

The only really parental figure in her life was her godmother Gemma. And Gemma had had such a horrible time the last few years she hadn't really been able to do that much with Freya. Visiting the school had been out of the question since the trial. Gemma didn't want to cause Freya any more problems than she already had.

Gemma still sent Freya letters and care packages. These small gestures meant a lot to Freya. Gemma would write such sweet letters in her florid handwriting and draw small pictures in the margins. Gemma was a really good artist.

She also mailed Freya chocolate raspberry biscuits that she would make herself.

Poppy would also drop letters into the care packages, giving her all kinds of advice on how to study, wear the school uniform, and which school clubs to join. Freya had taken to calling her 'Aunt Poppy,' which Poppy adored.

Freya was good-hearted, much like Gemma. But while Gemma would endure abuse, Freya would not. Freya had found herself widely disliked and unpopular with her classmates, especially after Gemma's criminal trial. She had grown to hate the school and counted the days until graduation when she would finally be allowed to leave. She had never told Gemma and Poppy what was really going on at school and how she really felt about All Saints. She didn't want to disappoint them.

LOUISE
Freya had only one friend: Louise. Louise was a shy girl from East Anglia, the daughter of an extremely wealthy farmer. She was also an only child. She was bad at sports and hadn't joined any of the school clubs. Louise had been placed in the 'single' room with her three years earlier because no one else had wanted to room with Freya.

Louise turned out to be a godsend.

'I suppose you have heard all about me,' said the blonde haired Freya when Freya entered their room on her return from Christmas break. 'Yes,' replied Louise nervously.

Freya looked at the tiny Louise and said, 'So, what do you think of me in the flesh? Am I an ogre?'

Louise hesitated and then responded, 'No. I think you are beautiful.'

Freya smiled. She had been too judgmental towards little Louise. She had seen her around school for the last couple of years, but, like virtually everyone else there, had never spoken to her. Now Louise was her roommate.

'I guess the school had felt it necessary to sacrifice a virgin to the Minotaur,' quipped one of Freya's classmates to another girl when she saw Louise unpacking her things in Freya's room as the two walked down the hallway of the school dormitory.

The blonde Freya was about 5'9". She towered over Louise who stood about 5'1". Louise reminded her of Poppy, except Louise was a strawberry blonde. Louise had shoulder length hair, but it was kept straight. Louise didn't appear to have ever attempted to style it at all. She was skinny and had brown eyes. She had a pixieish quality about her.

'Louise,' said Freya.

'Yes,' she replied.

'I think we will be great friends.'

Louise smiled. The first time she had smiled since entering the school two years earlier.

Louise was an average student; however, she excelled at writing. Freya later read some of her short stories and was impressed.

Freya was actually quite intelligent. She did poorly academically because she was so miserable. Part of her wished that she would be expelled for poor grades so that she could attend school elsewhere. Alas, her family had fought like tigers to keep her there.

Louise was very sweet. Freya learned that Louise's kind mother had died in a car accident when she was eight years old. Louise had been badly affected by her mother's passing. Her father had taken it even worse. That Louise bore a striking resemblance to her mother only made things worse for him. In turn, he chose to send her away to live with relatives who eventually sent her to boarding school in Sussex to be rid of her. Louise had always been aware of her family's feelings towards her, and it had taken a heavy toll on her. **After all, who wants to be unwanted?**

'First things first, Louise. I want to cut your hair.'

'My hair? Why?'

'Because there is a beautiful girl trapped underneath it, and I need to free her,' said Freya.

'Okay,' said Louise, and she smiled. (That was only the second time she had smiled since entering school.)

Freya washed her hair in the sink in their room and then cut her hair into a short chin-length bob. When Freya was done, she then led Louise to the mirror in their small room. Louise looked into the mirror.

'Well, what do you think?'

Louise started to cry.

'You don't like it?' asked a nervous Freya.

'I love it,' said Louise, and she smiled once again. (Only the third time she had smiled since entering school two years earlier.)

Louise had gone from mop-headed and mousy looking into an adorable school girl. The smile really helped, too…

Louise turned around and hugged Freya. 'Thank you, Freya. You are the only one here who has ever been nice to me. Thank you.' And Louise began to cry.

Freya knew just what to do: What her godmother would do. She smiled and told Louise that she would always be her friend and that nothing would ever change that.

Both girls had finally found a friend.

## Gemma— London—New Apartment

THE CITY
Poppy's boyfriend Brian helped Gemma find a small flat near the financial district at a moderate price (which means it was still expensive, but not as expensive as similar places in the area). The building owner, a fellow Old Harrovarian, had agreed to rent the small one-room flat to Gemma without a deposit and at a cut rate. Brian had made a Herculean effort to locate the small apartment, and it had paid off.

The apartment was in a large red brick and concrete building that had once been a warehouse. The two-storey building had been portioned into no less than 30 units. Each unit was tiny (400 square feet) and was composed of one small room with a built-in kitchen and a tiny white tiled bathroom. One wall of the tiny flat had been sheetrocked over and painted white, and the opposite wall was made up of a series of windows. The windows were divided into two halves: the lower half had been frosted and the upper portion of the window had been left clear. This was supposed to provide a modicum of privacy. Most of the residents had installed curtains. The hardwood floors had been sanded and resurfaced. They gleamed nicely. There was a metal door at one end. This block of flats was considered luxury housing in London.

Gemma was thrilled. 'Thank you, Brian,' said Gemma happily. 'I love it. And I'm close enough to the Gherkin to walk to work.'

'That will be quite a walk, Gemma,' replied Brian.

'I can walk to my office in only 20 minutes,' beamed Gemma. 'I like to walk.'

'But, Gemma, you can't walk home at night. This is London, not Sussex.

And even Sussex isn't all that safe anymore,' said Brian wistfully.

'I'll take the Underground at night. It's only two stops,' responded Gemma.

'Why not drive, Gemma?'

'Parking is expensive at the Gherkin. I want to save as much money as I can,' said Gemma, and she smiled.

'Alright,' replied Brian. 'Do you need any help moving in?'

'Almost everything I own is in my luggage,' said Gemma pointing to the two leather box suitcases sitting on the mattress in the corner of the room. 'And I have a box of bedding and housewares being delivered to me today that I ordered online. I'm all set.'

Brian smiled and nodded.

He turned and walked to the door. As he unlocked it, he turned to glance back at Gemma. She was tiny, 5'3" (at best), only slightly taller than Poppy.

Brian couldn't help but think that Gemma was somehow different than she had been just a couple of months ago. Gemma seemed even more fragile than she had been before. Like something had broken in her and couldn't be repaired. Gemma remained kind and friendly, but she was somehow much more guarded. Something had happened. Brian didn't know what. He wanted to ask Poppy, but he decided against it. Poppy was extremely protective of Gemma. Brian couldn't help but worry about Gemma.

Brian was aware of Gemma's former boyfriend, but he had never met him; neither had Poppy.

Brian said goodbye and left Gemma behind in her apartment. He felt guilty about the rent that Gemma was paying for such a tiny space, but it was half the price the other tenants were paying.

At least the building had a good security system.

## Gemma—London—Alone

### THE APARTMENT

Gemma was slowly getting settled into her new apartment. The first night had been a sleepless one. She alternated between lying in bed and pacing back and forth around her apartment. After three years of drifting, she was finally back in a space she could call her own. It was a strange feeling.

She looked down from her second floor window onto the street next to her building. Cars were parked up and down it. It was partially illuminated by street lamps. Beyond it, the London skyline flickered. London had changed a lot during Gemma's lifetime, but it was still her home. She could think of no place else she would rather live. And most importantly, this is where her friends lived.

Gemma's mind was filled with memories and flashes of emotion that night. It seemed that Gemma's brain had suppressed a lot of things in the last three years, and now, alone in her own apartment, they were emerging one by one. Sometimes Gemma would feel her face and realize that she had been crying; at other times she would lay in bed and just stare out the window or at the ceiling.

Gemma was a different person now. She missed the old Gemma, the carefree Gemma, the trusting Gemma, the happy Gemma. Gemma knew that nothing would ever be the same. Too much had happened. She had survived physically, but had been badly damaged emotionally.

Gemma still held out hope for a normal life. She wanted to find someone and remarry. Being married was important to Gemma; she didn't want to be alone. She couldn't have children, but she could still construct a home life with someone. Or could she? Had normality been stolen from her? Could she ever trust another man again? Or was she so damaged that that would be impossible? Why had fate given her George and Grey? What had she done to deserve all this?

Gemma was exhausted from pacing around the apartment. But she couldn't stop. At least she didn't have to work tomorrow. She wouldn't start work for five weeks. She had to use this time to pull herself together. Fate had given her one more chance. Perhaps this was her last chance?

One memory haunted her more than any other: that night with Grey. No other event had so traumatized her. Gemma wondered why she had reacted to it so slowly. Was it some sort of defense mechanism? Now the memory of that night came to her in painful jolts. Sometimes she would start crying uncontrollably. She took four showers that night. Or was it five?

## Gemma—London—Pistol

The glossy black car was idling at the curb when Grey exited his office in Primrose Hill. It was late. He opened the door and got in. Grey fastened the shoulder belt and nodded to the driver. The Audi A6 pulled away.

Grey had a lot on his mind. He had a lot to do before the meeting tomorrow night. He sat in the front seat in silence. The driver said nothing either. He was focused on the road ahead.

They left Primrose and made their way across central London, turned north and soon they found themselves moving through Croydon. By that time, it was late, and the streets were nearly deserted.

Grey reached into his coat and pulled out a handgun. 'Yugoslavian,' he said to the driver. 'I brought it back with me. I haven't fired this in a long time.' Grey turned the pistol over in his hands and examined it.

'Turn right at the corner,' he said. The driver complied. The driver signalled and the car turned. 'Pull over and stop,' ordered Grey. The driver did just that, but he left the car idling. The street ahead was partially illuminated by the Audi's headlights.

Grey scanned the street up ahead and behind. He took out a map and looked at it. Someone had marked it with red ink and yellow highlighter. 'There isn't any CCTV on this street. The CCTV cameras on this street have been disabled by the locals.' Grey smiled. 'I guess they don't want anyone to see what they are up to.' Grey scanned the map carefully. 'The next two blocks have had all of their cameras disabled too.'

Grey looked at the driver and said, 'Turn off your headlights. Drive straight, and then take a left. Go two blocks and then turn them back on.' Grey motioned to the driver and ordered, 'Go.' The car moved forward. Grey lowered the electronic window on the German sedan and his hand went up. Blam! Blam! Blam! Blam! Grey was firing the Yugoslav pistol out the window of the car and into the terraced houses that lined the street. 'Speed up,' said Grey calmly. 'Blam! Blam! Blam! After each shot, a window shattered.

The car reached the end of the street and turned. The headlights were still off. The car then accelerated. The driver turned on the lights and sped away.

'The pistol works just fine,' said Grey calmly.

The driver laughed. 'It's good to see you again, Grey,' the driver said in a Yorkshire accent. 'I would die of boredom without you,' he said with a smile.

The car made a clean getaway.

## Gemma—London—Winter returns

MARIA
After several weeks in Portugal, Winter finally returned to London.
He had purchased a small stone three-bedroom house in northern Portugal. It sat on two acres, had a stone well, and dozens of olive trees. The stone house needed work. It needed to have a new electrical system installed as well as having the plumbing upgraded. The house was located in the mountains. It was relatively cool in the summer and there was snow in the winter. He really didn't like hot weather, but Portugal was affordable. After all, he didn't have Grey's income. He had to economize where he could. And besides, the new electrical system could easily support air conditioning.

Winter had heard nothing from Grey while in Portugal. That was not unusual; Grey would often go silent for months at a time. This time Winter felt things were different. Grey had never acted in the manner he had been acting in when Winter last stayed with him in London. Gemma's departure from his life had affected him badly. Grey seemed to be lost in thought, perhaps dwelling on something. Most likely it was Gemma.

Yes, Gemma was an amazing girl. Winter had never met anyone like her. Winter had only wished that he had met her first. Then, perhaps, well... Nevermind.

Winter had gotten a lot of help from Grey's Portuguese housekeeper Maria. It was Maria that had spoken on the phone and written emails to the estate agency in Portugal. Winter wanted to do something to thank her for her help. He decided to give her a really nice gift. But what? Cash would be best, he thought. Yes, cash might be considered a bit vulgar, but in this economy, it was more appreciated.

Winter decided on an $800 pearl ring from Mikimoto (Maria deserved something really nice) and $2000 in cash. Winter was generous. His mother had taught him to be so.

Grey knew Maria's ring size ('Are you planning to marry my housekeeper?'), so buying the right size ring had not been a problem. Winter had had the blue leather boxed ring gift-wrapped in the dark blue wrapping paper and light grey ribbon of Mikimoto at the London Mikimoto store and had a white envelope of money wrapped with a blue ribbon.

Winter arrived at the house in Primrose Hill. He tapped in the security code, but the door failed to open. Grey had changed the code. (Who else could have done it?) Winter rang the doorbell, and Maria, clad in a black uniform, opened the door.

'Senhor. It's good to see you again. The house is ok?' asked Maria.

'Yes. Everything has gone through. I'm now the proud owner of my own Private Idaho.' The song reference was lost on Maria. She arched an eyebrow. Winter smiled. 'Americans are difficult to read sometimes,' thought Maria. She invited him in.

Maria was well educated, polite, and quite attractive. She came from a middle-class family in Lisbon. Beyond that, Winter knew very little about her. He didn't want to pry into her private life. Winter knew that Grey treated her well, and Grey had a degree of trust in Maria that he had in few others. He also knew that through Maria, Grey had become fluent in

THE INSEPARBLE GANG OF HAPPY GIRLS

Portuguese.

'Yes, he changed the code. He does that sometimes,' said Maria.

Maria was like a phantom, a ghost that appeared fleetingly. She had no set work hours. Grey would usually text her and tell her what days and how many hours a day she would work. The start and finish times were always different. Grey sometimes held business meetings at the house and he felt having Maria out of the house ensured confidentiality. Well, that's what Grey had told Maria.

Maria didn't mind. She was paid a flat salary of 40 hours a week. Grey paid on the dot and he gave her bonuses throughout the year. If she worked late, he paid her overtime and gave her money for a taxi home. Grey looked out for Maria. Maria was very loyal to Grey. Grey knew that. And loyalty was everything to Grey.

Maria loved the Japanese pearl ring, and when Winter handed her the envelope, she became emotional. 'This wasn't necessary, Senhor,' she said. Winter assured her that it was. Grey, being from the Carolinas, would expect nothing less from Winter, a fellow North Carolinian. No doubt, when—if—Grey heard about it from Maria, he would approve.

'What would you like for dinner, Senhor?' Maria asked happily. 'Please. Anything you like. I will make it,' she said in her nearly perfect English.

'How about a Portuguese dish,' replied Winter.


**Gemma—London—Bosnia**

BOSNIA SUMMER 1992
DERVENTA
Grey peered through his binoculars. It was difficult for him to see through the smoke that had engulfed the village in the distance. He could see half a dozen Serbian tanks smashing through houses and destroying them. Grey and the group of young soldiers around him could hear the steady rattle of machine gun fire and tank shells exploding in the village as the Serb tanks fired point blank into farmhouses and barns. He could see at least a

hundred Serbian regulars and irregular paramilitaries moving around the ruins of the village. The chetniks would be busy for awhile.

'So, this is 'ethnic cleansing,' thought Grey.

The international community had imposed an arms embargo on the Croatians and Bosnian Muslims. While the Serbs and Montenegrins were heavily armed and fully equipped, the Croats and Bosnian Muslims found themselves virtually defenceless. They were forced to fight with whatever weapons they could find.

Whatever the motivations of the international community were, only one thing was clear to everyone: Bosnia and Croatia had been abandoned.

The average Serbian or Montenegrin soldier was usually clad in body armor, often wore a steel or Kevlar helmet, carried grenades, a machine gun (with as much ammunition as they could carry), and often had a pistol. They also carried a wide variety of knives, which they used to torture and murder the unarmed and defenceless civilian population.

The average Croatian Catholic or Bosnian Muslim soldier usually carried a rifle and was lucky to have more than 30 rounds of ammunition.

So lopsided was the fire power ratio in favour of Serbia, it was miraculous that either Croatia or Bosnia had survived at all. It was a combination of Croat and Bosnian bravery and Serbian cowardice and battlefield incompetence that had spared both nations.

The average soldier fighting for Bosnia or Croatia rarely had any kind of body armor or even a helmet. They usually wore BDU camouflage, black leather combat boots, and a black t-shirt. Some wore berets, but most went bare headed. They also wore the leather and canvas ammo belts of the former JNA (Jugoslav National Army).

Grey's platoon was no exception. None of his men wore body armor or a helmet. All of them wore a variety of camouflage BDUs they had been issued in their former armies. Some wore berets (of The French Foreign Legion and British Paras). They all carried machine guns, but most had only a couple hundred rounds of ammunition (at best). All of their weapons and ammunition had been taken off of the bodies of dead Serbian 'soldiers' they had killed in battle. These were the conditions that Grey and his unit of foreign volunteers had been forced to fight under.

'Okay. All the villages in this area have been overrun by the chetniks. We have to make our way back to the river and try to escape. The front has completely collapsed,' Grey told his men matter-of-factly.

'Taffy,' Grey called out to the young Welsh volunteer. Taffy had been wounded in the arm by an exploding RPG round earlier in the day. Taffy, heavily bandaged, exhausted, and leaning against the wall of a house and standing in the shade of a large leafy tree, looked up at Grey.

'I want you, Andrew, Robbie, Eugen, and Alexandre to head for the bridge. Eric radioed me a few minutes ago. The rest of the platoon is already on the other side of the river. Only take weapons and ammunition. Leave the rest of your kit here. Stay off the roads. Move through the forests and behind the hedges. It will be dark soon. The chetniks don't like to move around at night. It will give us a chance to escape,' said Grey.

He motioned towards the group, several of whom had already been wounded and were bandaged, and they departed, heading towards the river.

He looked at a young American volunteer and a slender blond Englishman. 'You two, come with me.' He looked at the young Englishman (an ex-hussar) and said, 'Go get the car; you're driving.' The young athletic soldier from Yorkshire sprinted away towards the front of the house.

Grey looked over at the 23-year-old American. Winter had entered the fray for strictly moral reasons. The Serbs and their Montenegrin twins were involved in what they had euphemistically called '**ethnic cleansing**,' a term the chetniks had coined themselves. What it really meant was **mass rape** and **genocide**. Every fiber of Winter's being railed against it. He hadn't joined out of a sense of adventure, but of moral conviction.

(Though by 2006, when Montenegro declared independence, the way the Montengrins talked, you would have thought they had never even heard of Bosnia.)

'How are you, bad boy?' said Grey and he smiled. 'We're going to get Tommy from the field hospital, and then we'll head for the bridge too. If we are lucky, we'll have time to escape. If not, well, okay,' he said and Grey smiled.

'So, Winter, when did you graduate from college?' asked Grey.

'May,' answered Winter.

'So, how do you like life in the real world?' asked Grey.

'So far, so good,' replied Winter.

Grey smiled. He liked Winter. He was different from the others.

Grey, only 24 years old, had left the French Foreign Legion little more than a year earlier. He had spent last year fighting in Croatia against the Serbs, and now that the war had spread into Bosnia, he was here.

Grey was not very tall, but he was extremely fit and physically tough. His blue eyes radiated strength and confidence. Grey was wearing camouflage BDUs, leather JNA webbing, a Romanian bayonet in a bakelite scabbard, several fragmentation grenades, and the green French Foreign Legion beret with the metal circled winged armed dextrochere of the 2e REP.

Several of his former Legion comrades were serving in the ranks with him. A few of them were on the other side fighting against him.

The local Croatian military commander in Derventa had put him in charge of a platoon of two dozen foreign volunteers. Most of his unit was British, some of them former Paras. There were also several Frenchmen, one Dutchman, an Irishman, a young Austrian from Graz (who would be killed while leading a counter attack later that summer), and to Grey's surprise, a couple of other Americans. Which reminded him, where was Brandon?

Brandon, an American, was another interesting case. A former investment banker in his late 20s, he had ventured to Bosnia for reasons known only to him.

Grey never asked anyone why they had volunteered to fight here because he really didn't care. They were here, he was their commander, and they had a war to fight.

Brandon was easily one of the best soldiers in the unit, a true warrior. Grey was impressed. Brandon was a hyper-aggressive soldier. He was fearless. He often headed off behind the lines at night alone or took his Yugoslav sniper rifle and headed off to look for prey—all alone. Today was no exception.

The old Renault 4 pulled up and they got in. 'Okay, let's get Tommy,' said Grey. The compact car pulled out of the farmyard and accelerated down the tree-lined road. The sound of machine gun fire was intensifying. Artillery shells were literally whistling overhead. Smoke clouded the road.

'Faster!' shouted Grey.

The driver shifted gears and the white car bolted forward. The car headed down the road and then the driver noticed something: he was driving straight towards an oncoming JNA tank. He slammed on the brakes and turned the wheel sharply. The white Renault skidded off the road, through a wooden fence, and came to rest in a small farmyard. As the car stopped, a tank shell exploded behind them.

'Outta the car!' shouted Grey, and everyone exited and ran towards a small wooden barn. They entered the small structure and with their guns at the ready; they waited.

A few minutes later a group of Serbian paramilitaries appeared. Most of them were bearded and wore body armor. They were all heavily armed.

Grey motioned to the two men with him to wait.

The soldiers—if you could call them that —swarmed into the farm house shooting wildly. A grenade detonated inside the house and the windows on one side of it exploded outwards.

The Serbian chetniks exited the house. They looked shabby in their Yugoslav army camouflage uniforms. Many of them wore large black patches embroidered with white eagles and human skulls and most had mangy beards. These people were Serbian paramilitaries, not known for being either brave or having good hygiene.

They were talking amongst themselves while two of them started searching through the car. They found something in the backseat and started arguing over it. The other Serbs stood around smoking cigarettes.

Their apparent commander, a bearded and pot-bellied middle-aged man wearing a black šajkača hat embroidered with a human skull and crossbones, was shouting into his handheld radio. They were not a very professional lot. This was to be their undoing.

Grey made a few hand motions and then the three men in the barn opened fire on the group of Serbs with their machine guns. It was over in seconds. A couple of the Serbs had tried to run away, but were cut down before they could make it out of the farm yard.

The Westerners ran forward and quickly grabbed whatever clips of ammunition, grenades, and even machine guns and pistols they could find. They then turned, heavily laden with machine guns, grenades, pistols, and leather and canvas ammunition belts, and bolted.

The three men ran down a heavily-forested dirt path that ran behind a row small white houses. Machine gun fire seemed to follow them, along with a barrage of artillery shells.

Derventa had been lost. Now it was up to fortune to save them.

THE FLAG
Brandon had spotted the Croatian flag fluttering on top of the T-72 tank as he came over a small tree lined embankment. The Croatian tank had been knocked out. Its crew was undoubtedly dead. On top of the tank was a large Croatian flag fluttering in the wind. Brandon knew just what to do: He waited.

It wasn't long before a group of steel-helmeted Serbian soldiers came along. They approached the tank. One of them jumped up onto it and grabbed the Croatian flag—a trophy—just as Brandon had predicted would happen. He looked through the scope of his sniper rifle. He aimed, held his breath, and fired. The Serb holding the Croatian flag was hit, dropped the flag, and fell dead from the tank. Brandon then headed for the river.

He made it across just in time. So did Grey, Winter, and the young English soldier from Yorkshire.

Tommy did not.

## Gemma—London—Louise

EAST ANGLIA
December 2018
Louise was now 18. In just three years she had gone from lonely, shy, and plain to being outgoing, cute, and happy. She owed everything to Freya. Freya was the only friend she had ever had. And as far as Louise was concerned, if she was the only true friend she would ever have, that would be enough.

The train rumbled into the train station in East Anglia. It was cold— freezing cold. Louise carefully buttoned the warm wool petrol blue coat that Freya had given to her for Christmas the day they had left for winter break. It was probably expensive. Louise was also wearing her red, blue, and purple striped wool All Saints scarf and a pair of faded denim blue jeans.

Louise had made Freya a Christmas card two weeks before. She had sketched out the school buildings, the village church, the local post office, and a drawing of their 'single' room on the cover. Written on the front of the card was MERRY CHRISTMAS, FREYA. She had colored it with colored pencils she had purchased in the village store near the school.

Louise had spent two days working on it secretly in her room. She had kept it hidden in her drawer. She wanted to give Freya something special.

Louise took a photo of the two of them smiling in their room and glued it on the inside page of the card. In the photo, they were wearing their school uniforms (the red, blue, and purple tartan skirts and fitted white cotton blouses of All Saints) and sitting on Louise's bed together. The card had a simple caption:

*To: The girl who saved my life.*

*From: Louise*

Freya loved the card. When she opened and read it, she started crying and hugged Louise. 'Thank you, Louise. You saved mine, too.' Freya told her it was the nicest Christmas present she had ever received.

Unbeknownst to Louise, Freya now kept the card in a plastic envelope in her safety deposit box along with her platinum Cartier tiara in London.

Louise received a very small allowance from her father. He had neither seen nor even spoken to Louise, his only child, in over five years.

If it hadn't been for Freya's help, Louise would never have been able to do anything at school beyond eating in the dining hall and wearing the school uniform. It was Freya who bought her lunch at the village cafe. It was Freya who paid for train trips to London and theatre tickets in the West End. It was Freya who took her out to dinner at posh and popular London restaurants. 'I don't mind spending my money on you,' Freya would say with a smile any time Louise looked embarrassed or uncomfortable.

And it was Freya who told Louise how cute, intelligent, and talented a writer she was and it had filled her with confidence.

Now, after more than five years, Louise would be reunited with her father. Was this really such a good idea?

The train rumbled into the station. People disembarked and were greeted by waiting friends and relatives. Louise wandered around the train platform looking for her father.

She finally sat down on one of the benches on the platform. It was freezing cold. The crowd quickly dispersed. She was alone. Louise wrapped her scarf around herself a little tighter. She waited.

No one ever arrived to pick her up.

After three hours of sitting outside in the freezing cold, Louise used her smartphone and telephoned for a taxi to take her 'home.'


**Gemma—London—Freya spends the weekend**

VICTORIA STATION

Freya arrived at Victoria station that evening. She was excited. She hadn't seen Gemma or Poppy in almost three months. Or her mother.

What had been happening in their lives? Her mother had mentioned something on the phone a few weeks earlier about Gemma having become engaged to an American art dealer, but when she wrote and asked Gemma about it, Gemma had avoided discussing it at all.

Her letters the last few weeks had been strangely vague, and for Gemma, very short. Really, they were more like brief notes than letters. If Gemma were engaged to be married, why had she not mentioned it?

Freya disembarked from the train. She wasn't carrying any luggage; it wasn't necessary. She had a separate wardrobe at the house in the West End. She kept loads of clothes at her grandparents' home in Mayfair, as well.

The blonde Freya walked confidently across the station: more like a soldier than the granddaughter of a baron. She had inherited her military bearing from the soldiers in the family line.

The temperature seemed to be dropping by the minute. She looked out of the large front entrance of the train station; it was starting to snow. Freya was wearing faded denim blue jeans and a navy blue quilted Burberry jacket.

'Freya!' a voice called to her from behind. She turned around. Gemma. Gemma looked fantastic. She was wearing what looked like a new coat. It was knee length, dark blue, and had silver buttons. Gemma was also wearing faded blue jeans and a pair of black leather Chelsea boots.

Gemma radiated happiness. She smiled and approached Freya with her arms outstretched. 'Welcome home, Freya,' said Gemma happily. They embraced there in the middle of the station. When Freya looked at Gemma's face, she was crying.

'What's wrong, Gemmy?'

'Nothing. I'm just so happy to see you,' Gemma replied, and Gemma started to wipe her tears. Freya then touched her hand gently and said, 'Wait. Let me help you.' Freya dabbed Gemma's tears with a tissue she took from a small and slim cardboard container in her jacket pocket. 'It's a good thing you don't wear makeup that often, Godmother. Otherwise, it would be all over you,' said Freya, and Freya smiled.

'I'm alright now, Freya,' said Gemma. After regaining her composure, Gemma smiled and then asked, 'Where to first?'

'Could I stay the night at your new flat, Gemmy? I'd like to spend some time alone with you.'

'What about your mother? Violet is expecting you,' replied Gemma.

'She left a message on my phone. She's spending the weekend in the country. Something about shooting birds,' responded Freya, and she sighed.

Violet had never been an attentive mother. Gemma, however, never had an unkind word for Violet. She always hoped that Freya and Violet would be able to repair their relationship. Violet, was, well, Violet. Allowances had to be made for her. 'Hopefully Vava will come around one day,' thought Gemma.

Gemma smiled. 'Alright then, Freya. Let's spend the night at my house. It's tiny, but I think you will like it. It's in a brand new development. You can still smell the fresh paint in the building. And I have a great view of the street,' she said, and Gemma laughed.

THE CITY
Gemma drove by Violet's house, where Elizabeth was waiting with a small overnight bag for Freya. After exchanging hugs with the housemaid, they departed for the financial district in Gemma's white Peugeot hatchback.

Gemma was a cautious driver. She never drove fast and always wore her seatbelt. She also used her turn signal and never attempted to run red lights. Gemma played by the rules. Not that it had ever done her any good.

The white hatchback made its way through the snow, along streets decorated with twinkling Christmas lights and illuminated store window displays. London, at Christmas, was particularly beautiful. Gemma loved Christmas. Freya loved Christmas and Christmas lights and decorations, too.

Freya loved the new apartment. It was tiny, *but it was Gemma's.* She was happy that Gemma had started to turn her life around. Gemma had a new job—a good job—and a flat of her own.

Gemma had purchased a small ceramic Christmas tree that had arrived in the mail already decorated with multicolored lights and a white plastic star at the top. The tree glowed nicely when it was plugged in. Gemma liked to sleep with the tree on as a kind of nightlight. The blue, red and white lights cast a pleasant glow in the tiny flat. The foot tall ceramic Christmas tree now sat on the low white (and nearly empty) bookcase that served to separate the queen sized bed from the rest of the small open space that made up Gemma's flat. Gemma lived alone. This small ceramic tree was enough to make Gemma happy. Freya really liked it too.

Taped to the white bookcase were beautiful Christmas cards from Poppy and Brian, Poppy's parents, and her brother James and his wife. Freya and Louise had both sent handmade cards, which Gemma really loved. Vava and her husband had also sent a nice card. There were also half a dozen cards from former co-workers and other classmates from Oxford and All Saints.

Vava's in-laws (The 4th Baron and Baroness) had sent her a beautiful Christmas card, along with a smart wicker Christmas hamper from Fortnum and Mason (which included a soft, luxurious picnic rug) filled with wonderful things like raspberry preserves, pistachio and clotted cream biscuits, apricot, cranberry & port chutney, and Portuguese Wild Lavender honey. Whether it was a card, a wicker hamper, or a book, Gemma appreciated being remembered.

Gemma always remembered to send Christmas cards to her remaining friends. She enjoyed selecting cards for people. Sometimes she made the Christmas cards herself. Gemma enjoyed it. She was a good artist and would use colored pencils to decorate the cards she made. The friends she sent Christmas cards to now were the people who had not abandoned her during her downfall. A true friend was worth more than any amount of money. In the end, all that is really left is the love and friendship one shares with others.

Once they arrived, they both changed into flannel payjama bottoms (Gemma's were pale blue and white stripes with a white drawstring waist; Freya's were grey and had a white drawstring waist) and light grey slippers. Gemma wore her red hoodie and Freya a light blue v-neck cashmere top.

Freya was happy to be with her godmother again. She was also happy to see Gemma moving forward with her life again after so many reversals.

Occasionally Freya would hold Gemma's hand while she talked, or she would hug her. She couldn't seem to grasp that Gemma was now standing before her. And in Gemma's own apartment.

Freya took out her smartphone and waved her hand. Photos came up.

'Here is Louise. Isn't she cute?' beamed Freya happily. 'And here she is playing cricket on the village green. Well, she is trying to play,' laughed Freya. 'I think she just likes wearing cricket whites,' said Freya, and she laughed again.

'Louise is really cute; she reminds me of Poppy,' said Gemma. 'You look really nice in the school uniform,' said Gemma. 'I'm glad they haven't changed it. Tradition is so important. Oh. Is that who I think it is?' asked a startled Gemma.

'That's Külli Vahtra. Mummy said you used to share an alcove together. She told me that Külli had fallen out with everyone at Oxford. She said that she could never figure out why Külli had spent the last two years at Oxford University avoiding her former roommates. She said you all of you had been the best of friends at All Saints. Mummy said that she really missed her, and that without her, all of you felt somehow incomplete.'

'Your mother said that?' asked an astonished Gemma.

'Yes,' replied Freya. 'I know. One doesn't think Mummy would even take notice, but she has. Külli must have been special if Mummy misses her.'

'Külli is one of the school's more accomplished alumni. She came and spoke to us about entreprenuership. She is really tall, isn't she?' said Freya.

'Yes,' replied Gemma. 'She was the captain of the school volleyball team. She was the best athlete the school had ever fielded,' said Gemma. 'I really miss her,' said Gemma reflectively.

'She drove a new Porsche Cayman to school. It was silver. It was beautiful. I was thinking about asking for one, but since I will be attending a rather dismal uni next year, I decided not to,' said Freya.

'I didn't buy a car until after I graduated from Oxford,' said Gemma. Cars are just extra work. Best to buy one after you graduate. 'Have you decided on what you will study?'

'History,' replied Freya.

'That's good.'

'I'm still going to become a flight attendant,' said Freya. 'I like the uniform and the idea of jetting around the world on airliners. Mummy can't understand why I want to work at all. She thinks I should just find a wealthy husband and marry right out of uni.'

A look of saddness suddenly came over Gemma's face.

'I'm sorry. I didn't. I mean...'

'That's okay,' responded Gemma. 'I know your heart.'

'I'm sorry, Gemmy. There is nothing wrong with marriage.'

Gemma smiled faintly. How could she blame Freya for avoiding marriage right out of uni? Gemma's own marriage had been disasterous, even ruinous. What kind of example did Gemma really set for anyone? Gemma had become a cautionary tale.

Changing the subject, Gemma smiled and said, 'What would you like to have for dinner? You must be famished.'

'Anything, Gemmy,' answered Freya smiling. 'I'm just happy to be with you.'

Gemma walked over to the narrow silver SMEG refrigerator (which had come with flat) and opened the door. The refrigerator light came on and Gemma peered inside. It was filled with all kinds of ingredients she had purchased just the day before.

'How about...'

'Steak!' they both said at the same time, and laughed. 'Yes! Good idea, Godmother! Everytime we have steak at school, I think of you,' gushed Freya happily, and Freya smiled.

Gemma and Freya spent the next hour preparing ingredients and cooking dinner. The flat was filled with the aroma of delicious food. Finally, they placed the assorted dishes with steak, salad, bread, and soup on the kitchen counter. They served themselves and carried their porcelain plates to the small dinner table in the middle of the apartment that also served as Gemma's desk.

'So, tell me. What did Külli talk about?' asked Gemma while they were having dinner.

'She gave a presentation on her company. She talked about her father and how he had come to England as a refugee from the Baltics after the Second World War. He had started a small business making leather boots and shoes. It was Külli who expanded the business into clothing and kit. She also showed us a few photos of her days at school.'

THE PRESENTATION AT ALL SAINTS
'My father always stressed to me the importance of getting a good education,' said Külli.

Külli was standing on the stage in the school theatre. She pressed the remote control and the Power Point image changed. It was a black and white photo of a prosperous pre-war Estonian family. Her father's parents looked happily into the camera. Külli's father, a young boy of about eight or nine, smiled happily, too.

'My father grew up on an estate in Estonia. My grandfather owned a large workshop producing leather footwear. He taught my father how to make boots himself. My father said my grandfather had been one of the best bootmakers in the country. Before the war.'

Külli reflected to herself for a moment. What she didn't tell her youthful audience was that her grandfather, a highly decorated former soldier who had served as an infantry officer in the Imperial Russian army during World War One and later fought for Estonian independence, had been taken away by the Soviet Red Army in 1939 and never seen again.

'Learn as much as you can, girls. Go to university, but also, *learn a trade, too.* It's important you have the ability to earn a living. Be flexible. Learn foreign languages; then you can work anywhere.'

Külli stood ramrod straight. She was still beautiful. A strict diet, proper skincare, and exercise had kept her looking surprisingly young at forty. She attracted longing gazes from more than a few Sussex school girls in attendance. Külli smiled knowingly, and a few in the audience smiled back.

Külli continued the presentation.

'I modelled while at Oxford, and after I graduated, I moved to France and continued my modelling career. You might ask, how did modelling help me run the family firm? Well, whatever you do, wherever you go, you can learn something. I learned as much as I could about the fashion industry and even photography. Never miss an opportunity to learn something from your betters. I never have. By the time I left modelling at 24, I had learned a lot. I returned to England with knowledge and list of contacts I would call upon in the future.'

Külli showed the girls a few of her fashion photos. One of her with honey blonde hair drew a lot of attention from the assembled school girls. 'And here is one of me in Paris for Chanel in 2001. It was my last show.'

Külli pressed the button on the remote and a photo of her in the school uniform appeared on screen. She was only 17 when the photo had been taken. The girls were transfixed. Here was one of their own.

'I learned so much here in Sussex,' said Külli. 'I can honestly say that my time here was the happiest of my life.'

Külli pressed the button on the remote once more, and another photo appeared. It was of Poppy, Violet, and Külli. They were on the playing field and dressed in the school's blue cotton tracksuits (with three white stripes down the sides of the track pants).

'I had so many good friends here,' said Külli as she turned back to face the audience. 'These photos are all so precious to me,' and then Külli pressed the remote button once more.

'Photos take you back to a certain place in the past. They help you remember. It's like travelling back in time,' she continued.

Külli then turned back to look at the photo that had appeared on the screen while she had been talking. It was of her and Gemma. *How did that get in there?* Külli froze momentarily. She looked at the photo of her and Gemma. They were at the bottom of a snowy hill. They had just sledded down it together. They were still sitting on the sled together; Gemma was in front and Külli sat behind her hugging Gemma. They were both laughing. Külli felt tears welling up in her eyes. 'Be calm, Gula,' she said to herself. The power; the effect, the spell that Gemmy still held over her was incredible. It wasn't magic. It was something pure: love.

Külli fought like a tiger to regain her composure. She turned back to the assembled school girls. She stood fozen. Overwhelmed by memories, Külli could only nod and say, 'Thank you.'

The girls applauded enthusiastically.

THE APARTMENT

'The photo of you and Külli was amazing. I gasped when I saw you on the screen. You were so young *and happy*. I've never seen you smile like that, Gemmy. Sussex must have been amazing back then.'

'Yes. It was,' answered Gemma quietly.

THE STREET

Just beyond the second floor windows of Gemma's new flat was a glossy black Audi. It was parked in the shadows, faraway from any of the intermittent street lamps which lined the pavement. Behind the wheel was a slender middle-aged driver wearing a black leather jacket.

Standing next to the car was Grey.

So this is where Gemma now lived. He scanned over the building. He then saw Gemma's white hatchback parked along the edge of the street. He approached and looked at the parking sticker: UNIT 9A.

**Gemma—London—Breakfast at Gemma's**

THE APARTMENT

Gemma awoke to the smell of frying bacon. Freya was standing next to the stove wearing gray flannel pyjama bottoms and a white t-shirt. Along the counter were plates of scrambled eggs, sausage, baked beans, fried Portobello mushrooms and tomatoes, and toast: a proper English fry up—albeit unhealthy.

'Almost done, Godmother,' said Freya as she glanced over and noticed Gemma raising her head from the oversized white pillow. Gemma inhaled deeply and smiled. 'That's *marvellous,* Freya. Thank you.'

On this particular morning, Gemma had not awoken to rain and overcast skies, but to glorious sunshine flooding into her flat. The skies were blue with only a few white clouds moving slowly across the London skyline.

'It's the least I can do, Gemmy. Did you sleep well?'

'Yes. And you?' she asked.

'I slept very well, Godmother.'

'I'm glad you stayed over. It's good to have you back, Freya. I missed you.'

'Not as much as I missed you, Gemmy.'

Gemma smiled. She was so happy to have her goddaughter back with her. Freya was a sweet, kind, good-hearted, thoughtful girl. She was also brave. Gemma admired her bravery. Gemma hoped that Freya would find a husband that made her happy. Freya deserved to be happy.

Gemma felt terribly guilty about all the trouble Freya had gotten into because of her. It really bothered Gemma. Freya had never told Gemma how isolated and miserable she had become in Sussex because of the fallout from Gemma's trial. But Freya *had told* Karmen, her Croatian nanny.

Freya knew that Gemma was being crushed by the trial and the betrayal of so many of the people around her; she didn't want to add to her burden. But Freya had to talk with *someone*. Freya knew that Violet was incapable of providing her a shoulder to cry on; it just wasn't Violet's nature.

Freya had made many tearful phone calls to Karmen in the field behind her dormitory, hidden behind a screen of trees that separated the dormitories from the school chapel. When Freya spoke to Karmen it was always in the flawless Croatian that her nanny had spoken to her growing up.

Karmen was now employed raising the children of the 4th Baron's only daughter.

Karmen was always kind, understanding, and, sympathetic and Karmen's words always had a calming effect on her. Freya had begged Karmen to never tell her godmother about her phone calls to her. Karmen had agreed, but last year when she met Gemma at the baron's house in Mayfair, she broke down and told her. Karmen felt that Gemma should know. She wanted Gemma to know about Freya's fierce loyalty and the misery she had endured because of her.

Gemma had been aware of some of what had been going on at All Saints, but not the extent. Gemma took the news badly, but she was grateful that Karmen had told her. She was grateful to Freya for her absolute loyalty and devotion.

'We raised her right, Gemma,' Karmen said in her accented English.

Now Gemma was doing all she could to make it up to her. She loved Freya more than any being in the world—even more than Poppy, Violet, and Gula. *Freya was hers.*

'Gula. Where have you been all these years?' She thought to herself as looked across the room at Freya, who was happily preparing them both breakfast. Gemma thought about her every day. She deeply regretted that Gula had missed out on having a relationship with Freya. They would have gotten along swimmingly—Gemma was sure of it.

Freya had the same underlying toughness that Gula had. Both girls were good-hearted, but they didn't suffer abuse helplessly like Gemma. Gemma was gentle. It wasn't in her nature to fight back.

Freya finished cooking the bacon and placed it onto a folded paper towel on top of a plate. She then took a porcelain plate from the drying rack and brought it over to Gemma, who was still lying in bed.

'Breakfast is served, Madam. But, serve yourself,' said Freya with a smile.

'Thank you, Freya,' replied Gemma happily. 'You're a good goddaughter, and I'm sure, an excellent chef.'

## 6 GREY IN GANGLAND

**Gemma—London—Tommy**

MANCHESTER

December 2018

'The French Foreign Legion is like no other unit in the world. No combat formation is as well-trained, well-disciplined, or well-equipped. We are the most efficient fighting force in the world. And what sets us even further apart from other combat units is that we are loyal to the legion, not any country. 'The Legion is my country.' Isn't that right, Grey?' said the man in Slavic accented English.

'Yeah, I suppose,' answered Grey nonchalantly.

'And it is loyalty to each other that makes us special. Different,' the man continued. Sometimes when he spoke, he would throw in the occasional French or Serbo-Croatian word. 'Don't you agree?' he asked.

'That's how it should be,' replied Grey.

'We served in the Legion together. We were in the same battalion, the same platoon.'

'But different squads,' added Grey casually.

'Yes. But a platoon is a small unit. We trained, ate, slept, and even bathed together for years. I know you well, Grey.'

'You think so?' replied Grey.

'Yes,' answered the man.

'Do you remember your corporal?' asked Grey.

'My corporal? Ah, I had a few, Grey,' the man replied.

'No, you didn't. The three years you served in the platoon with me, you had only one corporal. I can't believe you don't remember his name.'

The man looked around nervously. 'Oh, yes. You mean Tommy?'

'Yeah. Tommy. An Englishman. From Blackpool. So, you do remember him,' replied Grey.

'Yes,' the man answered, smiling nervously. 'I remember him.'

'He was fair to you. He was a true professional. A true soldier. A true legionnaire,' said Grey sharply.

Grey then looked directly into the fat Serb's eyes.

'Why did you torture him to death?' asked Grey nonchalantly.

'Torture?' the Serb retorted. 'I have never tortured anyone. Whoever told you that is a liar,' the Serb replied. There was a definite air of desperation in his voice.

'No. No, you tortured Tommy to death in Derventa in 1992. He had been shot in the shoulder. You found him lying bandaged up on one of the beds in the house near the school. You found him there. Wounded. And you and your men dragged him out of the house and started torturing him. You cut him up alive. You have bragged to so many people about doing this ever since. More than one of them has told me the same story you told them. You bragged that Tommy survived torture for almost two hours. He was tough as nails, wasn't he?' asked Grey.

The man Grey was talking to was on his knees. His hands had been bound behind him with rope. Several of the fat Serb's tobacco-stained fingers had been broken. He was shirtless. He had been savagely beaten. One of his eyes was badly swollen and blood was still coming from his broken nose and bloody mouth. He also had a deep gash in his forehead. Blood covered his face. His body was covered in an array of Serbian White Eagle tattoos and Serbian Chetnik emblems and slogans. He was fat, bull necked, and his balding head was shaved. He had tattoos on his neck as well. He was in his early 50s, but he looked much older. A life of excess had taken its toll on his body.

'They are all lying, Grey. You know me. *You know me.* I was in Derventa with my unit. But Tommy wasn't there. He was never in Derventa. I would have found him and helped him if he had been there,' replied the fat Serb.

'I know he was there,' said Grey casually, as if he were talking about the weather. 'I know he was wounded.'

'That's not true, Grey. Whoever told you that Tommy was in Derventa is a liar. A legionnaire would never betray one of his own.'

'I know he was there,' said Grey.

'Grey. Please listen to me. Tommy was nowhere near Derventa. I heard he was fighting in central Bosnia, not Derventa,' replied the fat Serb.

'Every time one of you chetniks opens your mouth, a lie falls out,' said Grey. 'I have never met a more two-faced, deceitful group of backstabbing bottom feeders like you in all my life. How your kind has survived this long, I will never know.'

'Grey. You have to believe me. Tommy wasn't there. I swear on my daughter's life.'

Grey looked at the fat lump who was on his knees in the basement of an abandoned factory outside of Manchester. He sighed. 'I know Tommy was there.'

'No, he wasn't, Grey! I swear it! I swear it! I swear it on the life of my daughter!' the fat man said desperately through tears.

'I was the one who took him to the field station to be treated,' said Grey.

The fat Serb froze. He looked at Grey. Tears streaked his bloody and badly swollen face.

'I was on the other side of town when the Serbian army rolled in. We were heavily outgunned, outnumbered, running out of ammunition, and being overrun. We were ordered to retreat. I tried to make it back to Tommy, but

I was told by the others that the Serbian chetniks—you—had already captured that part of Derventa,' continued Grey without the slightest trace of emotion.

'So, all of this has been about Tommy? You lured us out here to get revenge?' the fat Serb asked through broken yellowish-brown teeth.

'Nah,' said Grey. "I lured you and your gang out here to get your share of the loot.'

'You have it,' replied the fat Serb. 'You have all of the jewellery,' he said.

A few feet away from the fat Serbian gang leader were four of his heavily-tattooed Serbian gang. They had all been badly beaten and were bleeding profusely. They were all bound and gagged. They had all been stripped down to their underwear. They were lying on the filthy concrete floor of the abandoned factory. Their mouths had been duct taped closed. One of them was trying to scream, but his cries were heavily muffled.

Surrounding Grey and the heavily bound Serbian gang members were four other men. They all carried Kalashnikovs and wore ammo pouches. Two of them had pistols as well. They all wore body armor over there civilian clothes. They stood motionless, like pieces of iron. These were some of Grey's men. All of them had fought alongside him in Bosnia. All of them had known Tommy.

'I don't have all of your money,' said Grey. 'I want all of it.'

'Grey. I don't have any more money. You have over four million dollars in jewellry right there.'

'Two million. Tops,' replied Grey coldly. 'I want the rest. I want the cash in your secret bank account. Yeah, I know about it.'

'Grey,' pleaded the fat Serb. He was in a lot of pain. He was losing blood. 'I don't have a secret bank account. I'm just a humble man.'

Grey slung his machine gun over his shoulder and took out a small notebook. 'Here is the account number. I got it from one of your former comrades—who you stabbed in the back and left to rot in jail in Spain. He gave me the account number. He said you had memorized the bank code. He said there was at least a million dollars in it.'

The fat Serb looked at Grey and started to cry. 'Grey, please believe me. I don't have a Swiss bank account.'

'Who said it was Swiss?'

The fat Serb looked down. 'Please, Grey. You have all of the loot. Just let me go. Please.'

'I want your money.'

Grey picked up a shovel and walked towards the Serb. 'Give me the bank code number, and I won't smash in what's left of your face,' said Grey matter-of-factly.

The fat Serb looked up. 'Grey. So, this is about business? Right? And we are businessmen. Right? So, let's make a business deal.'

Grey yawned.

'If I give you the bank codes, will you let me go?'

'Sure,' answered Grey.

'Really?'

'Sure. I just want money.'

'You don't want revenge for Tommy?'

'So, you admit you butchered him?' asked Grey.

'Yes,' replied the fat, heavily-tattooed Serb.

'Okay. You give me the bank codes, and I'll let you go. A deal is a deal in my book. Everyone knows that,' replied Grey.

'Thank you, Grey.'

'You're welcome. The codes.'

The fat Serbian recited the bank codes from memory. One of Grey's men tapped it out on an expensive tablet computer. The man looked up at Grey. 'Transfer complete,' the man said with a Dutch accent. 'Four million dollars, Grey.'

Grey looked down at the fat Serb.

'Kill them,' Grey said nonchalantly.

Two of Grey's men picked up the recently purchased pickaxes they had brought with them and calmly hacked the four bound Serbs to death. The fat Serb screamed the entire time. When the four gangsters were dead, the fat Serb was crying, screaming, and begging for his life.

'Grey! We had a deal! We are businessmen!'

'We are gangsters,' replied Grey calmly. 'And you murdered our comrade,' said Grey coolly.

Grey picked up the shovel and started swinging it at the fat Serb. He didn't stop until the man had been decapitated.

'Alright. Let's bury them as quickly as possible. I have to meet someone for lunch tomorrow in London,' said Grey.

And Grey felt better.


**Gemma—London—Grey reverts to type**

PRIMROSE HILL
December 2018
Grey had had a good week. He had tied up some loose ends, killed some people who just needed killing, and had made a lot of money doing so.

He sat at his desk in his office in London and gazed out the window. The Park outside was windswept, filled with leafless trees, grey, and dismal. Winter in London was not exactly wondrous. But there was one element of this godforsaken city that Grey liked: Gemma.

Grey at fifty-one had survived the unsurvivable; achieved the impossible, and surmounted the insurmountable. His grasp had exceeded his reach. He had punched above his weight and won.

And yet, Grey felt hollow. He was alone. Grey had spent decades alone. It hadn't bothered him when he was younger; he always had women when he wanted them. But he had never had a woman worth keeping.

Gemma was from another world.

It had been lust at first sight for Grey. But, then, well, something changed in him. Gemma had a nature that he liked: gentle, intelligent, well-educated, cultured, and *posh*. Gemma was one of those unattainable women that men dream about having. Only, in Grey's case, he had captured one. And then he went and wrecked everything.

Grey opened his desk drawer and took out the Purple Asprey bag he had purchased almost three months earlier. He opened the bag and took out a purple box. He opened it. Inside was a bracelet made of a colourful variety of precious stones set in 18 carat white gold. The bracelet's name: Chaos.

Grey examined it carefully. What craftsmanship. And, all things considered, what an apt name for the relationship he had had with Gemma. Chaotic was the best way he could describe it.

Grey was ambitious. He was in the process of expanding his ~~business~~ criminal empire. He had dozens of reliable and battle-hardened men he could call on at anytime. He had connections in Scotland Yard who tipped him off to any potential investigations. They also supplied him with invaluable information on rivals. He had access to millions of dollars, and, most importantly, a respectable facade as a successful businessman.

**Yes, a facade**. He was a fraud, like *hordes* of others in London. Grey wondered if anyone would ever see through it. And if they did, would they even care? **As long as the money kept flowing**, no one really cared in this city. That was the fundamental truth that Grey had used to get everything he had wanted in London. Everything, that is, except for Gemma.

This was the interesting part about Gemma. As far as Grey was concerned, *he had purchased her.* Gemma's friend had set them up hoping that the rich

American would fall for her and marry her. Take care of her. Pay her bills. Grey had wanted a wife straight out of Burke's Peerage, a member of the English nobility, and he had been offered one. She was for sale.

He was hoping for a decent looking woman with a nice accent. 'She graduated with me from Oxford.' So, she would probably have a posh accent. Grey hadn't really expected that much from Violet's description; his expectations had been low. **However.** When he met her, he couldn't believe his luck. Luck? No. This was fate. *This was meant to be.* Grey had met the woman that he had always dreamed of having. No. Gemma was beyond what he had ever hoped for. She was ~~attractive~~ beautiful—stunning, articulate, well mannered, well educated, posh, and **a member of the club**—that is, of the nobility. Gemma was a blue blood. And, there was something more about her. Gemma was fragile. She was unique. There was something about her which made her desirable. Grey couldn't quite quantify it, but he knew that unidentifiable quality was within her. And he wanted it. And he wanted her.

And, as far as Grey was concerned, *they had made a deal.* She had agreed to marry him. He had spent money on her. Gemma was an investment —his greatest investment. Yes, Gemma was his. *He had a right to her.* Gemma was the one who had broken the contract, not Grey.

Grey stared out of the window of his office. He saw a young woman getting out of a silver Volvo. She was blonde and was helping her young daughter out of the backseat. The woman looked *posh.* That was the kind of woman he wanted. And he wanted to have a daughter like the little girl that the woman was now holding hands with and walking to the front door of her house across the street. He wanted the life of the man who lived in that house. And Grey decided then and there that he would.

**Gemma—London—Social Media**

LONDON
Grey sat at the computer in his office. He never used social media. He knew better. Social media served no other purpose than to destroy one's privacy and invite trouble.

Grey had acquired sophisticated and expensive software that allowed him to freely access social media platforms. The software had paid for itself many times over. Grey used it to track his enemies, select victims for home invasions, and locate people.

Grey had also learned something else: that even if some of his rivals were smart enough to avoid using it, their children were not. And his enemies weren't always savvy (or watchful) enough to keep their children off of it.

Maxim had been one such individual. He had been one of the Russian mafia's most vicious enforcers in London. A former FSB agent, he had known better than to use any kind of social media. He knew his enemies were looking for him. But his daughter Mila wasn't as clever.

He had told her not to use social media, but he had never checked up on her. She had ignored him and was on several different platforms and bragged constantly about her family's wealth, beautiful homes, and expensive cars.

Every time that spoiled brat got a new tattoo, a piece of jewellery, or a handbag; Mila would rush to post it on half a dozen social media sites. Mila couldn't have a meal or even drink a cup of coffee without downloading a photograph of it on the Internet.

She loved using the real-time features offered on the platforms. The 'look at me' mentality of that little braggart was insufferable. It had been useful to Grey.

Mila had supplied enough information on her father's whereabouts that Grey and his gang were able to track him, his new girlfriend, and Mila to a restaurant in Central London.

Mila had been live-streaming, bragging to her followers about how expensive the meal had been, when bursts of machine gun fire from across the street had riddled her father and his young Montenegrin girlfriend with bullets.

Mila had also been hit. She bled to death on the street. Her smartphone landed at an angle just inches from her head when she collapsed and it had live-streamed her death onto social media. Mila's slow death went viral.

Now Grey was using this illegal and dangerous software to find information on Gemma. Gemma didn't use social media, but Violet did. Freya had set the page up for her mother so that she could stay abreast of her activities at school. Violet rarely, if ever, accessed it. Violet had never posted anything, and her media page listed only three followers. One of them was her strikingly beautiful daughter Freya. Grey hadn't known that Violet even had a daughter before he found her online. Gemma had never mentioned her to him.

Freya was extremely active on social media, posting a lot of photos on her page. There was only one photo of Violet. There were a lot of Freya and a petite strawberry-blonde girl named Louise in their school uniforms at Freya's posh boarding school in Sussex. Freya appeared to be as posh as her mother Violet. And while the blonde-haired and blue-eyed Freya bore a resemblance to her mother, she had a warmth about her that Violet lacked.

There were also pictures of Freya and Gemma with an attractive blonde woman who looked to be in her mid-30s—Poppy. Poppy appeared in several photos with one or the other, or all three of them together. Each photo had additional information posted under each of them. There was one of Gemma, Poppy, and Freya standing in front of Poppy's silver Citroën hatchback. That had been extremely helpful to Grey.

There were several photos of Gemma, Freya, and a woman named Karmen. These photos drew Grey's attention more than any of the others.

There must have been dozens of photos featuring Freya at various stages of her life.

One was of a very young and intensely beautiful Gemma holding the infant Freya, wrapped in a pink blanket, in her arms. Gemma radiated happiness. She was smiling. Grey had never seen Gemma smile like that.

Another photo showed a very young Freya wearing a school uniform. Gemma and Karmen were standing on either side of her and holding Freya's tiny hands.

The slim and attractive Karmen was wearing a brown uniform with white gloves and a brown hat with a large 'N' embroidered on it.

In another, Karmen was adjusting an elementary-school-aged Freya's bright yellow raincoat in the stone entry hall of a house. Karmen was wearing the same brown uniform. Grey recognized it as the kind worn by graduates of England's premier nanny training college.

There was only one of Violet. In it she was walking with Freya outside of a stable. They were both wearing blue hunt jackets and beige breeches—fox hunting outfits. Violet wore beige gloves and was carrying a hunting whip. Freya must have been about 11 or 12. Violet and Freya both looked uncomfortable walking next to each other. Freya looked like she would rather be anywhere but there.

In one photo that Grey particularly liked, Freya—she looked to be 5 or 6 years old—was wearing soft pink pyjamas and sitting in Gemma's lap and gazing happily up at her. Gemma was reading her a bedtime story. Gemma looked serenely happy. (Something Grey had never seen himself.) Yes, Gemma was a natural mother. Grey looked closely at the photo; she was reading Cinderella.

Finally, there was one that looked quite recent. Freya, Gemma, and Poppy were dressed warmly and were standing in front of a modest semi-detached house. There were all hugging each other and smiling. Gemma's white Peugeot hatchback was parked in front of the house.

These photos and posts were more than enough to piece together a clear picture of Gemma's life, especially of the people who were closest to her.

It was obvious to Grey that Gemma and Freya loved each other.

**Gemma—London—Freya and Louise in London**

LIVERPOOL STREET STATION
December 2018
Freya was waiting on the platform when the train from East Anglia pulled into the station. It was freezing cold; a light snow was falling.

Freya was happy. She had been reunited with her godmother and aunt Poppy. Her mother was still off in the country. She would return the following day and Freya was expected to stay with her after that.

Tonight, would be Freya's last night with Gemma and Poppy. Louise would be staying with her at her grandparent's house in Mayfair from tomorrow. In a few minutes, Freya would be reunited with her best (and only) friend from school. Then her circle of friends would be complete.

The train came to a halt. Passengers poured onto the platform. Freya scanned it for the diminutive Louise. Ah! There she is! Freya moved through the crowd. When she she made eye contact with Louise, she smiled.

'Welcome to London, Louise,' said Freya. Louise smiled and hugged Freya.

'It's so good to be back with you, Freya. I missed you so much,' replied Louise.

When Freya released her from her embrace, she looked at Louise. Her eyes were filled with tears.

'What happened?'

'My father didn't even bother to meet me at the station. I waited in the cold for three hours. I had to take a taxi home,' said Louise, trying to suppress her emotions. 'He was in his office when I arrived at the farm, continued Louise as she choked back tears.

'Let's take a black cab to Poppy's house, Louise. You can tell me what happened on the way,' said Freya gently. Freya then picked up Louise's leather box suitcase, put her arm around her, and walked with her out of the train station and into the snowy streets of London.

## THE FARM
Louise was riding in the back of the silver taxi cab when she spotted the farm under a white layer of snow in the distance. Five years had past since she had seen or spoken to her father. Nine years had passed since she had seen the farm.

It looked the same. The main house and three large outer buildings sat on four thousand acres. There were at least a dozen other buildings on the property. Some held tractors and farming equipment. One housed farm labourers who came mostly from Eastern Europe. Others were for storage and yet others were used to pack the produce for shipment to London.

Louise's father had exclusive contracts to supply London's premier department stores and hotel restaurants with fresh produce. His business acumen had made him a very wealthy man.

But money had not bought her father happiness.

Louise had mixed feelings. On one hand, she wanted to see her father. He was, after all, her father. On the other hand, he had sent her away and had never bothered to so much as telephone her. He paid her school fees and sent her one hundred pounds a month in pocket money. It was a pittance.

Louise paid the taxi driver and carried her leather box suitcase through the snow to the front door. She knocked. No answer. She turned the doorknob. It opened, and she entered her family home.

The interior had not changed since her childhood: hardwood floors and white walls. The furniture was the same as well.

The house was immaculate. Her father had been an officer in the Coldstream Guards. He kept everything in military order. Cleaning was a form of relaxation for her father. It calmed his nerves and gave him something else to focus on.

The sun was going down. The lights in the house were already on.

'Father? Are you home?'

'Louise?' a masculine voice barked from inside the house.

'Yes. It's me,' replied Louise nervously. Her heart beat quickly. She hoped that her father would be happy to see her.

A tall, clean-shaven and fairly muscular middle-aged man entered the room. He had a sharp and crisp appearance. He was handsome in a soldierly way. He looked like a soldier, even in civilian clothes. He was wearing faded blue jeans, a white dress shirt, and a silver Omega dive watch secured to his wrist with a black rubber strap. His hair had already turned white.

Louise was a bit startled by his appearance. He had aged well beyond his 48 years. He looked down at his only child.

'You know where your room is. Go and unpack. The housekeeper has left dinner for you on top of the stove.' And with that he turned and walked back into the interior of the house.

Louise, at first deeply saddened, fell into a terrible state of despair. 'This is my father?' she said to herself in barely a whisper. He had never been a kind or loving person, even when her mother had been alive, but this had all been too much for Louise.

What had she done wrong? She didn't deserve this. Freya had spent the last three years repairing her psyche. Freya, dear Freya. Louise wished she had never come home. It was her paternal aunt that had suggested it. Now Louise suspected the suggestion had only been made to avoid having to host Louise at her home for another gloomy Christmas.

'Mummy? Why did you abandon me?' Louise asked the cosmos. Tears filled her eyes and then rolled gently down her cheeks.

The worst moment of her life had been when her father told her that her mother was dead. This was the second worst moment. The moment she realized that she was alone in the world, an orphan, not in name, but in reality. Any chance Louise had ever had of having a family had perished along with her mother on a rural road during a heavy rain.

Louise avoided the kitchen and made her way to her old bedroom. She entered. It was the same. The housekeeper had regularly changed the bedding and vacuumed the room, but otherwise it was the same. The white shelves were still lined with the toys her mother had purchased for her.

Louise's mother had truly loved her. She had told her that every day. Louise had inherited her mother's strawberry blonde hair, brown eyes, and diminutive height. She had also inherited her kindness. And for that, Louise was grateful.

Louise was no longer the empty shell her family had abandoned in Sussex. Freya had instilled strength in her. Louise knew that she was loved. Not by her family, but by Freya. That was enough.

Louise never unpacked. She called a taxi with her smartphone. The driver took her back into town. Louise spent the next two days at a small inn using the money Freya had secretly placed in the pocket of her new petrol blue wool coat (which had also been a gift). Louise slept, ate in silence at the inn's restaurant, and thought about her future.

Louise's father didn't even bother to telephone her. She had left without notice, and her father hadn't cared. Louise decided she no longer cared either. One more term at All Saints, and she was off to university. She would never contact her father again.

That suited both of them.

**Gemma—London—St Albans**

SAINT ALBANS CHURCH
December 2018
Gemma always sat in the very back of the church whenever she went. She had stopped attending Anglican Church services years ago. Gemma had grown tired of so many things. She finally admitted to herself that she really didn't like a lot of the people who attended church with her—for a myriad of reasons.

Gemma had once enjoyed attending church. It had been spiritually fulfilling. The sermons often answered questions she had been pondering just days or even hours earlier. It was uncanny. Divine.

Now Gemma sat in the last pew of St Albans, a relatively small Victorian era stone structure. It had been built through the generous donations of British colonists in colonial India.

The doors were said to have been made from wood imported from Indian jungles. Each door had once been decorated with The Star of India. Both emblems had been removed in the 1970s. All that remained was discoloured wood where they had once rested. However, engraved in each wooden door was the former motto of the British Raj: Heaven's light our guide.

The Portland stone walls had once been decorated with flags of The East India Company, the Viceroy of India, the British Raj, the Union Jack, dozens of Indian army regimental flags, and even the banners of private companies that had once thrived in colonial India. Now, because of political sensitivities, they had all been taken down and placed in a storage room somewhere. All that remained were the metal mounts where the flags had once been inserted. The bare walls seemed to radiate that they had been stripped and left exposed.

The stained glass windows had each been dedicated to individual British colonists. Some had fallen in battle, some had been felled by disease, and some had died of old age. Each one was remembered here. A small brass plaque under each window was engraved with a few details of each life. All of these people had been long forgotten by virtually everyone.

The British Empire had been swept away. Now all that remained of it were entries in books and places like this.

Gemma liked coming to this small nearly-forgotten church in central London because it was usually empty, save for a lone caretaker who only seemed to appear when he unlocked the doors in the morning or when he secured them at night. Gemma had spoken to him a few times. He had a small office in the building. The office was located through a door in the side of the church near the entrance where Gemma usually sat—alone.

St Albans had been Gemma's sanctuary during the trial that destroyed her life and reputation. She used to sit in here alone and cry. No one had ever disturbed her.

She would sit in the small stone church and pray and ask God for help, to please save her. Had he listened? Gemma really didn't know. All she knew for sure was her life had been ruined and the guilty had walked away without so much as a parting glance. How could that be possible?

Today, on this cold wintery day, Gemma found herself alone in St Albans again. She could hear the sound of the traffic outside. She rewrapped her grey and white scarf around her neck and shoulders. Much better.

Gemma's phone pinged. She had received a text. She took her smartphone out of her coat pocket and looked at it. Her blood ran cold. It was from Grey:

**Gemma. I need to see you again. —Grey.**

Gemma ignored the text and put her phone back in her coat pocket. Her phone pinged again:

**Gemma. This is important.**

She ignored him and put her phone away. The phone pinged again. Gemma did nothing. She sat in the pew and stared at the Gothic ceiling overhead.

Ping…Ping…Ping…

Gemma would have liked to have turned off her phone, but she couldn't because she didn't want to miss any important calls from friends.

Ping…Ping…Ping…

Gemma sighed.

'Leave me alone, Grey,' Gemma said to herself.

Ping…Ping…Ping…

'I don't even have peace in St Albans,' thought Gemma. She took out her phone again and with a few hand gestures, she blocked him.

Ping.

Gemma looked at her phone. It was Poppy. Gemma smiled.

**Gemmy, please come to Covent Garden at 6pm tonight. We are having an impromptu get together. Freya is bringing Louise. It will be nice to finally meet her. Freya is going to the train station to pick her up now. Let's have a pyjama party tonight :)**

Gemma smiled. This is just what she needed. Gemma texted back happily:

**Sure :) I'll be there in an hour. See you.**

Gemma felt that this happy text from Poppy was perhaps some form of divine intervention. Gemma sighed at the thought. It would have been better if God had kept Grey away altogether.

**Gemma—London—Pyjama Party**

BLACK CAB

The cab ride from the train station to Poppy's house had been very emotional for both of the girls. Louise told the story of her return home in tears; Freya listened and was barely able to keep her composure. Little Louise was a sweet girl who deserved better than life had given her. **It seemed life was good at cheating people out of a lot of things.**

As the black cab moved slowly through the heavy evening traffic and closer to Covent Garden, Louise felt her resolve strengthening.

'Freya,' said Louise. 'I'm glad this happened. It made me think carefully about my life and everything that has happened. I realized that while sitting in my room at the inn in East Anglia that I had everything I needed back in my room in Sussex.' Louise looked at Freya and said, 'Thank you, Freya. You saved my life. You are the truest friend I have ever had. I know that.'

The girls embraced tightly. Both were crying. The black cab made its way through the traffic and the quickly darkening streets of London. They both sat back in the large backseat and held hands for the rest of the journey to Poppy's house in Covent Garden. By the time they arrived, it was dark.

Freya paid the cab fare and carried Louise's leather box suitcase to the front door of Poppy's semi-detached. There was a thin layer of snow on the ground and it was snowing lightly as they approached the front door.

Freya knocked on the door and Poppy opened it. She smiled and hugged Freya. She looked at Louise, smiled and said, 'It's nice to finally meet you, Louise. I've heard nothing but good things about you. You are even cuter in real life than in photos. Welcome to my home. I'm Poppy.'

Louise was thrilled to finally meet 'Aunt Poppy.' Louise started to extend her hand in greeting when Poppy moved forward and hugged her. They were roughly the same height, Poppy being only slightly taller. Louise was deeply moved. This was the greeting she had hoped her father would have given her.

Poppy ushered them inside and closed the door behind them and locked the door.

The house was a typical Edwardian era house: small. It was two storeys high and a large window facing the street. The hardwood floors had been restored when Poppy purchased the house at the turn of the century.

Poppy took Louise's suitcase and put it into a bedroom which was off of the living room on the first floor of the house. Poppy had turned the small side room into a guest room. 'Alright girls, let's change into our pyjamas for tonight's sleepover,' said Poppy happily.

Freya and Louise went into the first floor guest room and Poppy headed upstairs. The girls all changed into modern sleepwear: Poppy put on a pair of pale blue flannel pyjama bottoms with a white drawstring waist and a navy blue hoodie. Freya wore a pale blue cashmere v-neck top and grey cotton pyjama bottoms (also with a white drawstring waist). Louise wore blue and white striped flannel pyjama bottoms and a beige cable knit sweater that she had purchased on sale at Zara that fall.

They all wore white socks and beige slippers (the footwear being provided by Poppy). The slippers were all made for petite girls like Gemma, Poppy, and Louise. Freya looked at Poppy and said, 'Aunt Poppy? Do you have nothing that can fit a girl like me?' And she laughed. 'I'm surrounded by elves.'

'Wait. I have a pair of slippers I bought for Brian that he has never worn. I suspect he doesn't like the color—even though he won't admit it.' Poppy went upstairs and came back down with a shoe box. Inside was a brand new pair of purple velvet slippers. They fit Freya perfectly.

'What's wrong with purple?' asked Freya.

'That's what I said. I told him I would keep them here for when he sleeps over,' replied Poppy. Then Poppy thought about what she had said and smiled. The girls laughed and hugged Poppy.

Girls' night had begun.

## THE APARTMENT

Gemma packed her leather overnight bag quickly. She went into the small white tiled bathroom and grabbed her tooth brush and a few other things and put them all in a small rubberized canvas pouch she had purchased the day before. She walked back to her bed and put it into her overnight bag. She zipped it up.

She changed into a pair of faded denim jeans and a white cotton blouse.

Gemma was running late. It was already dark. The Underground had been crowded and she had to wait and catch a second train at each transfer. She looked at her watch: 6:33pm.

She put on her blue wool Burberry coat and buttoned it. She went to the window and looked down on the street to see if any black cabs were about. She didn't see any. She saw only a row of parked cars up and down the street. A thin layer of snow blanketed the street and the cars.

Gemma grabbed her bag and headed out. She went down the stairs and into the brightly lit lobby. It was painted white and had highly polished concrete floors. CCTV cameras were located inside the lobby and outside the entrance. The front double doors were metal, left over from the building's days as a warehouse. She approached them and took her magnetic security card out of her wallet. She punched in her door code and then waved her card over the security lock. The double doors clicked, and Gemma pushed one door open.

It was still snowing lightly. Gemma walked out and closed the door behind her. The electronic doors clicked behind her. Gemma turned left on the pavement and started to walk towards the tube station.

She passed by a young couple and continued walking. Then, ahead of her, a slender man of plain appearance and a black leather coat got out of a black Audi sedan. He stood in her path and smiled.

'Hello, Gemma,' he said.

Gemma stopped. She quickly scanned around the streets hoping to see other pedestrians. There were none. Gemma said nothing. She stood on the darkened pavement and weighed her options. **Grey**. He must be here too. Her eyes darted around: nothing but darkness broken intermittently by the narrow and gentle illumination of the street lamps. Was Grey standing in the shadows waiting for her? Her heart was in her throat. It was as if her heart had stopped beating, and she had stopped breathing.

'Grey wanted me to give you something,' the man said with a Yorkshire accent. He smiled slyly as if he was the only one in the room who had been in on a joke.

He walked forward as he raised one hand. Gemma could see a small purple box in his right hand. She was frozen. He stopped and held it up to her.

Gemma then noticed a policeman walking up the street. She exhaled. 'Thank you, God,' she said to herself.

'Tell Grey I don't want it. Tell him to leave me alone.'

The driver smiled and answered, 'It's from Asprey. You should accept it.'

The young policeman stopped; his yellow reflective jacket glinted in the street lamp illumination. His police radio let out occasional chirps, static, and official chatter. He looked at them.

'Good evening. Is everything alright?' asked the young police officer.

Before Gemma could speak, the driver spoke. 'She won't accept this nice gift from Grey. He bought it just for her.'

The policeman looked at Gemma and spoke. 'Why not accept his gift, ma'am? You mean a lot to Grey,' the policeman stated in a professional manner. It was if he was mocking his own profession. Well, he was. Wasn't he?

Gemma froze once more. She couldn't believe it. Her first impulse was to run, but she found herself rooted to the pavement.

The young police officer took the purple box from the driver and held it out in front of Gemma. 'Please accept it, ma'am,' he said and the policeman smiled.

Gemma felt tears welling up in her eyes. She felt as if all the blood was rushing into her head—it probably was. She looked around. No one else was there. No one, but the two men standing before her.

She grabbed the box and then pushed past them. She brushed both of them as she passed and continued to walk quickly away from them. The two men started laughing. She burst into a run and sprinted until she came to the end of the street and encountered several other people.

Some of the pedestrians looked at her; one said 'Why the rush?' and laughed. Was he also one of Grey's men? Gemma wondered. She was breathing hard. She was terrified.

Grey had orchestrated all of this to scare her. It had worked.


**Gemma—London—Chaos**

CHAOS
Gemma made her way into the tube station and boarded the train. She sat in a seat. She was still trembling by the time the train had reached Convent Garden. She had placed the purple box in her leather overnight bag without opening it.

She made her way up the stairs of the station and onto the crowded street. Thank God it was crowded. Gemma looked around, nothing but a sea of Christmas lights and unfamiliar faces. No Grey.

Gemma walked through the lighly falling snow towards Poppy's house. It was close to the station. Gemma constantly looked over her shoulder as she made her way to Poppy's. When she arrived at the house, she looked around and then darted to the front door and knocked on it until someone answered.

'Oh. Hi Gemma. Come in,' said Poppy as Gemma pushed past her. Poppy was a bit surprised.

'What's going on, Gemma?'

'Shut the door,' said Gemma. The panic was obvious in her voice. Poppy quickly closed the door and locked both locks and the deadbolt.

'Where are the girls?' asked Gemma in a hushed voice.

'In the kitchen making popcorn.'

'Come upstairs with me. I need to tell you something.

Gemma headed up the steps, and Poppy followed her up. Gemma entered her former bedroom and put her overnight bag on the bed.

'Shut the door.'

Poppy closed the bedroom door. Gemma looked terrified.

'What's wrong, Gemma?'

'Grey.'

'What happened?'

Gemma sat down on the bed. She breathed hard and then explained what had happened on the street outside of her apartment. Poppy occasionally shook her head as she listened to the astonishing story Gemma was relaying to her.

'Surely he couldn't have been a real policeman, Gemma.'

'He was real. I have no doubt about that. Grey had hinted at these connections when I was with him. He wants me to know how extensive they really are.' Gemma started to tremble again, and she started to choke back tears when she spoke again. 'Grey won't let me go, Poppy.'

Gemma, tiny and fragile, sat on the edge of the bed. Poppy could see the terror in her eyes. Poppy had never seen anything like it. She had never expected anyone she knew to ever experience anything like this. Especially Gemma.

'Let's go to the police. They can't all be working for Grey, Gemmy.'

'No. It only takes one police officer that does to report what we are doing to Grey. And Poppy, what proof do I have? None. That's the way Grey engineered this. He knows exactly what he is doing.'

Poppy exhaled and sat down next to Gemma. She held one of her hands and said, 'Gemma. Let me talk with Brian. He knows a senior detective in Scotland Yard. They went to Harrow together. He will help you for sure.'

'No. Grey would find out. He is fully anticipating me to go to the police. He has already planned a response. He is highly cunning. I sensed that before; now I know my instincts were right.'

Gemma unzipped her overnight bag and took out the purple box. It was marked Asprey. She opened it. Inside was a beautiful bracelet made of colourful precious stones mounted in white gold. It was beautiful.

Poppy looked at it. She had seen that exact bracelet at Asprey's in London. A family relation, a viscountess, had purchased one for her daughter earlier in the year. Poppy's cousin Morgan now wore one just like it.

'Chaos,' said Poppy. 'The bracelet's called 'Chaos.''

Gemma breathed hard. She looked at it for a moment and then placed it back in the purple box and put it on the nightstand.

'Chaos. For sure,' replied Gemma quietly as she shook her head.

There was a knock at the bedroom door. Gemma jumped.

'Gemmy? What are you two doing in there? Come out! I want to introduce you to Louise. And we have a lot of popcorn for you. Oh, and we have a movie about vampires we would like to watch,' said Freya excitedly.

'Just a minute, Freya. We'll be right out. I'm changing,' said Gemma calmly.

Gemma looked at Poppy and said, 'We can't tell the girls. I don't want to ruin this night. I have to stay calm, Poppy.'

Poppy put her arm around Gemma. 'Gemmy, I'm scared. I don't want anything to happen to you. I want you to come with me to the house in the Lake District tomorrow. Spend Christmas with me and the family. My parents haven't seen you in ages. You will be safe at the house. Father has a collection of shotguns and rifles. We will be safe. You can stay with me in my room. I'm a crack shot.'

'You are?'

'Yes.'

'Really?'

'Yes, Gemmy.'

Gemma suddenly smiled. 'I feel safer already. You are right, Poppy. There are more good men at the Yard than bad. Let's talk with Brian after the holidays.'

'Brian is going to be staying with me at the house. Father has invited him. He likes Brian, even though he attended Harrow. All the men in my family are Old Etonians. Father said he is willing to make an exception and allow me to marry Brian.' Poppy smiled.

'Thank you, Poppy. You always save me.'

Gemma changed and headed downstairs with Poppy. She met Louise. It was love at first sight. Gemma hugged Louise and welcomed her into the fold. The girls were a set.

They watched the movie about vampires ('Is this a Christmas movie, Freya?') and ate popcorn. They drank a variety of unhealthy soft drinks and even ordered a large pepperoni pizza (which they devoured while watching the movie). They all had a great time.

Eventually they all fell asleep on camping mats that Poppy had laid down on the living room floor in front of the television. The girls all seem to disappear into a sea of white cotton pillows, duvets, and white sheets. They all slept soundly.

The next day, Freya and Louise headed off to spend Christmas with Freya's family at her grandparents' house in Mayfair.

Gemma, Poppy, and Brian boarded a train for the Lake District and the baronial country seat of Poppy's family. As the train pulled away from the station, Gemma felt as if everything would be alright and her that problems were ebbing away from her the farther the train moved away from London.

She was wrong.

# 7 THE LAKE DISTRICT

**Gemma—London—The Lake District**

NORTHWEST ENGLAND

December 2018

Gemma didn't want to ruin everyone's holiday, so she asked Poppy not to mention her problems with Grey to anyone until after Christmas. Gemma felt it was best to discuss it with Brian, and perhaps even Poppy's father and brother, the day before they returned to London. Gemma felt that for the last three years, all she ever brought people were problems. Gemma didn't want the few remaining friends she had to view her as a collection of troubles. Gemma had felt her life had reached a turning point; that is, until Grey re-entered it.

Poppy was wearing a knee-length pike-grey wool overcoat with a black bear fur collar. She also wore black knee-high leather boots. Her shoulder length glossy blonde hair rested on her black fur collar. The contrast made for a striking display. The glamorous Poppy looked every inch a member of an ancient baronial family.

Who would have guessed that her family had to save every penny they made? That the family had only managed to save their ancestral lands because of the prompt payment of rents by the few remaining (and quite successful) tenant farmers still residing on their land? The family had been blessed with a long line of frugal ancestors who carefully maintained strict household budgets and had never taken out any loans or made any risky investments.

Poppy's ancestors had maintained several traditions. One was for the males to attend Eton and Oxford (preferably Christ Church). Another was a short service commission in the Life Guards. The most important (after loyalty to King and country) was to be frugal.

Poppy's family had been forced (like most noble families) to sell off some of their ancestral land because of the savage taxes imposed by successive Labour governments after the war. Before the war, the family could boast over 10,000 acres of land. By 1970, the family had less than a thousand.

The family had also been forced to sell off its once rather extensive art collection; a collection that had been built up by the family over hundreds of years. It was the art collection that had saved the family home more than anything else. Today, the family had very little of the collection left. Most of the paintings in the home had been commissioned and painted in the last 100 years.

Poppy's family was an ancient one. The 12th Baron could trace the family back over a thousand years. There were several generations of knights, then baronets, and finally barons. The family had participated in virtually every war (and civil war) that England had fought in. Poppy's ancestors had fought in the crusades. The family still had suits of armour and a collection of medieval weapons that had once belonged to these men. They now adorned the walls of the family library.

The manor house was not ancient. The family's current residence had been built in the 1890s. It wasn't even that large. It was a two-storey stone structure. It had half a dozen bedrooms and a rather nice library at one end of the house. The house, architecturally, was not particularly special. It was well-built and relatively easy to maintain. That is what the 10th Baron (Poppy's great-grandfather) had wanted: something he could afford.

Poppy's father had told everyone that if worst came to worst, they could sell off most of the remaining land and keep the house. The house was rather modest and so solidly built that it wasn't that expensive to maintain. However, he didn't expect a situation like that to arise anytime soon.

The family castle still existed. It was on a hilltop a short distance from the house. It was in ruins. Poppy used to play in it with her friends when she was young. Gemma, Poppy, Violet, and Gula had explored it each time they came home with Poppy on holidays. Poppy loved playing tour guide and would happily regale them with the same stories her father and late grandfather (the 11th Baron) had told her repeatedly. Gula had liked walking up the stairs to the top of the last remaining tower and enjoying the view of the valley. Gemma had often joined her.

## THE INSEPARABLE GANG OF HAPPY GIRLS

Gemma also came from an ancient family. She was descended from a long line of knights, baronets, and eventually barons.

Gemma's baronial home in Sussex had been lost to bankruptcy in the 1990s.

Gemma had managed to save some things from the bailiffs: a collection of old photos, some family documents, including her family's original patent of nobility, an Anglican prayer book from the 1700s, and a medieval sword that one of her ancestors had wielded at Agincourt which was now on loan to a museum in London. Virtually everything else had been taken from the family pile and auctioned off.

When the baliff's arrived at Gemma's house in London a liitle over decade later, none of her husband's valuables were taken, only Gemma's. George had quietly removed his valuables a few days before the bailiffs arrived. He had not warned Gemma about their coming arrival. George had known that the bailiffs would seize Gemma's things for his debts, and he had said nothing.

Violet came from an even more illustrious family of viscounts. Her family had not only maintained its pre-war wealth, it had managed to further enrich itself. Violet had also married into an immensely wealthy noble family that continued to make money in mining and agriculture.

Külli, of mixed Estonian-German ancestry, was considered a commoner in England. In fact, she also had a few Baltic knights, barons, and high-ranking Czarist army officers in her family background. Though the blood of Baltic German nobles ran through her veins, in England, Külli was just another commoner.

Külli had never really said much about her family. Her family had been destroyed by the Soviets long before she had been born. Her aged father had spoken often and fondly of her grandparents, none of whom had survived the Soviet invasion of Estonia in 1939. They had all been taken away by the Communists. They had become what Stalin liked to call 'Former People.'

Her father had only survived because, as a teenager, he had been hidden by surviving family members who had arranged to have him smuggled out on a ship to Scandinavia. He never learned what happened to those who had stayed behind.

## THE TRAIN TRIP

Gemma wore her new blue, wool, knee-length Burberry coat—the same coat she had worn to pick Freya up at the train station a few days before. And to keep warm, she was wearing the fur hat she had worn to Freya's birthday three years before. Looking like a Russian Grand Duchess, Gemma had arrived at the train station with two suitcases.

Gemma was still strikingly beautiful at forty. She attracted the gaze of both men and women as she ~~made her way~~ glided down the railway platform to her waiting train carriage. Gemma, in spite of everything that had happened in the preceding three years, was still beautiful. She still had the air of a Sloane: well-spoken, well-educated, cultured, and posh. Gemma's inherent nobilty still shone through. This is what attracted so many to her. It's also what had drawn Grey.

Poppy and Gemma met Poppy's brother James and Brian on the platform.

James was only around 5'9". He had the same blond hair as Poppy. He bore a strong resemblance to his younger sibling. His almost feminine attractiveness reminded Gemma of George. He was wearing a charcoal grey Savile Row suit, white dress shirt, black necktie, black leather wingtips shoes, and a black overcoat with a light brown fur collar.

He smiled as they approached. 'Gemma! It's so good to see you again!' James said happily.

'Hello, James. It's good to see you, too,' replied Gemma, and she smiled.

James had always been kind to Gemma. He never shied away from appearing with her in public after her ruin. James was fearless and loyal like Poppy and Freya. Gemma loved him for it.

It was James who had taken her out to dinner with his wife and young son and daughter (twins) after her acquittal.

His children both referred to Gemma as 'Aunt Gemma.'

James' wife Helen was also good to her.

But it was James who had escorted Gemma home after her first humiliating court appearance. It was James who held her hand as they left the court house. She would never forget that.

Brian stood on the railway platform next to James. He was a little taller (about 5'10") and athletic. He had played cricket at Harrow. He was also quite good at tennis. He was handsome and surprisingly shy around women.

Brian was a banker, like Poppy. They had met in The City at a seminar. As Poppy told it, it was love at first sight. Poppy was giving a presentation on gold ETFs when she met Brian's gaze. She stopped talking for a moment as her heart skipped a beat. She smiled at him and then continued with the presentation. Brian made his way to her afterwards and they had been together ever since.

Brian held out his hands and received Poppy's. 'Thank you for inviting me, Poppy. This means a lot to me,' he said.

'The whole family invited you,' answered Poppy. 'We all love you,' she continued, and Poppy smiled.

Brian smiled and he picked up Poppy's lone suit case.

James tried to pick up both of Gemma's, but she stopped him and said, 'Just one, James. Thank you.' Gemma grabbed the other.

The cobalt blue private railway car was all burl wood, leather, wool carpets, and sterling silver. The private train car was more suited to the Orient than the Midlands.

The 12th Baron had arranged for the railway carriage to be attached to a train heading for the Lake District.

The owner of the train carriage was a relatively wealthy cousin of the 12th

Baron, a viscount, who had recently moved back to England with his family after a long sojourn abroad.

The viscount's only child, a 15-year-old daughter named Morgan (also a 'Hon'), was expected to enter the posh and exclusive All Saints in the fall of 2019.

They all boarded the railway carriage and made their way to their private cabins. The private railway car's burl wood and sterling silver interiors gleamed in the dim glow of the small berth lamps.

Brian was sharing his cabin, two doors down from Poppy and Gemma's cabin, with Poppy's older brother James (The Honourable James). James' wife and children were already at the country house with his parents, the 12th Baron and Baroness.

The girls quickly settled into to their cabin and changed into their pyjamas. Gemma and Poppy then climbed into their respective berths.

'Good night, Poppy.'

'Good night, Gem. Please don't worry. Everything will be alright.'

Poppy went to sleep quickly in the lower berth's bed of white Egyptian cotton sheets, a large white pillow, and a soft light grey wool blanket that was edged in dark blue silk.

Gemma rested her head against the large soft white pillow in the upper berth and stared out the window into the dark night, as the train rumbled north up the tracks towards the Lake District. Gemma was happy to rest in a luxurious and private sleeper cabin with Poppy.

The train had left late that evening. It was pitch dark as the train pulled out of the station. A cold front had moved in and snow was falling as the train headed out of London.

Two days before, Gemma felt she had a bright future. Now with Grey back in her life, she had never felt more trepidation and uncertainty.

'Please, God. Don't abandon me. Help me,' prayed Gemma as she lay in the upper berth of the railway cabin. The natural patterns in the burl wood seemed to almost swirl and move in the moonlight that flooded in through the window of the railway carriage as the train steadly moved north.

Gemma, warm under layers of soft white Egyptian cotton sheets and thick wool blankets, eventually fell asleep too.

## Gemma—London—The House

### THE TRAIN STATION
The 12th Baron was waiting at the small train station with Hector, a tall and powerfully built member of the household staff, when the train arrived. It was early in the morning, dark, snowy, and cold. It had only stopped snowing less than an hour before their arrival.

The baron, wearing a long black coat with a large light brown fur collar, smiled as he saw his children, future son-in-law, and Gemma step down from the train. He walked in their direction to greet them. He hugged Poppy first, and then James, hugged Gemma, and shook hands with Brian.

The baron was not a tall man, roughly the same height as James. He kept his white hair cut like a British army officer. His blue eyes were not fierce; they were kind. Both of his children had inherited his eyes. They had also inherited his kind heart and manner.

'It's so good to see all of you here. I'm glad you could all join us for the holidays. The children are excited to see everyone, especially their aunts Poppy and Gemma,' said the baron.

The baron then turned to Brian and said, 'Brian, thank you for coming to stay with us for Christmas. The whole family would like to become better acquainted with you.' Brian smiled and replied, 'Thank you, sir. Thank you for inviting me.'

And with that, the baron led the small party to two waiting vehicles: a five-door dark blue 1984 Range Rover and a silver 1975 Bristol 411 motor car.

**A Bristol motorcar.** Gula had driven Gemma in her dark blue 1977 Bristol to Violet's country house for the foxhunt during their first year at Oxford more then 20 years ago. Gemma could barely turn around these days without encountering something that didn't remind her of Gula. Was all of this some kind of sign?

'Alright, James and Brian will ride with Hector; and Poppy and Gemma will ride with me in the Bristol. You must all be tired after the journey. Your rooms are waiting for you.'

They all climbed into the respective vehicles and drove away from the small rural train station and towards the baron's estate. Car headlights illuminated the road ahead of them.

Gemma sat in the black leather back seat of the Bristol; Poppy sat in the front and chatted happily with her father. Gemma looked out the car window as it motored down the dark country road.

The countryside was covered in a fresh blanket of snow. The branches of the trees sagged under the weight of it. Gemma was glad to be away from London—and Grey. She felt safe here.

THE HOUSE

The family pile was situated near the center of the estate. It was relatively small, even modest compared to most country houses, but it was also beautiful. The stone structure had a flat roof that was ringed by a decorative parapet. The entrance was a set of large gleaming and glossy black double doors. The facade of the house was made up of two rows of large sash windows, top and bottom. There were also several stone chimneys.

It must have been around 3am by the time they arrived at the stone house, which partially illuminated in moonlight, appeared to be moored in a thick white blanket of snow. Gemma noticed that several of the first floor windows had lights on inside.

It was freezing cold, and everyone moved quickly across the snow-covered drive after exiting the vehicles. The driver and another servant took care of the luggage while everyone entered the house through the large double doors.

WARMTH

It was warm inside the house. A wave of warmth washed over everyone as they crossed the threshold. James shut the doors behind them. The entry hall was dimly lit.

The baron informed Brian that he would be staying in a corner room upstairs and that Gemma would be staying with Poppy in her room.

'You must all be very tired,' the baron said. 'Good night. I'll see everyone in the morning.' He then nodded and ascended the stairs.

'Good night, Brian,' said Poppy. She was tired, but managed a smile for him. Brian moved to kiss her good night, but then stopped midway and looked at James. James smiled, 'It's alright.' Brian looked a bit embarrassed; everyone was staring at him. He smiled and gently kissed Poppy on the cheek. Poppy smiled. 'Good night, shy one.'

Gemma thought the episode was really sweet. She envied Poppy. She had found a good person. At least Gemma hoped she had. She wanted Poppy to be happy, and hopefully, become a mother. Gemma could sense that Poppy would be a good mother.

Poppy and Gemma ascended the stairs. Once they reached the top, Poppy turned and smiled once more at Brian. Poppy and Gemma then headed down the dimly illuminated white walled hallway to Poppy's bedroom.

James and Brian followed them up the steps a moment later and James led Brian down the hall to the guest room that had been allotted to him.

Exhausted after a long night of travel, they all slept well.

### Gemma—London—Castle Ruins

SNOWY MORNING

Gemma woke up next to Poppy. Outside, there was a light snow falling.

Gemma got out of bed and went to the window. The fields around the house were blanketed in a fresh but thin layer of snow. In the distance she could see the family's ancestral castle. The main walls, gate house, and one tower were still largely intact; the rest was in ruins. Gemma hadn't been in the ruins since she was a school girl in Sussex. She decided that a trip to the castle, even on a frozen day like this, was exactly what she needed.

She went into the bathroom and filled the rather large white enameled iron clawfoot bathtub with hot water. She moved around the bathroom grabbing a white bar of expensive vanilla scented French soap and deciding to try some Japanese shampoo she found on a small white shelf in the bathroom. She added some bubble bath to the tub and stirred it with her soft manicured hand.

The bathroom was tiled in pre-war white and blue tiles. At one end of the narrow room was a large window which looked out on the castle ruins.

At the other end of the bathroom was a tall folding screen made up of three panels that was meant for people to undress behind. The screen had a white and blue Art Deco pattern from the 1920s. Poppy loved it. 'It came with the house,' she had told Gemma the first time she had visited over 25 years ago.

After a few minutes, Gemma took off her dark blue pyjamas (with white piping), laid them over the top of the Art Deco screen, and then slowly lowered herself into the bath. '*Heavenly*,' thought Gemma as she relaxed in the warm water. She rested her head against the back of the tub and closed her eyes.

Gemma allowed her body to completely relax in the warm water; her mind followed.

Gemma couldn't say she had had a happy childhood. Her father had been violent and abusive, especially towards her older brother and mother. They moved out of her father's house and in with her maternal grandparents when she was eight years old. Her mother had died when she was 12. Her father hadn't even attended the burial. Her brother left for Hong Kong the day after their mother's funeral.

Gemma had begged him not to abandon her, but he only shook his head. 'I have no happy memories of this place, Gemmy. I'm sorry. I have to go. I love you, Gem.'

And as her brother grabbed his suitcase and as he turned to leave, he looked back and said, 'I love you, Gemmy.'

He stared at his much younger sister for a few moments. Gemma was crying; her brother walked back to her and said, 'I'm sorry. Too much has happened to me here. Please try to understand. I'm not strong, Gemmy.'

The future 9th Baron looked at her and said, 'You will never see me again.'

He gently brushed her hair, and then he turned and walked out of the room. She hadn't seen or heard from him since.

Gemma's grandparents sent her to All Saints in Sussex a year later. It was felt a change of scenery would do her good. She would board with a group of young and energetic girls from England's best families. Gemma would be among her own kind.

It worked. Gemma flourished in Sussex. She would spend the next five years happily living in an alcove and studying with her friends. She had only happy memories of her days at All Saints. Gemma wished that she could go back and relive them exactly as they were.

There was a gentle knock on the door.

'Gemmy? Breakfast will be served in half an hour. Oh, and your luggage is here. I found it outside the door this morning,' said Poppy. 'And Gemmy, please hurry up. I would like to take a bath too. If you stay in there too long, I'll be tempted to join you.' Poppy could be heard laughing outside the door.

'Join me, Poppy! I don't mind!' laughed Gemma.

Poppy opened the bathroom door and stuck her head in. 'Hurry up, Gemmy!' And Poppy laughed.

BREAKFAST
The girls dressed in their country tweeds. Gemma wore a pair of light brown and navy blue checked wool trousers and a white blouse. Over that she wore a rum-colored wool jacket with a blue suede collar and blue piping.

Gemma also put on a pair of brown leather shoes and leather gaiters. Gemma was going exploring today. She would need them to protect her shins.

Poppy wore a pair of brown wool trousers, a pale blue cotton blouse, a dark blue wool coat, and a pair of brown leather Chelsea boots. She looked at her silver watch. 'We are running late again, Gemmy,' and she smiled. 'We always seem to be running late.'

'Yes, but that has always allowed me to spend more time with my friends. I wouldn't have it any other way,' said Gemma and she smiled.

Poppy looked tenderly at Gemma. She felt like crying. Gemma had suffered so many reversals. Poppy smiled and then hugged Gemma. 'That's just one reason out of a million that I love you, Gem.'

'One day, I would like you to list all of the others,' laughed Gemma happily.

The girls made their way down the hallway and then down the stairs into the entry hall. Gemma knew the route. They turned right and headed through the large drawing room and to a set of double doors. They opened them and stepped into a narrow hallway which led them to a single glossy white door. They could hear voices and smell delicious food.

Poppy opened the door and the people seated at the long, polished burl wood table all looked in her direction.

'Good morning, girls,' said the 12th Baron cheerfully. 'Sleep well?'

'Yes, Father,' replied Poppy.

'Gemma! Poppy!' cried the twins excitedly. They smiled brightly and rushed around the table to greet and hug both girls. Gemma was with young children again. She was back in her element. She knelt down to hug them both along with Poppy.

Helen, James' wife, smiled and greeted them. She waved her butter knife and said, 'Hurry up, girls, or the men will eat everything,' and Helen laughed.

Poppy's mother, the baroness, sat at the end of the table.

'Good morning,' said Gemma happily.

Gemma walked around the table and kissed the baroness on the cheek.

'It's good to see you again, Gemma,' said Poppy's mother. She was slim and had grey and white hair. She had the same kind demeanour as the rest of the family.

Gemma had always envied Poppy for her happy family more than anything else. Poppy had been truly blessed.

Brian and James were sitting on either side of the baron at the other end of the table; the baroness sat at the other end with Helen and the happy twins. Poppy and Gemma took their respective seats on either side of the baroness.

The maid, a young Croatian immigrant wearing a simple black dress and white apron, poured Gemma a cup of coffee. 'Hvala (thank you),' said Gemma in Croatian, and smiled at the young brunette. The housemaid was a bit surprised, but responded with a happy nod.

Gemma had learned quite a bit of the Croatian language from Freya's nanny Karmen. Freya spoke the language perfectly. It was Freya's secret language.

The small household had only four permanent staff. The two young Croatian servants worked full-time; additional and temporary staff was hired as needed. Expenses had to be kept to a minimum. The family had a good reputation, so finding staff had never been a problem.

Gemma enjoyed a leisurely breakfast with the family and soon-to-be member of the family, Brian. She was happy. Ensconced in the baronial estate of her loyal and true friend, Gemma felt safe. She wished that she could stay there forever.

'What are your plans for today, Gemma?' asked the baroness, who was also clad in tweed.

'I would like to visit the castle today,' replied Gemma politely.

'In this weather, Gemma? Well, dress warmly,' said the baroness.

James, wearing a smart charcoal grey tweed suit and white dress shirt, looked down the table at Gemma and said, 'Could I join you? I haven't been to the castle in ages. It would be nice to explore it today. A vigorous walk in the cold air would do me some good.'

'Wear your overcoat and boots, James,' said Helen.

'It's supposed to warm up a little this afternoon,' said the baron. 'If you find any lost treasure, please notify me immediately,' he added happily, and the baron smiled.

## THE CASTLE

The weather had warmed up considerably by noon. The Sun peaked out from behind the clouds. It was a nice winter day. Gemma, Poppy, James, and Brian all trekked through the grounds towards the castle ruins. The thin layer of snow crunched underfoot. Within 15 minutes, they reached the outer walls.

'Let's go through the main gate,' said James. He led the way, followed by Brian, Poppy, and Gemma.

The castle wasn't very large at all. It had probably only held a couple of hundred men when fully garrisoned. The walls, built approximately 900 years ago, were still largely intact. Of the five towers, only one remained standing. The others had collapsed long ago. The stones had been carted away to be used on other structures over the centuries, including the current house which stood close by.

All that remained of the internal structures were foundations.

In summer, a smooth grass lawn filled the former courtyard of the fortress. It had been carefully picked clean of debris. The lush green lawn around the castle was also always well maintained.

The baron enjoyed having tea in the castle grounds with his many friends.

James and his friends clad in cricket whites had played cricket on the green next to the castle while on holidays from Eton and Oxford. James missed playing cricket with his friends. He had promised himself that as soon as his children were old enough, he would teach them to play.

But today, the grounds were covered in a thin sheet of snow.

Brian had never visited the castle and was deeply impressed. 'Your family owns this?'

'Yes, we do,' answered Poppy. 'It's been in our family for around 900 years, give or take a few decades.'

'Come here, Brian. I want to show you the cistern,' said Poppy. Poppy led Brian by the hand away from Gemma and James.

'Let's go up the tower,' said Gemma. 'I want to see the view from the top.'

James and Gemma entered the small door and went up the stone stairs that spiralled up the insides of the stone tower. The wooden floors of each level had all been carefully restored.

ENGLAND
When they reached the top floor, James went up the ladder which led to a wooden hatch and the rooftop. Gemma followed him. Once they were both on the rooftop, they stood at the battlements and looked out on the wintery Lake District which stretched out before them.

Gemma placed one of her beige leather gloved hands against one of the snow-capped battlements and slowly breathed in the cold air. The vast almost phantasmagoric snow-covered landscape lay before her. Rays of sunshine poured through the gaps in the clouds. It was an impressive sight.

'It's glorious,' said Gemma. 'How beautiful England is,' she said quietly.

The astounding beauty and tranquility of the English countryside was the only cathedral Gemma ever truly needed or desired.

James was admiring the view when he said, 'To think: my ancestors have been looking out from this tower for over 900 years.'

Gemma and James enjoyed the spectacular view. They pointed out different terrain features and talked about the history of the castle: how many times it had been besieged and how many cricket matches and teas it had hosted.

Gemma's thoughts now returned to Grey: such an unpleasant thought. She wanted to discuss the situation with James, but decided against it. 'Let everyone enjoy Christmas,' she thought.

Gemma had been through so much.

And even after all that she had been through, she never thought she would ever encounter someone *as menacing* as Grey. What exactly was he? What was he involved in? Was he some kind of government operative or a gangster? Perhaps he was just a corrupt businessman? There were a lot of those in London these days.

The encounter with the driver and the policeman had been really unsettling. Why had Grey orchestrated something like that? Gemma could not even begin to understand someone like him. It was beyond her.

Still, Grey was a problem. She had to decide what to do. Was Grey dangerous? Or perhaps, the question should be: How dangerous was he?

**Gemma—London—Crack shot**

MANOR HOUSE

Poppy led Gemma into the library. The library was at one end of the house and the plaster patterned ceiling relief hovered two stories above them. The white ceiling contrasted nicely with the grey stone of the walls. The stone used to construct the walls of the house had all come from the ruins of the family castle.

The first storey of the room was filled with wall mounted book shelves. The second storey of the room was filled with large windows. The wall on the front of the house also had large windows as did the far end. The back wall of the house was windowless and had been left bare so that a tapestry could be hung from it.

The richly embroidered tapestry was quite unusual. The tapestry depicted a group of knights on armoured warhorses charging into battle in the ancient Kingdom of Jerusalem. Latin words had also been embroidered onto the wall hanging.

'That was brought back from Jerusalem around nine hundred years ago. It had once hung in my ancestor's palace in the city. When one member of the family returned to England, he took the tapestry with him. We have had it ever since,' said Poppy.

She stopped in front of it and pointed out some of the details to Gemma. 'The knight with the large shield out front is my ancestor. You see, our coat of arms is on his shield.'

Gemma's ancestors had also fought in the Crusades. However, most of the family's collection of medieval weapons, armor, and other objects related to the crusades had been either sold or later auctioned off in the 1990s to pay off her father's debts.

Gemma sighed. So much of her ancestral heritage had been lost. Maybe it really didn't matter; she was childless and so was her brother. The family title would probably go extinct when her older brother died. Even if the family had managed to have kept more of the family silver and other artifacts, there would be no one left to inherit it.

Gemma had managed to hang onto a shield that had been used during the crusades and had returned with her ancestor. It was on loan to a museum in London (The same one that had her ancestor's sword that had been wielded at Agincourt).

There was also a medieval history book, an illuminated manuscript, filled with gold paint and elaborate and ornate calligraphy. It had been produced in the Kingdom of Jerusalem specifically for Gemma's ancestors. The first page had been decorated with her family's coat of arms. It detailed her ancestor's activities during the crusades. It was now deposited on loan to Oxford University.

Gemma was glad that at least Poppy's family had managed to hang on to as much as they had, even though they had also been forced to sell off much of their family's treasures to maintain the house and ancestral lands.

A few medieval weapons and shields decorated the walls of the library, and in one corner, there stood a suit of medieval armor.

There were two large tables in the library and several high-back chairs. The library was filled with thousands of books. Many of the really old books were kept in a glass case near the tapestry. Most of the books on the shelves were less than a hundred years old.

Gemma had visited the library quite a few times and each time Poppy insisted on giving her a tour of it. Gemma happily agreed because Poppy always remembered some new detail of her family history that she had neglected to mention to her before. Gemma was never bored when Poppy played tour guide. She loved Poppy's country house and being with Poppy.

Poppy was fully aware of Gemma's illustrious family history. Their ancestors had fought side by side in several famous battles going back a thousand years. They had also always fought on the same side.

Poppy turned to Gemma and said, 'Now I'm going to take you into the secret room, Gemma.'

'Secret room?'

'Yes. It's the family's secret room. You mustn't tell anyone,' said Poppy gravely. And then she smiled. 'I have a key.'

Poppy walked over to the bookshelf next to the tapestry and took out two books. In the space was a circular brass plate embedded in the shelf. She put her key in the lock and turned it.

'Open Sesame,' said Poppy happily.

The lock clicked. Poppy turned to Gemma and said, 'Come hither, Honourable Gemma'.

As Gemma walked over to Poppy, Poppy opened the secret door. The bookshelf opened outwards. Beyond it was darkness. Poppy took out her smartphone and turned on its light. She entered. Another click, and the electric fluorescent lights came on inside. The small room was fully illuminated.

Gemma entered. The room was gray stone and had a stone floor (as opposed to the hardwood floors of the library). The ceiling was not high. The room was windowless. Along the wall was a polished burl wood glass cabinet filled with rifles and shotguns. This was the family's arms room. At either end of the room were small tables and some folding metal chairs. There were also three filing cabinets at one end. The room was not ornate. It was quite utilitarian.

Poppy searched her key ring. Once she found the right key, she opened the gun cabinet. She took out a Lee-Enfield rifle. 'This rifle saw military service in India, Afghanistan, and Flanders. My great grandfather kept it and brought it home with him after the Great War. We have maintained it in perfect working condition. You see, right here: it still has the markings for the Imperial Indian Army.' Poppy worked the bolt of the rifle expertly. She then returned it to the cabinet. There were no less than four Lee-Enfield rifles in the long, polished wood gun cabinet.

Poppy put it back and then took out a flint lock rifle. It was beautifully polished and made of dark rich wood. It had been engraved with ornate patterns. Poppy held it out to Gemma. Gemma carefully took it from her and looked at it. The flint lock rifle was rather heavy.

'The flint lock was at Waterloo. It belonged to a member of Napoleon's Old Guard,' said Poppy. 'The 7th Baron fought at Waterloo and brought it back with him. He also brought back a beautiful gold sword that had been wielded by a Napoleonic officer at Waterloo. The sword is now in a glass cabinet at James' house in London.'

After Gemma had finished looking it over, she gave it back to Poppy and she carefully put it back in the cabinet.

She then took out a Webley Mark IV revolver. It was also well maintained. It was in its original leather holster and the pistol belt was still attached. 'My maternal great grandfather was issued this pistol when he was serving in

India. He served in a hussar regiment,' said Poppy.

She then picked up a box of bullets. 'We still have several hundred rounds of ammunition for it.' After returning the box of pistol bullets to the cabinet Poppy continued the story. 'He eventually rose through the ranks to become a general. He retired after The Great War and lived out his days in London. That's where his only child—my grandmother—met the 11th Baron.'

'Go on, Gemma. Try it on,' said Poppy happily. Gemma hesitated for a moment and then took the belt and holstered pistol from Poppy. She put it on and tightened the belt. It fit.

'He had a small waist,' said Poppy. 'It really suits you, Gemmy.'

Gemma laughed. 'Poppy, stop it.'

Poppy then went back to the cabinet and took out a beautifully polished wooden rifle. The metal parts had all been beautifully and ornately engraved. 'This rifle is from Austria-Hungary. The 10th Baron had it commissioned in 1905 when he was a military attaché at the British Embassy in Vienna.'

The rifle was truly a piece of art. It gleamed in the fluorescent light of the ceiling lamps.

Poppy then took out a highly polished wooden box. She carried it to the small table at the end of the narrow room and set it down. She opened the pistol case and inside was a pair of flint lock pistols set in blue velvet. Poppy took one out and handed it to Gemma.

'These were used in the English Civil War. They still work quite well,' explained Poppy. 'These are my favorite pistols in the entire collection. The ancestor who used these was killed in one of the last battles of the war. The family hid the pistols and his sword until the Restoration.'

Gemma examined the pistol carefully. It was heavier than she had expected it would be. She handed it back to Poppy, and Poppy returned it to the case.

After she closed the case, she placed it back in the gun cabinet.

'Let's use this one,' said Poppy as she took out another rifle. It was a different Lee-Enfield. It was also perfectly- maintained. 'This one saw action in World War Two. We use it to practice target shooting more than the others.'

Poppy then helped Gemma take off the pistol belt. Poppy returned the Webley revolver to the gun case.

She then took out a leather ammo pouch and filled it with bullets taken from a cardboard box inside the cabinet. She locked the gun case and then turned to Gemma.

'Okay, Gemmy. Let's see what you can do,' said Poppy, and Poppy smiled.


**Gemma—London—Target practice**

THE SNOWY FIELD
Poppy lay flat on the ground. Well, not *exactly on the ground*; she had laid down an old army surplus canvas sleeping bag on the frozen ground, and then lay down on top of that. She was wearing a navy blue quilted Burberry coat and cashmere Burberry scarf; it's beige, black and red tartan wrapped carefully around her neck for warmth.

She looked through the sights on the Lee-Enfield rifle. She looked down range. The paper target was tacked to the wooden target stand and fluttered slightly in the gentle breeze.

It was cold; the breeze made it that much colder. There was a light layer of snow on the ground.

Poppy aimed at the target, held her breath, and fired. Blam! Blam! Blam! Each time she worked the bolt and ejected a shell casing. After three rounds she stopped firing and looked up at Gemma, who was standing beside her.

She motioned with her hand towards Gemma. Gemma removed her ear plugs, and said, 'Shall we check?'

Poppy got up and shouldered the rifle. She took out her ear plugs and said, 'Let's go and see how I did.'

They both walked across the snowy field, snow crunching underfoot. When they arrived at the wooden stand, they both examined the paper target.

'Bull's-eye! Bull's-eye! Bull's-eye!' exclaimed Gemma. 'Poppy! You're fantastic!' Gemma smiled and looked at Poppy in amazement.

'I told you, Gemmy,' and Poppy flashed an impish smile. Poppy stood ramrod straight in the snowy field. She was wearing beige wool trousers and dark brown leather shoes with dark brown leather gaiters. She looked like she was on safari in a very cold climate. Her blonde hair was now intertwined with her Burberry scarf.

'You belong on the cover of Tatler, Poppy,' said Gemma. 'Wait,' said Gemma, and she took out her smartphone. Click! Poppy's smiling and angelic face appeared on the screen of Gemma's phone. She showed it to Poppy. Poppy smiled.

'Gem, please send that to me immediately. I want to send it to Brian. He should know that his future bride is not only quite fetching but also extremely dangerous.' And Poppy smiled.

'You are dangerously cute, Poppy,' said Gemma. 'But you have always been dangerously cute. I think that is the deadliest weapon in your arsenal,' said Gemma.

Gemma touched the screen and Poppy's phone pinged a moment later.

Poppy forwarded the photo of her holding the Enfield rifle in the snow with her Burberry scarf and jacket off to several different people simultaneously. They responses came back quickly:

**Poppy! You look marvelous! What have you done with your hair? It looks fantastic! And the rifle! Who is your stylist? :) —Freya**

**You went shooting without me, Poppy? Where are you on the estate**

exactly? I want to join you. —James

Poppy—You become more beautiful with each passing day. I look forward to our future. BTW: You aren't going to carry that down the aisle when we marry, are you? —Brian

Poppy, does Brian know what a Pandora's Box of talents you truly are? You must go hunting with me next year. Mummy misses you. Gemma will have to come too. I'm sure Gemma will look quite dazzling in tweeds and hunting kit. I have an extra shotgun she can use. —Vava

As Poppy's smartphone pinged, Gemma and Poppy looked at the responses and laughed.

Poppy then handed the rifle to Gemma. Gemma held it nervously.

'Don't worry, Gemma. Just do as I told you and you will be alright. Now, let's walk back and you can try it.'

They walked back to the canvas sleeping bag. Gemma laid down carefully and got into position. She aimed the rifle, held her breath, and fired. Blam! Gemma looked down range.

'Did I hit anything?'

Poppy looked through a set of small German field binoculars she had taken from the leather pouch that was sitting on the folding camp chair she had set up next to the canvas sleeping bag.

'No. Nothing. Are you sure you are aiming at the target, Gemmy?' and Poppy smiled.

'That's not funny, Poppy.'

'I'm only teasing, Gemmy. Okay. Try again.'

Gemma got back into positioned and fired again. Blam!

'You missed again.'

Blam! Gemma worked the bolt and another shell casing was ejected.

'No. Try again, Gem,' said Poppy while looking through the field glasses.

Blam. This time the bullet was true—well, kind of. The bullet struck one of the wooden legs of the stand and it splintered; the tripod fell over into the snow.

'You hit, Gemmy!' said Poppy excitedly, and then she laughed.

'I'm sorry, Poppy. I'll buy you a new stand,' said Gemma apologetically.

'No need to Gemmy. We have plenty of extra legs in the garden shed. It happens all the time.'

'Really?'

'No. Not really.' And Poppy laughed. 'But, it's true; we have extra wooden legs in the garden shed—just in case something like this happens.'

'It's not funny, Poppy,' sighed Gemma.

'Don't worry, Gem. I'll make you a top-notch sniper in no time.'

And Poppy smiled.


### Gemma—London—Andrew

LONDON

Andrew had served in the British Paras. After his discharge, he had ventured to Croatia in 1991 and joined the Croatian army. In 1992, when the war spread to Bosnia-Herzegovina, he had followed. He had been wounded twice in battle.

After the war ended in 1995, he returned to London. But he was no longer the man he once was. Traumatized by his experiences, Andrew slowly descended into alcoholism.

He married a local girl from the East End and had a daughter with her, but the marriage failed after a few years and Andrew found himself living in a tiny, rundown council flat.

Andrew worked as a day labourer—when he could find work, or get out of bed. What little money he made was spent on his daughter and alcohol. Andrew was a wreck and he knew it.

When he heard Grey was living in London, he sought him out. When he appeared at Grey's office, Grey had mistaken him for a homeless person. Andrew was unrecognizable: emaciated, shabby, and unshaven. He was a far cry from the sharp young former Para he had known in Bosnia in 1992.

'Come in, Andrew.'

Andrew sat in Grey's office and told him about his ruined life. Grey listened. Andrew had only one concern: his family. He asked Grey to look out for his ex-wife and daughter. Andrew said he couldn't. He knew he would never recover and the fate of his only child had left him particularly upset. Andrew had nothing to offer Grey in return.

'Andrew. I want you to put your life back in order. And I want you to stop worrying about your family. I'll look out for them. I promise.'

Grey opened his desk drawer and took out a white envelope. He counted out some cash and then handed it across the table to Andrew. 'Two thousand pounds. Please accept this. It's only the beginning, Andrew. You saved my life in Bosonski Brod. I haven't forgotten that. But I want you to keep on living. Do it for your daughter. She needs you. What's her name?'

'Sharon,' replied Andrew. Andrew coughed badly every time he spoke.

'How old is she?'

'Nine,' he replied, and then Andrew covered his mouth and coughed.

'Andrew. Give me your ex-wife's address and phone number. I would like to contact them, if that's alright with you.'

'Why?'

'Because I'm going to look after them for you while you recover,' answered Grey.

'Thank you, Grey.'

'You're welcome. The address and phone number?'

Andrew wrote down the information on a piece of paper that Grey had handed him. He handed it back to Grey along with Grey's sterling silver pen.

Grey then walked Andrew to the door and out onto the street. He hailed a black cab and then he hugged Andrew. 'Andrew. Everything is going to be alright. I'm here for you.'

'Thank you, mate. I really appreciate this. It's for my daughter, Grey. I hate to ask you for anything. But it's for Sharon. You understand? She's all I have left.' Andrew started to cry.

'Andrew. Please. I hate to see you like this. We are comrades. I swear I will look after Sharon. Now go and get your life back in order. I'm going to come by next week with some more money for you. I think you need to spend some time at the seaside. The ocean air will do you good. I'm going to find a place for you at the beach. You'll stay there for awhile. Okay?'

'Thank you, Grey.'

The black cab pulled up, and Grey helped Andrew into it. Andrew drove off in the cab. That was the last time Grey ever saw Andrew again. Two days later the police found his lifeless body in the kitchen of his home. He had died of a heart attack.

Grey paid for the funeral.


## Gemma—London—Sharon

SCHOOL GIRL

Grey met Andrew's ex-wife and nine-year-old daughter Sharon at Andrew's funeral at the Anglican Church in the East End where Andrew had married Sharon's mother a decade earlier. Sharon was a rundown looking little thing. She had cried her eyes out during the funeral. Her mother, once quite attractive, had aged well beyond her years.

Each month, Grey would visit Andrew's widow's small council flat and hand her an envelope with a thousand pounds. That amount supplemented the widow's pay cheque enough for her to get by. He would often have groceries delivered at his expense.

He always chatted with the young blonde Sharon and handed her an envelope with a hundred pounds in it. Sharon, usually dressed in her blue school uniform, would smile and very politely say, 'Thank you, Uncle Grey.'

## UNCLE GREY

Sharon was a friendly and outgoing young girl. Grey liked her. She was polite, unlike a lot of children he encountered. She had had a rough life in the East End. She wasn't really good at her studies. Her mother wanted her to attend university, something no one in her family had ever managed to do. The allowance that Grey gave Sharon had allowed her to do things like go to the cinema, buy decent clothing, shoes, and later on, cosmetics.

Grey would visit the home at least twice a month. He always took Sharon out for walks in the local park when the weather permitted it. Sometimes they even visited Andrew's grave and Sharon would lay flowers on it. Grey would also take Sharon out to lunch at least once a month.

Sharon was good at track and field. She enjoyed swimming. She had even won competitions at school. Grey praised her often. He encouraged her. Grey didn't really know anything about parenting, but he knew that Sharon was Andrew's daughter. He made the effort.

It seemed to be all for naught.

Sharon was a member of England's abandoned white underclass. She found herself part of a harassed and isolated minority at her rundown school in the East End. Sharon, blonde and Christian, was shunned by her hijab-clad classmates. Her classmates spoke a myriad of foreign languages around her. She was often bullied. She was virtually alone. She eventually grew to hate school.

Something was broken in Sharon. Maybe it was the social isolation at school. Maybe it was her upbringing with a single mother who hadn't had the time to spend with her. Maybe it was her father's death. Maybe it was just fate. Sharon eventually left school without attaining any A-levels.

She had developed a violent streak and would often get into fist fights, which she usually lost. She also started drinking and smoking. Grey had tried to discourage her from that, but she wouldn't listen. She had also discovered boys, or rather, they had discovered her.

Sharon was drifting. She was unskilled and seemed condemned to work at fast food restaurants or stock shelves at supermarkets for minimum wage for the rest of her life. Sharon was directionless. She felt hopeless. She turned to the only other person (besides her mother) in her life that truly cared about her: Grey.

One day she showed up at the front door of Grey's Primrose Hill house. She was 18.

'Uncle Grey. I want to make money. Real money.'

'Doing what? Hey, is that a tattoo?'

Sharon rolled up her sleeve to reveal a human skeleton inked onto her forearm. It was quite elaborate and it coiled around her arm.

'Is that what you spend your money on?' asked Grey.

Sharon, slim, above average height, athletic, and fairly attractive, looked sad.

'Uncle Grey. Teach me to shoot.'

'Guns?'

'Yes.'

'Why?

'I want to work for you?'

Grey's eyes narrowed. **This was a serious security breach.** How they hell did she figure this out? Grey sat across from Sharon who was sitting on his couch. At first, he was alarmed, and then he saw potential.

'I'm an art dealer, Sharon.'

Sharon didn't blink. She showed no emotion. She looked at Grey stony faced and replied, 'There are a lot of men like you in London. I grew up around them. I went to school with them. I have sex with them.'

'Okay, Sharon. I don't even want to hear about that.'

Sharon continued to speak without a trace of emotion. 'I know you are one of these types of men. Uncle Grey, I don't want to end up another poor single mother in London, on the dole, drunk, and hopeless. I don't have the brains for school work. I wish I had, but I don't. But I know I can do certain things. I am my father's daughter.'

'Your father wasn't a gangster, Sharon.'

'I know that. I'm proud of him for that and many other things. I know he was a good man. Life had been hard on him. But I know he tried. Please, Uncle Grey. I have no other options. I really don't,' she said as her voice trailed off and Sharon started to cry. 'Please, let me join you. I will be **loyal** to you. Just give me a chance.'

**Loyalty.** If there was one word that Grey revered, it was loyalty.

Grey became lost in thought. He stared past Sharon and out the window of his house. Beyond it was a beautiful park filled with beautiful *posh* people. Sharon wasn't posh, *nor would she ever be.* Sharon was what her countrymen would call a *chav*: the complete opposite of someone who was *posh*. With her working class accent, mannerisms, fashion sense, and tattoos, Sharon was definitely working class.

Grey's gaze refocused on Sharon. He studied her for a few minutes. She was physically fit. (She would have to stop drinking and smoking full stop.) She was fairly attractive. (Grey would send her to an upscale hair salon and see what they could do with her.) And, oh, yeah, a good dentist. Grey knew one of the best dentists in London.

'Alright. But on one condition: you do exactly as I tell you. You never disobey me or question any of my orders. You understand?'

'Yes.'

Grey rattled off a list of everything Sharon must stop doing (drinking, drugs, and smoking) and everything she must start doing (exercise, kick boxing, and going to the rifle range). Oh, yeah, and no more boys. Grey would arrange for her to stay in a tiny flat in central London. He wanted her out of her old neighbourhood.

Sharon agreed immediately. She smiled and then stood up, went over to Grey, and hugged him. She had tears in her eyes.

'Thank you, Uncle Grey. I won't disappoint you.'

SHARON
The salon employed miracle workers. Sharon was made over and looked stunning. **It never ceased to amaze Grey what money could do for someone.**

He bought her a gym membership and she became toned. Kickboxing made her muscular. He took her to the rifle range and taught her how to shoot a variety of rifles and shotguns. He took to the countryside and taught her to fire handguns and machine guns. She was good at shooting, a real natural.

She ate healthy and her complexion glowed. The dentist fixed her teeth, and when she smiled, everyone assumed she must be American. Sharon was beautiful. Her confidence grew stronger every day. For the first time in her life, Sharon was happy.

He paid an instructor to train her how to ride high speed motorcycles. He bought her a Japanese racing bike. Sharon was extremely good at racing. She was a natural. She had found her hidden talent. In fact, she was so good at it that she wanted to become a professional racer and join the racing circuit. The last year and a half had seen her life transformed. For the first time in her life, Sharon had dreams.

Grey, however, had other plans for her.

NORTH LONDON
The black Ducati racing bike weaved through evening traffic. It was a beautiful bike. It responded perfectly to the rider. The rider expertly handled the bike as it accelerated and braked in heavy traffic. It had been stolen just an hour earlier. The owner hadn't even noticed it was gone yet.

The rider was wearing a pair of faded denim jeans, a black leather racing jacket, a black motorcycle helmet (with a black visor) and black leather boots. She also wore a small black backpack. Inside the helmet, the rider was talking through an electronic earpiece.

'I'm approaching them now. I can see the silver Aston Martin. I'm almost there,' said the now 19-year-old Sharon.

'Alright,' said Grey into Sharon's earpiece, 'Pull up on the passenger side. He's on that side.'

The motorcycle engine revved and Sharon expertly moved through traffic. Traffic was at a crawl, and then the glossy silver Aston Martin stopped at a red light. Sharon could easily drive up the center lane whenever she wanted. The path was clear.

One side of the street was a river of white luminous headlights, and in the other direction, a stream of red tail lights. Just five cars ahead of her was the silver Aston Martin. Inside it was the man Grey had ordered her to kill.

This was not her first assignment. Sharon had already killed three other people on his orders.

She had wanted to become a professional motorcycle racer, but first she had to fulfill her obligation to Grey. 'It's only fair, Sharon. I have invested a lot in you. Just do a few more assignments for me, and I'll let you go.' Sharon agreed. After all, Grey was right.

All of a sudden, Grey's voice burst into her head via the earpiece, 'Go!' Sharon accelerated forward down the center lane. Her bike was illuminated by the street lights and the head and tail lights of the cars on both sides of the street.

She pulled up alongside the Aston Martin, took a semi-automatic pistol from her backpack and fired it point-blank into the car. The passenger side window shattered; the next five rounds struck the passenger and the driver in their heads. Both men died instantly. Sharon returned the pistol to her backpack and sped away.

Unfortunately for Sharon, CCTV cameras had pinpointed her location and followed her as she tried to escape. She found herself being pursued by police cars, and eventually, even motorcycle-mounted policeman. Sharon gunned it; at certain points during the chase, she was going over 100 mph down London streets.

As she tried to turn onto a bridge crossing the Thames, she lost control of the Ducati and slammed at a high rate of speed into the stone railings of the bridge. Sharon broke her neck on impact and died instantly.

The police were able to identify her by her tattoos. Her mother later identified her in the morgue.

It was probably for the best, thought Grey. After all, girls like Sharon never really stood a chance anyway.

Grey paid for the funeral (which he did not attend) and for her to be buried next to Andrew.

Grey always told himself that he would place flowers on both of their graves at least once a month. He never did. Soon, Sharon was just a faded memory. A few months after she died, Grey seemed to have forgotten about her entirely.

### Gemma—London—Gula in winter

MARBLE ARCH
Külli was lying on the bed across from the fireplace in her upstairs bedroom. The glow from the fire illuminated her. Her head was propped up on a pile of white pillows. She looked out the window and could see the snow falling outside. It was night. The light from the street lamp cast shadows into her room. Külli was deep in thought. She was also completely naked.

'What are you thinking about, Külli?' asked the slim young brunette with waist length hair. She was standing by the window. She was also completely naked.

'Nothing,' she replied.

'Come on. You have to talk to me. I turned down Christmas with my family in the Cotswolds to spend it here with you,' she replied, and the young girl smiled.

'I'm thinking about my past, Daphne.' And Külli looked up at the ceiling.

Daphne approached slowly. When she reached the edge of the bed she got in and crawled over to Külli. She lay down next to her and placed her head on her shoulder. She smiled.

'Your past,' replied Daphne, 'is in the past. I am here in the present. Aren't I enough for you?'

'The past is important,' responded Külli.

'You have had a fantastic life, Külli. You are the kind of woman who has everything. What else could you possibly ever want with the past?'

Külli sighed.

Daphne was such a silly girl. She was only twenty and an undergraduate majoring in fashion design at one of England's second tier universities. Külli really couldn't expect too much from her. She was, however, quite sweet and Külli was happy with her. Daphne was also beautiful and rather warm-hearted. And warm. Külli liked her and had always been kind and generous with her.

Generous. Oh, that reminded her.

Külli got up slowly. Daphne moved her head and placed it firmly on the pillow. Külli got out bed and walked to a dresser next to the window in the dimly lit room. Gula opened the top drawer and took out a wrapped gift.

She turned around and walked back to the bed. She got back in and made her way back to Daphne. She held the box out in her right hand. 'Merry Christmas,' Külli said softly. Daphne's face lit up. She popped up quickly and looked at the box and then into Külli's eyes. 'For me? Really?'

'Yes,' answered Külli softly, and she smiled.

Daphne gently took the present from her hand. It was wrapped in beautiful white paper with a red ribbon stamped 'Cartier'. It was sealed with a red wax seal.

'Külli. I didn't expect anything like this,' said Daphne sincerely—yes, sincerely—Külli knew Daphne's heart. She was a good person. And Külli knew that Daphne truly loved her.

Külli only wished that she could somehow love her as much. Külli's heart had been lost to Gemma decades ago. She knew she would never love anyone else the same way. But still, Külli was human and she needed affection, even love. Daphne made her happy. She would never do anything to hurt her feelings.

She had arranged for her to intern at a fashion magazine the summer before, and now she was interning with Külli at her own company. Daphne showed promise. Külli would do everything she could to help her be successful.

'Go on. Open it,' said Külli happily. She smiled.

Daphne placed the gift on the white bed sheets and looked at it.

'It's so beautifully wrapped. I hate to unwrap it,' she replied softly. She looked at Külli and smiled gently.

As beautiful as Daphne was, in no way did she remind her of Gemma. Külli wished that she had.

Külli had had half a dozen relationships over the last twenty years. Each time she hoped she would find *another true love* and Gemma's spell over her would be broken. It had never happened. She had had her heart broken at 19. Külli had been careful to avoid doing the same to others. Gula knew how truly terrible a broken heart could be.

The girls she had had relationships with had all eventually found boyfriends, married, and had children. Gula had let each one go gently and told each one how much she loved them. There had been no more broken hearts. Gula had seen to that. And she had managed to stay on good terms with all of her exes. Gula was privately proud of that. The only one left with a broken heart had been Gula.

Daphne was a particular favorite.

Daphne opened the present slowly. Cartier really did wrap things beautifully. Eventually she managed to remove the red ribbon and white paper and retrieve the red leather box. She opened it. Inside was a stunningly beautiful diamond bracelet. Daphne looked at it, and then looked back at Gula.

'I can't accept this,' she insisted while shaking her head. 'It's too expensive, Külli.'

'It's yours, Daphne. I had it made just for you. I want you to have it.' Külli smiled innocently, then seductively.

Gula was still alluring. She had worked hard to maintain herself. She knew the power she had over women, and she used it. (Power, that is, over every woman except for Gemma.)

Daphne took it out of the box and put it on her slim wrist. It was beautiful.

The fire in the fireplace reflected off of it. It looked like her wrist was shimmering in orange light.

'Thank you, Külli. I'm afraid the present I have for you pales in comparison.'

'Whatever you give me, I will love.'


## Gemma—London—Christmas in Mayfair

### VAVA ARRIVES

Violet returned from the country late in the afternoon. It had started to snow in London just as the train pulled into the station. The train trip back in the family's private train car had been exhausting. She hadn't been able to sleep at all. By the time she arrived at the 4th Baron's house in Mayfair, London was blanketed in a thin layer of snow, and Vava was barely able to keep her eyes open.

When she entered the house, she was wearing a white cotton blouse, a navy blue wool jacket (with a fur collar), a slate grey pair of wool trousers, and black leather Chelsea boots. Behind her were two servants carrying her luggage (well, at least some of it).

Vava was only 40. She had long glossy blonde hair and was remarkably slim; she could still wear the same outfits she had worn while at Oxford. Vava was still attractive.

Unlike most of her Oxford classmates, she had married right after graduation and had a baby less than a year later.

Many of her classmates had remained unmarried and childless. The ones that did have children usually waited until their thirties to have them. Vava was glad that that part of her marital obligation had been fulfilled. When she thought of her Oxford classmates chasing five-year-old daughters around in a nursery at forty, it made her shudder.

Her husband was in the entry hall talking on his smartphone. Violet looked at her white-gold watch; it was 4:34pm. Time to go to bed.

'Yes, Freya, I miss you too. Why don't you come downstairs? We're home,' he said, and The Honourable Hugh (Hughie to his friends) smiled.

Ten seconds later, Freya and Louise, both clad in faded denim blue jeans, appeared at the top of the stairs. 'Daddy!' said Freya excitedly.

Freya's father was in his early fifties. He was tall (6'4") like his father and blond like his Rhodesian mother. Her father was not particularly handsome. He was rather average looking, but he was still slim and always sharply-attired. He employed a valet who ensured he was always well dressed.

He had been working for the family firm since graduating from Oxford. A life spent mostly overseas overseeing mining operations across the globe (in mostly third world countries) had meant being separated from Freya and his wife.

His older brother (the future 5th Baron) had no interest in mining and instead had focused on expanding the family's agricultural ventures. Hugh had been left to run the mining end of the family firm alone. His father had turned the reigns over to him years ago due to ill health. Both brothers had a reputation for efficiency; they were also known for their integrity and fairness.

Freya loved her father. He was always been kind to her. Hughie deeply regretted that work had taken him away from his small family.

Hugh loved Violet, flaws and all. Hughie knew what Gemma knew: that Vava had a good heart. It was just that her strict upbringing had left her unable to relate emotionally to other people. That and her sheltered existence had left her personality a bit warped. Vava was an extremely attentive wife. 'Are you comfortable, darling? Can I get you anything else? No, don't wear that tie; wear this one.' Vava was also loving and affectionate with him.

He couldn't understand why Violet had so little interest in their daughter. Vava lacked motherly instincts. Hughie was grateful that Gemma had filled that void (along with Karmen). As a result, Freya was a bit of a stranger to Violet. Their relationship had always been strained.

If Freya resented her mother for lacking interest in her life, she had never expressed it (at least not to him). Freya seemed content with Gemma and Karmen.

Violet, for her part, had never expressed any jealously towards either woman. Vava was probably glad (but probably not grateful) that Gemma and Karmen had so happily and effectively filled the role that she should have played.

Freya moved down the stairs like a panther. She had inherited that from Vava. Louise stayed at the top of the stairs, smiling, but unsure of what to do.

'It's good to see you, Daddy,' said Freya. She hugged him, and then she turned and looked up at Louise. 'Come on, Louise. I want to introduce you to my father.'

Louise smiled and carefully walked down the stairs. She was nervous. Older men made her nervous. Her own father was cold and indifferent. Louise didn't know what to make of a kind-hearted father. His behaviour seemed quite alien to her.

Louise finally reached the bottom of the stairs. She was tiny. Her natural strawberry blonde hair was still kept in the chin length bob that Louise had given her three years before. Louise's face was framed by the sharp edges of her hair. Her strawberry blonde hair contrasted nicely with her clear pale complexion and her dark brown eyes. Louise was wearing a cream cable-knit v-neck tennis sweater with blue and red colored bands along the neckline and cuffs, faded blue jeans, and light brown leather shoes. She was terribly cute and obviously shy and a bit intimidated.

Hughie could sense this, and so he decided to do what he could to make Louise feel at home. He smiled and said, 'Hello, Louise. I've heard such nice things about you from Freya. You're right, Freya. Louise is really quite stylish.'

Louise blushed and smiled. Freya melted. Louise was so sweet and innocent. Here was Louise, her dearest (and only) school friend. She loved Louise. Louise was a true friend. She knew that Louise had had a terrible childhood, and it grieved Freya.

Louise felt that Freya had saved her life; truth be told, the opposite was just as true. Freya had been rescued by Louise from near total social isolation. Her pariah status had remained unchanged for the last three years; however, with kind and loyal Louise at her side, it didn't matter. Freya had an intelligent and good-hearted confidant. Freya would do anything for Louise, and Freya knew that Louise would do anything for her.

At 18, both girls were poised to launch off into adulthood. Next year, however, Louise would be attending a different university. Louise's second tier university was in London. Freya's third tier uni was in the Midlands. Freya regretted that she had not studied harder. She also regretted that her poor school discipline reports had affected her ability to enter a better university. She wanted to stay together with Louise and attend university with her friend like her mother had with hers.

Vava had led a riotous existence at Oxford University. Everyone was surprised when she actually managed to graduate with a degree in art history. The Honourable Freya, who was much more academically gifted than her mother, had ended up in one of the country's least regarded universities. Oh, the misery of it all.

'It's nice to meet you, sir,' said Louise. 'Thank you for allowing me to stay with you during the Christmas holidays. I really appreciate it,' and Louise smiled.

'I'm happy you could stay with us. You are always welcome in our home,' answered Hughie.

Violet then approached and greeted Louise. 'It's nice to finally meet you, Lulu.'

'It's Louise, Mummy.'

'Yes, Louise. You are as "dangerously cute" as Poppy was at your age,' said Violet. 'Freya tells me so many nice things about you. I'm glad you came to stay with us,' she said, and Violet smiled.

Violet looked at Freya and said, 'She really does remind me so much of Poppy.' Violet then looked back at Louise, smiled, and asked, 'Have you met her yet?'

Freya was shocked. Her mother was actually being really nice to Louise. She had been worried her mother would embarrass her. She hadn't. She was as grateful as she was ~~surprised~~ stunned.

'What a poppet you are, Louise,' gushed Violet. 'I'm so glad Freya has finally brought a friend home for us to meet.' Violet smiled and then said, 'Well, I shall return to my lair. I'm sure Freya has told you what a dragon I am. So now I'm going to go upstairs and rest on my pile of gold.' Violet smiled, nodded, and glided (like a true Sloane) up the stairs.

Freya and Hughie stood in the entry hall looking astonished.

Louise turned to both of them and happily said, 'Your mother is so nice— and witty. She is really sweet,' and Louise smiled.

'Daddy. Did Mummy hit her head on something?'

'I'm not sure. I'd better take her round to the doctor's tomorrow and check.'


## Gemma—London—Oxford 1998

VAVA IN 2018

Vava exercised almost daily. She also enjoyed outdoor activities like hunting (a variety of wild animals) and horseback riding. She enjoyed wearing the required outfits (usually purchased from Külli's company—'Gula has always made the most stylish outfits!') that went with it. Vava thought that she looked particularly attractive wearing a leather bandolier of shotgun shells (that she *always* purchased from Külli's company—'Because G makes the finest kit in England!) and a shotgun (which she had purchased from Holland and Holland).

Vava only wished that Gula would be friends with her—and the rest of the gang—again. Violet's memories of Gula pained her. Vava had never come to terms with Külli's sudden break with the group. Gemma had been devastated by it, but she had always refused to really discuss it.

OXFORD in 1998

Violet made her way across the grass quad quickly. It was a cold autumn day. The leaves had turned and Violet was crushing golden leaves underfoot as she made her way to class. She was late for a lecture—again. She had stayed up all night talking with Hughie on the telephone—again. And in due course, she had overslept—again. Now she found herself rushing to class with her notebooks and her leather-cased portfolio. Suddenly, Violet spotted a ghost: Külli.

Külli was walking alone. Her long glossy brown hair had been intricately braided into a single sort of pony tail down her back. ('Probably something peasants do in the Baltics,' reflected Violet. 'How quaint,' she thought.)

Külli was headed in the opposite direction of Violet's lecture, but Vava hadn't seen Külli in almost a year. She seemed to stay away from Somerville and all of the gang's former haunts. Here was a chance for Violet to find out what had happened between her and Gemma. She looked towards the lecture hall, and then she looked at Külli walking away from her. Vava pivoted on the heels of her flats and bolted after her.

Vava wanted to call after her, but she was afraid Külli might dart off into a building or down an alley. Vava chose to surprise her. She picked up the pace and eventually broke into a sprint as Külli turned and disappeared down one of Oxford's ancient alleyways.

Vava reached the alleyway and turned. Standing just a few meters away was Külli. She had stopped to search through her leather book bag. Her back was to Violet. 'Gula!' shouted a breathless Violet. 'How are you, G?' Violet was breathing hard. She leaned up against the ancient stone wall and tried to catch her breath.

Külli lowered her book bag and slowly turned around. Külli was beautiful. Vava had always considered Gula beautiful, but her absence from Violet's life for almost two terms seemed to have amplified her beauty. Or was it Külli's exotic appearance? Vava wasn't sure. But, after all of the drama, she was *dying* to know what had happened between her and Gemma.

Külli was wearing a long, dark blue, pleated wool skirt, a white blouse, and over that a light grey blazer piped in white, and her platinum wrist watch. She looked like a model that had stepped from the pages of a fashion magazine.

Külli stared at Violet for a moment, and then she turned and started to walk down the cobblestone alleyway.

'Oh, no, you don't, Gula!' exclaimed Violet, and she grabbed Külli's arm and spun her around. Külli was surprised by Violet's aggressiveness.

'Gula, I've known you for seven years! I lived with you for five! We were the best of friends in Sussex! And now, at Oxford, you refuse to even speak with me! Really, Gula! How can you treat me—us—like this?!' Violet wasn't angry, she was upset and confused.

Violet was still holding Külli by the forearm when Külli finally spoke. 'What did Gemma tell you?'

'Very little. Gemmy said you had had an argument and that *she had said terrible things to you*—**which I find impossible to believe**. That's not Gemmy's nature. And besides, I know that Gemmy was always closer to you than anyone else. She loves you, Gula. She loves you even more than she loves George.'

Gula was taken aback. As much by what was being said as *by who was saying it* (and *how* she was saying it). Vava had never been much for emotional outbursts or displays of affection. Vava's behaviour at this moment was uncharacteristic for Vava. Gula realized she had entirely misjudged her. Vava had a heart after all…

Gula reflected for a moment on Vava's words. Gemmy had taken the blame for everything; when the blame had been entirely Gula's. Gemmy was a good friend, true and loyal. She hadn't revealed anything. Gula's secret was safe. **Of course, it was**.

Külli's mind seemed to shift in another direction and she felt suddenly overwhelmed with emotion. Külli started to physically tremble. Violet, holding Külli's sleeve, noticed. Vava looked (up) at her and realized that Gula was crying. Vava had *never* seen her do that. It was almost unnerving.

Violet's demeanour changed. She released Külli's arm and suddenly Violet appeared to have a gentle air about her. *Gula had never seen that.* Gula was still crying when Vava spoke.

'G, please come back to us. Whatever has happened can be overcome. Gemmy and Poppy want you back. Gula. I want you back. I need you too.' And Violet began to cry.

Külli had not thought Vava was capable of crying. The last few minutes had been incredible. Külli was deeply moved. Yes, she missed her friends: The Inseparable Gang of Happy Girls.

Külli started crying even harder. She moved forward and hugged Violet. She cried on Vava's shoulder (well, more like the top of her head; Vava was about 5 inches shorter than Gula). After a couple of minutes, Külli pulled back. She wiped her eyes. Vava was still crying.

'Gemmy did nothing wrong. I'm to blame. I'm not surprised Gemmy fell on the sword for me. That's her nature. But, I'm the guilty party,' Gula said softly.

Violet held out her hand to Gula. 'Come on, G. Come with me. Let's walk back to Sommerville together right now. *We need you.*'

Külli almost followed her. She had started to raise her hand to grasp Vava's, but, at that moment, inexplicably, something came over Gula, and she lowered it. An emotional reunion would change nothing. Gemmy would still be engaged to George. Gula would have to endure it all. It was too much for her. **She couldn't bear it. She couldn't.**

Choked with emotion, barely able to speak above a whisper, Külli spoke. 'I'm so sorry, Vava. I can't. And I can't explain why. Please don't ask me. I'm sorry. Vava. I'm the weak one; not Gemmy.'

And with that, Gula turned and retreated down the alley.

Vava made no attempt to follow.

## Gemma—London—The Frozen Lake

THE FROZEN LAKE
Poppy decided that today would be a good day to take Gemma on a drive through the countryside and stop at a lake that they used to swim at when they were still attending school in Sussex. The idyllic summers at Poppy's country house were happy memories for all of the girls.

Poppy drove the silver Bristol 411 along the road leading away from the house. As soon as they crested the hill near the castle ruins, Poppy began to speak. She was excited and happy.

'Gemmy! I have something to tell you! Brian made it official this morning! He formally proposed to me!' Poppy said excitedly and happily. Poppy was beaming.

'Poppy! That's fantastic! I'm so happy for you! This is great!' Gemma paused for a moment and then asked, 'How did he propose to you?'

'Brian asked me to give him a tour of the library—I had promised him I would back in London. I hadn't expected he would propose to me there. I was telling him about the tapestry in the library when he took out a small box from Van Cleef and Arpels. Brian then told me that the first time he had seen me he knew that he wanted to marry me. He told me that he regretted not asking me to marry him immediately after my presentation on gold ETFs.' Poppy smiled and laughed. 'I asked Brian, 'Was the presentation really *that* good?' Brian smiled and told me that it was.'

'So, what did you say?'

'Gemmy! Of course, I said yes!'

Both girls laughed.

'When we get to the lake, I'll show you my ring. It's so beautiful, Gemmy! I can't believe it! Finally! After all these years, I'm going to get married!'

The Bristol hummed along the road at a slow pace; the roads had patches of ice here and there. Poppy was careful.

'Gemmy, the engagement ring is so beautiful! I never thought I would ever get married. I had almost given up until I met Brian at the conference. Today seems surreal. Is this really happening?'

'It's happening, Poppy. And I'm happy for you.'

The silver Bristol 411 motorcar drove across the frozen landscape. As they came closer to the lake, memories came rushing back to both of them. For Gemma, the disappointments of adulthood had made these happy memories all the more poignant.

The car finally arrived at the edge of the frozen lake. The snow-covered landscape was broken only by the lake, which itself was covered in a thin layer of ice.

After she had turned off the engine, she raised her hand to show Gemma her engagement ring. It was a stunningly beautiful Perlée solitaire diamond ring set in white gold. The ring sparkled on Poppy's hand. Poppy smiled. Gemma was visibly impressed.

'It's really beautiful. Brian selected the perfect ring,' said Gemma.

The girls then got out of the silver car and stood at the lake's edge. They stared out across the ice for a few minutes. Neither of them spoke. Both were lost in thought.

Poppy was filled with hope and could only dream of the happy future that lay ahead for her with Brian. Gemma, conversely, dreaded the uncertainty that the future now offered her. Gemma felt safe here, surrounded by friends and happy memories of the past, but she would return to London soon. What would the future hold for her?

## Gemma—London—Wagner

A SMALL TOWN

The American South

Grey enjoyed opera. His father had listened to it often, especially in the evenings. His father had never once invited Grey nor ever allowed him into his home office to listen to it. It didn't really bother Grey. He had, perhaps, inherited his father's indifference. Nonetheless, Grey used to sit on the stairwell outside the door and listen for hours while growing up in a small town in North Carolina. Grey found it soothing, even uplifting.

He would often go to the local public library downtown and listen to opera records on the headphones supplied by librarian in the audio/visual room on the second floor. It was at the local library in the foothills of North Carolina (of all places), that Grey had discovered Wilhelm Richard Wagner.

Wagner had had a profound effect on the young Grey. It instilled in him a sense of adventure and destiny—of the possibilities of human greatness. It made him want to adventure and engage in warfare. It filled him with bloodlust. Grey felt inspired. It was Wagner that had driven Grey to bypass college and enlist in the French Foreign Legion.

Grey had never been close to his father. His father had been indifferent, cold, and distant. It should have bothered him, Grey supposed, but it really didn't. Grey didn't think much of his father. He was often violent and abusive towards him and his mother. Grey didn't think much of his mother either. She was almost as indifferent to him as his father. At least she cooked dinner.

Grey's family had once been quite prominent in North Carolina. His ancestors had all served as officers in the Confederate Army, something that Grey was extremely proud of. His family had owned a plantation that covered over 500 acres, and the family had owned almost a hundred slaves. After the Civil War, most of them had left the plantation, but, strangely enough, virtually all of them had legally adopted Grey's family name as their own. Not out of any sense of loyalty, his grandfather had once explained to him, but out of pride. They were proud of their association with Grey's family. So, it wasn't unusual for the teenage Grey to meet black people with his family's extremely rare name in his home county as well as many of the adjacent ones.

The family had been forced to sell off their land in the decades following the Civil War until eventually, all that remained was the main house. Financial mismanagement by Grey's grandfather had forced the family to sell the house in the early 1960s.

By the time Grey had been born, the family was living in a modest house in a middle class neighbourhood a mile away from the family's former plantation house in a small town that had been built on land that had once belonged to his family.

The town's main industries were textile mills and tobacco farms, neither of which paid a living wage. Most of the town's roughly 1,800 residents lived barely above the poverty line.

The plantation house, once surrounded by hundreds of acres of farmland, was now located on a side street at the edge of town.

The plantation house had been purchased by an unsavory and crass lawyer. He lived there with his wife and two daughters.

The large ornate plantation house was the only structure in the entire town that could be called beautiful. The rest of the town was made up of nondescript single-family homes, and the small downtown area was filled with uninspired architecture, much of it built in the 1940s. The only notable features of the town were the faded RC Cola signs and the former plantation house.

Grey's mother had repeatedly cautioned him to never speak of the house to his father; the unspoken warning was that merely mentioning the house would provoke a violent response from him. That didn't bother Grey either. He never mentioned it to him. Truth be told, Grey rarely said anything to his father.

While growing up, Grey used to walk across town several times a year and gaze at the house from the park that was across the street from it. Grey didn't know what to think or feel about the large antebellum structure. It had once belonged to his family.

Grey's family had once produced great men. Grey's father was nothing. He had attended a mediocre state college and worked as a mid-level state auditor. The family was now just middle class. The family name was still well known locally and to historians. That the family had sunk so low really bothered Grey. Grey's father was a failure. He had never done anything with his life. He had barely left the state and had never left the country. Grey's father had never even had a passport. His father was pathetic. Grey swore that he would never end up like his father.

Grey wanted to restore the past glory of his family. He sometimes dreamed about purchasing the plantation house and restoring it to its former glory. However, Grey didn't have any money. And there was another problem: Grey wanted to leave North Carolina and never come back. Grey felt that, like one of the heroes in a Wagnerian opera, he would have to leave home to seek his fortune. Perhaps, like a character from an opera, he would become a king. There would then be no need to ever return home.

Fate had been hard on Grey. It had pushed him very hard. But Grey felt it had all been for a reason. He had been funnelled in a certain direction. Fate was not finished with Grey. He was destined for greatness. Grey had the blood of warriors in his veins.

Just before Grey graduated from high school in 1986, he used some of his savings (over a thousand dollars in cash) to purchase a one-way plane ticket to France. He had also applied for and received a passport just before graduation. (Something he did without informing his parents.)

IMMOLATION
The night after Grey graduated from high school, he put some clothes in a duffle bag, and wearing jeans and a t-shirt, left the house in the middle of the night. He walked alone through the deserted streets until he reached his family's former plantation house.

There was still a light on in an upstairs bedroom when he had arrived. He waited for over an hour in the park across the street. He watched the light in the window until it was turned off.

Grey then looked around. No one. Such a warm and humid summer night. Grey walked across the street. He opened the metal gate on the side of the house and entered the garden. He was carrying a gas can.

Grey had decided that the people who lived here were unworthy to own his former family home. Honor demanded purification. Grey splashed gasoline on the side of the house in several different spots. He set the empty gas can down on the steps leading up to the backdoor and stood back. He gazed at the house. Yes, this was the right thing to do. Grey lit a match and threw it. He then turned and ran.

He ran through the park and down a back alley until he reached the center of town. He crossed the street and walked to the local bus station. He heard the sirens of the fire trucks of the local volunteer fire department as he entered the small rundown bus terminal.

He turned around and looked in the direction of the house. A short distance away there was a huge orange glow and smoke filled the air. Many of the townspeople had been roused from their sleep by the sirens and had come out of their houses to investigate what was happening.

'One ticket to Raleigh,' said Grey calmly at the heavily-scratched ticket window. He passed the money to the clerk, and the fat, slovenly, bespectacled clerk pushed a small white ticket back through the window.

Grey took it and then sat down in one of the blue plastic chairs that were attached to a long metal frame in the terminal. The floor of the waiting room was covered in vinyl tiles, many of them chipped and cracked. The paint on the walls was peeling and water-stained.

This building seemed to embody everything about this town that Grey hated. It had been neglected, left to rot. It barely functioned. Grey's hometown was populated with people who had given up, or like his father, had never even tried. The very room Grey found himself sitting in repelled him. But it was exactly what Grey needed: a final reminder that he was leaving nothing behind that he would miss. This place was toxic, poisonous, and hopeless.

The large cracked glass windows of the dilapidated bus terminal looked directly out in the direction of the burning plantation house.

He said nothing. His face was expressionless. Grey felt nothing.

He took a Walkman cassette player out of his duffle bag and put on the headphones. He played Wagner's Tannhäuser Overture as he watched the glow of the fire a few blocks away. Grey watched the glow grow stronger, and then slowly weaker as the flames were put out. About that time, a large silver bus stopped in front of the terminal.

'Boarding for Raleigh!' shouted the lone clerk, a middle-aged, fat, and bald man with glasses who had never lived anywhere but this town.

The teenage Grey picked up his duffel bag, and still listening to Wagner, boarded the bus for RDU airport and his future.

AFTERMATH

The house had been gutted by the fire. No one in the family had escaped the flames. Investigators had quickly concluded it was arson. The motive? The local police suspected the father, a prominent lawyer, had cheated one too many of his former clients and one of them had most likely sought revenge. No suspects were ever named. The crime went unsolved.

Grey's parents knew immediately who had done it. They said nothing. Not out of loyalty to Grey, but to protect themselves. They never reported their only child missing. They avoided discussing him with neighbours (not that anyone ever asked about him), and they made no attempts to ever locate him. Privately, Grey's father was proud of Grey. For the first, last, and only time in his father's pathetic life, he was proud of his son. Grey had done the right thing.

Grey entered the French Foreign Legion, served a tour, and received an entirely new identity upon leaving. He told everyone that his name, Grey, was just a nickname.

## 8 GEMMA AND POPPY

**Gemma—London—Church of England**

ST GEORGE'S

2018

On Christmas Eve, the baron's family and house guests attended church at the village church a few miles away from the estate. The whole family was Anglican, as well as both house guests.

Gemma had once been a regular churchgoer, but had stopped going years ago after the trial. Her notoriety had followed her into church and, contrary to what she had hoped, she found herself unwelcome by most of the congregation. The priests had been kind and supportive, but Gemma knew that any further attendance would only add to her misery.

On this Christmas Eve, Gemma found herself sitting in the front pew with the baron and his family.

Poppy's family had paid for the construction of the small stone church in the 1300s. In the 1400s the church had gone from being Catholic to becoming Anglican. If one looked closely at the ceiling, they could make out the Latin words engraved in the stone walls.

The church only seated about 100 people, at best. Those who did attend sat on red velvet cushions on long wooden pews. The local noble family, as a courtesy as well as out of custom, always sat on the front pews. Church attendance at the church averaged about thirty, including the baron and his wife. On holidays, attendance usually surged to around seventy. This evening, the church was filled to capacity. Some parishioners had to stand at the back of the church.

The newly installed heating system (a gift from the baron) worked well.

Everyone dressed formally: the men in coat and tie, the women in dresses or country tweeds. The church cloakroom was filled with a wide variety of wool jackets—some with fur collars, the baron's long wool coat, a few parkas, waxed and quilted jackets, and even a couple of fur coats.

The parish priest of St George's church and his altar boys performed the service flawlessly and the local choir sang very well. The service had been a happy and relaxing experience for Gemma. She had missed the services, if not necessarily many of the congregation, back in London.

After the service, everyone walked from the small church to the church annex—a single story wooden building that had been constructed in the 1930s. There the attendees could choose from a selection of turkey, beef, pork, or lamb slices. There was also a wide variety of cheese, bread, and non-alcoholic drinks. One small side table offered slices of cake, pie, and sliced fruit.

The annex's main room had been decorated with Christmas lights and paper decorations. There was a Christmas tree at one end that illuminated the dimly-lit room. The main sources of light in the main hall that night were candles and Christmas lights.

Gemma thought it was all quite beautiful. At first, she had been nervous about chatting with the locals; most of them knew exactly who she was. She was afraid someone would say something and there would be a scene; however, everyone was nice and seemed to go out of their way to be pleasant to her. She was extremely grateful. She almost felt normal again.

The baron and baroness exchanged Christmas greetings with the locals. The baron and his wife especially liked to greet the children and see how much they had grown. They also met a few new additions to some of the families. The baron had always been popular with the local villagers, as had his late father, the 11th Baron, and his grandfather, the 10th Baron.

Poppy happily introduced her fiancé Brian to everyone. Poppy and Brian made a nice couple.

James and his wife chatted with some of the villagers, too, and the twins

238

had a good time playing with the local children.

The highlight of the evening was the arrival of Santa Claus. This year it was felt that an outsider should play Santa, so Brian was drafted to do it. He was a rather slim Santa, but he did a good job with the children. He arrived with a large bag of wrapped toys and stockings full of candy. He sat in a large chair and handed out the gifts and stockings to the children one by one. Brian seemed to really enjoy it.

Gemma, who was standing behind Poppy, whispered in her ear, 'Brian will be a great father, Poppy.'

Poppy turned around to Gemma and smiled. 'I think so too. I hope so.' And then Poppy held Gemma's hand and said earnestly, 'Gemmy. When— if—I have a baby, Brian and I would like you to be godmother. It would mean so much to us.'

Gemma hadn't been expecting that. She stared for a moment and then hugged Poppy. "Thank you, Poppy. That would mean a lot to me too.' The two Happy Inseparables looked at each other and smiled; they then hugged each other again.

Gemma deeply appreciated the gesture. Fate had rendered her childless, but it has also given her Freya, and now Poppy's future child would enter her orbit (though she knew the bond would never be even close to being as strong as Freya's was with her; Poppy would be a good mother).

Gemma and Poppy returned to watching Brian play Santa. They had an enjoyable evening.

Afterwards, everyone made their way through the snowy cold night and back to their warm homes.

Everything seemed normal.

**Gemma—London—Christmas Day**

POPPY'S BEDROOM

Gemma had slept well. She had crawled into bed, snuggled up with Poppy, and went to sleep. She woke up next to her warm friend. Gemma felt serene. The trip to the Lake District was just what she had needed. Here, in this house, surrounded by those she loved, and who loved her, she was happy and safe.

Gemma was covered in soft white sheets and a white duvet. Her head was buried in a large, soft, white pillow. Her shoulder-length brown hair rested on her pillow and sharply contrasted with the whiteness around her. The sheets and pillows gave off the intermingling scents of Gemma and Poppy's cold creams.

She looked up at the white plastered ceiling. She scanned it for details. There were many. The room, once done up in rococo, had been redone in art deco by one of the daughters of the 10th Baron in the 1920s.

The ceiling and crown molds were done in what could best be described as Egyptian Art Deco. The room's ceilings and walls were entirely white. The details were difficult to detect at first, there being no variation in color. The room was edged in a wide plaster crown mold depicting Egyptian hieroglyphics. The ceiling was more of the same. The bedroom was made to resemble the interior of an ancient temple.

The lighting was set along the edge of the walls, hidden behind the plaster crown molding. It flooded out and across the ceiling when the lights were turned on. The lighting had two settings: dim and full. The first switch turned on only one of three bulbs. The glow those few bulbs emitted cast long shadows from between the hieroglyphs carved into the crown moldings. The effect was hypnotic.

The furniture in the room had been purchased in Germany in the 1920s. It was most likely Bauhaus, or at the very least, an inspired copy of it. All of it was made from polished Circassian walnut. It must have been enormously expensive. But, as Poppy had told her many times in the past, the family still had real money back then.

The maple bed was older; it was late Victorian. It had been purchased at the same time as the house was built. The mattress, however, mercifully, was modern.

Gemma had spent many nights in this bed. She remembered her first night in it; she had shared it with the entire gang. All four girls had slept together. She had awoken in Gula's embrace. At fifteen, she had thought nothing of it. Even now, the memory remained a happy one.

This house was filled with happy memories; like ghosts, they appeared and then faded away, only to reappear later. They always made Gemma smile— and yearn for those happy, innocent days of her youth.

Gemma enjoyed the near silence this morning offered her. Peace and calm. Gemma ~~wished~~ prayed that her problems with Grey would come to an end quickly, and that he would let her go. Grey. He had once again intruded into her thoughts, like a stone being thrown through a glass window.

'Please, God. Help me,' prayed Gemma to herself.

Gemma reached over and picked up a silver necklace from the nightstand. She held it in her small soft hands. Suspended from the slim silver chain was a sterling silver cross of St Albans, her patron saint.

The cross had been a gift from her mother. Gemma's kind and protective mother had always called Gemma by her middle name—Ophelia. That was the name that had been engraved on the back of it. Gemma had only managed to avoid having the small silver cross taken by the bailiffs because she had left it hanging off of the bathroom mirror in Poppy's flat after a brief visit a few days before the bailiffs arrived.

Gemma felt that God, or perhaps her mother's ghost, had saved it from being taken. The small ankh like silver cross of St Albans was Gemma's most prized possession. Gemma put the silver necklace on and lay back down.

Poppy stirred next to her. She reached out and felt around. She felt Gemma and then stopped. She caressed Gemma's shoulder gently. Her head slowly rose from the pillow and Poppy's kind blue eyes, surrounded by golden blonde hair, met Gemma's gaze. Poppy smiled.

'Merry Christmas, Gemmy,' she said softly.

Gemma smiled and replied, 'Merry Christmas, Poppy.'

'The twins should be up soon; then Christmas morning will begin in earnest,' declared Poppy.

Poppy crawled across the king sized mattress and then got out of bed. She was wearing the pink silk nightgown that Brian had given her for her birthday a few months before. She stood and stretched. She spun around and faced Gemma, who was still laying in bed.

'Okay, I'll take a bath first. Don't worry. I'll save you some hot water, Gemmy.' And Poppy smiled.

THE FAMILY
Breakfast was served in the wood-paneled dining room. The two Croatian maids, far away from home, had elected to work on Christmas (at double pay). The family chef, Edward, young and still unmarried, had also volunteered to stay. The last remaining member of the staff, the estate manager, Hector, was married and at his home in the nearby village, enjoying the day with his family.

The long polished dark walnut table was covered in a white tablecloth and the family's finest silverware and porcelain. Breakfast was laid out on the sideboard.

The twins had wanted to skip breakfast and open their presents immediately, but their parents insisted that they have breakfast first.

Everyone ate breakfast and chatted happily. The twins sat on either side of Gemma and excitedly told her what they hoped to get from Santa. Gemma listened attentively; she loved the seven-year-old twins. If only she had been able to have had children of her own…

After breakfast, the entire party headed into the drawing room where a large Christmas tree had been set up and decorated by the entire family. The gifts were placed around the base of the tree.

Gemma had purchased history books for the men, Folio books (each book by a known favorite author) for the Baroness, Poppy, and Helen, and soft plush toys and sweaters for the children. The gifts were not really that expensive. No one here usually spent much on gifts. It was the thought that mattered most. Gifts should be something that someone could enjoy. In this family, it meant books.

Gemma also loved books. She had once had a large collection of books in both French and English. Some of them were first editions. A few had even been autographed by the authors. All of them had been seized and auctioned by the bailiffs.

Gemma received French cookbooks from the baron and baroness, a black leather Mulberry handbag from Poppy ('I love it! Thank you, Poppy!'), a beautiful limited-edition book with gilt edges on Byzantium from James and Helen, and an expensive black leather Montblanc briefcase from Brian ('For the City,' Brian had said with a smile). The children each gave Gemma Christmas cards they had happily made for her. Gemma loved all of her Christmas gifts. She always did anyway, no matter what they were.

She had even loved the dark brown leather open-end cartridge belt from Holland and Holland that Vava had given her for Christmas when they were 16. Gemma never wore it—shooting had never interested her. Gula, however, found the workmanship to be amazing. Gula wore it around the alcove room at school, studied it carefully, sketched it out in one of her notebooks, and later used it to pattern her own line of cartridge belts at her family's outfitters. Gula never missed an opportunity to learn something.

**Gula**. There she was again. Gemma couldn't shake her from her thoughts. Gemma didn't want to shake Külli from her thoughts. Most of her memories of Külli were happy ones. Mostly. Mostly.

The morning was a happy one. It ended with the three couples: the baron and baroness, James and Helen, and Poppy and Brian seated together and holding hands. Gemma was on the floor of the drawing room playing with the twins. All were happy. All had had a Merry Christmas. All felt the future held happiness for them, even Gemma.

## Gemma—London—The Golem

THE MURKY LAMP

Gangsters are a peculiar bunch. Some criminals spend as much time rationalizing what they do as they do committing their crimes. Some criminals don't even bother.

The one common thread they do share is their belief that they understand 'how the real world works.' This is one of their fatal flaws. Professional criminals—gangsters—don't really have even the most basic understanding of how the real world works. They only understand gangland. This basic flaw in their mentality leads them to miscalculate and most of them eventually end up either incarcerated or dead.

Very few escape the consequences of their actions. The few that do are extremely dangerous; not because of what they might potentially do in the future, but because they inspire other members of the criminal classes into believing that they can do the same.

**Grey had never been caught**. He had never spent a day in court. He had never been questioned by the police. No suspicion had ever fallen upon him. At fifty-one years of age, Grey was virtually unique in gangland. Not only had he never been caught, he was almost entirely unknown in the criminal underworld. While there were rumors of someone like him swirling around London, nothing had ever been confirmed.

Grey had managed to fly under the radar for over two and a half decades.

He had kept his operation small. His gang was crewed with comrades from the Legion, the battlefields of the ex-Yugoslavia, and the former Soviet Union. They were a highly unusual and tight-knit group of men.

Most of his men were in their forties and fifties. Most were still physically fit and and all those in his gang were all still mentally sharp.

Most of the alcoholic or drug addled among his former comrades had died years ago. Grey never let those men into his inner circle. To them, he was just a former comrade who had been highly successful. Grey was generous, he often paid their rent and gave them cash. Why not? He could afford it. And, at one time, these men had served him loyally. A couple had even saved his life in combat. And besides, maybe, one day, he might need their services. Gratitude would compel them to agree to do almost anything.

And many of his comrades had something else Grey could use: their children. Yes, most of these men had children. The men in his inner circle all seem to be on their second or third marriage. Or, at the very least, they had had children with girlfriends (and ex-girlfriends). Some of these children had served (or were serving) in the military, attended (or were attending) university, or had even become police officers. Yes, Grey had a very unique and highly loyal network around him.

Most of the children had no idea what their fathers really did for a living. The ones that did figure it out either broke contact and moved away or they asked to join. The ones that joined Grey's gang were highly valuable commodities to him.

The children of ex-girlfriends were the most valuable. **None** of the children he had recruited used their father's family name. They used the mother's. The father's name did not appear on their birth certificates. That allowed for legal and societal distancing from their fathers. Grey had created a gang that consisted of cells, just like a revolutionary organization. This made it much more difficult for Scotland Yard or Interpol to put the pieces together—with or without a computer database.

Grey had learned many things over the years; one was that technology had its limits. Another was that technology could easily be turned against its creators and users.

## GANGSTER MENTALITY

However, a flaw remained: Grey felt that he understood how the universe worked. *He didn't.* He only really understood gangland. This flawed way of thinking had led him to misjudge many situations and miscalculate reactions. Grey, however, had been extremely lucky. In spite of all of his mistakes, he had never been caught or killed. This had only served to embolden him and make him believe he was somehow infallible.

## A GOLEM

**Grey was a product of his times**: a product of the wars of the 90s and the breakdown of the old international order. Countries had collapsed and disappeared. New countries had been created from the wreckage. And from the ruins, waves of human wreckage had also appeared. Everyone is shaped in one way or the other by their experiences, for better or worse. Grey had been no exception. Grey was a monster, for sure. However, Grey was a golem walking on thin ice.

## NEMESIS

It was only a matter of time now. Grey's arrogance—his hubris—would lead to his eventual downfall. The question was: how many people—innocent and guilty—would he take with him?

## Gemma—London—Violence Contained

## GREY

Grey had spent the last few weeks training at a private gym. Grey had gone back to kickboxing. He was good at it. And, as a consequence of the hard training, he had slimmed down considerably. His appearance had changed. He looked brutal. With his fresh Legion-style haircut, he looked every inch the soldier he really was. Grey felt good.

He wanted to get back in shape for this new phase of his life. Grey was branching out. He was planning to go head-to-head with rival criminal gangs, that, without exception, were completely unaware of Grey's existence.

Grey had managed to cultivate the image of a successful (and entirely legitimate) businessman. Grey was 'an art and antiques dealer.' Very few people outside of Grey's criminal gang knew the truth. That's how he wanted it. He needed that element of surprise.

Grey knew a lot about art. He was a quick learner with a nearly photographic memory. Grey was intelligent. He also spoke three foreign languages fluently (which included the near perfect French he had learned in the Foreign Legion) and could get by in a couple others. He lacked many of the social graces. Being around Gemma had made that abundantly clear to him. Grey was not charming. Grey could carry on an interesting and intelligent conversation (especially with men), but he was at a loss in many regards. Grey was a work in progress.

**And this is where Gemma would come in.** Gemma could teach him a lot of things, such as how to navigate London society. Gemma was damaged goods. Her reputation was in ruins. A lot of her kind refused to associate with her. That didn't matter to Grey. The nobility in England seemed to be largely bankrupt or at best, treading water just to stay financially afloat. They had lost most (if not all) of their money—like Gemma.

And they were whoring themselves out to parvenus like Grey just to survive. Just like Gemma.

No, the 'London society' that Grey was thinking of was the *new one.* The London society made up of gangsters, movie and television stars, footballers, and the hordes of nouveau riche (who were mostly foreign) that had flooded into London in the last decade. They all wanted to be part of 'The Set.' So did Grey.

Many of 'The Honourables' now worked for these people. They hated it. They hated the reduced circumstances they had found themselves in, but what choice did they really have?

Many Sloane Rangers worked as personal shoppers, event planners, and even DJs. Oh, and more than a few of them aggressively sought out rich foreign men to marry so that they could live the lifestyles their grandmothers (or great grandmothers) had had.

Grey thoughts now returned to Gemma. She was beautiful and intelligent. She was *posh.* She would be Grey's wife, the mother of his children, and play hostess to his clients and business associates. Grey could now clearly visualize Gemma emerging from a silver ~~Audi~~ Volvo with their daughter. Gemma would learn to accept her role in his life. Eventually she would fall into place like so many other things had throughout his life. Grey now had momentum.

Grey also knew something else: **He was in love with Gemma.** Well, was it really love? Or was it inordinate lust? Grey really wasn't sure. He only knew that Gemma **had to be his.** This one thought was set in his brain like a piece of iron. After all, Grey had already had her. That was ownership.

## Gemma—London—Boxing Day

REFLECTION

The day after Christmas had found Gemma filling the white porcelain bathtub with hot water when she noticed the first flakes of snow to fall outside the bathroom window. The view from the window was spectacular, the hills and forests spread out before her, a vast panorama in white. Within minutes, the hot water from the bath would steam up the windows and obscure the view entirely.

Completely relaxed in the warm water of the bath, Gemma was deep in thought. She reflected on how difficult the last three years had been for her.

Three months ago, she had hit rock bottom. She was down to less than a hundred pounds in the bank and was struggling to find even part-time work. In a fit of desperation—panic really—she had agreed to meet a wealthy American suitor at the suggestion of Violet.

Grey had turned out to be worse than George. And, most worryingly, Grey was refusing to let her go.

George had been many things, but at least he had never been physically violent with her. George had never even been verbally or emotionally abusive towards her while they were together.

George's true nature had remained completely hidden until the day the police had arrived with the bailiffs at their Notting Hill home. Gemma had been completely blindsided. George had been kind and charming right up till their last morning together. It was only when Gemma received a desperate telephone call from the house maid informing her of the bailiffs' arrival at the front door, did Gemma have any notion that something was wrong.

The shock of discovering George's other life had driven Gemma into the depths of despair. She had telephoned, texted, and emailed George asking him for answers. Gemma wanted to know how he could do what he had done to her. How could the man she had loved so completely—trusted so completely—have betrayed her so completely? Had she done something wrong?

Gemma's life had been completely destroyed in a single rainy afternoon in London. Gemma stood in the living room and cried as the bailiffs catalogued everything in their house. She broke down completely when the movers arrived and started to remove everything. She had begged the bailiffs to let her keep her family heirlooms—they had pointedly refused.

Poppy left work early and hurried over to Gemma's home to console her and protect her from the hordes of photographers that had arrived to document the baron's downfall.

But George wasn't even there. After a pleasant breakfast with Gemma, he kissed her gently and told her he would be home for dinner like always. He then headed out the door with his umbrella to the bank. Well, that's where he told Gemma he was going.

George never spoke to Gemma again. He never responded to any of her emails, texts, or phone calls. (In fact, he had had his phone disconnected that very day.)

Gemma became tabloid fodder. George's sordid private life was splashed across the front page of the papers. Fleet Street had struck gold. Gemma was portrayed by the press as a toxic wife whose profligate ways had driven her husband to embezzle millions from the bank to support her lavish lifestyle. Gemma had been universally villainized and condemned in the British press.

The truth was just the opposite. Gemma had used her salary to support George's lifestyle, and she would later discover, the daughter he had had with one of his colleagues. George's secret daughter with another woman had been the biggest shock of all. And the most hurtful.

Gemma, bankrupted by the court proceedings, moved in with Poppy. Gemma cried herself to sleep for months. It was Poppy who sat at her bedside and consoled her. Sometimes Poppy would sleep next to her and hold her. Without Poppy, Gemma was sure the trial would have killed her. Poppy had saved her. Poppy always saved her.

The next time she saw him was in the courtroom several weeks later. George Howard had destroyed her life completely, and he hadn't even had the courage to look in her direction. Gemma was devastated. How could he do that to her? How could he?

Gemma had managed to hang onto her position as an assistant editor at a London fashion magazine until a mass cull of the staff six months ago had led to her sudden and unexpected dismissal. She had only been able to keep her job because the head editor had been a good friend who had stood up for her at senior staff meetings. Now they both found themselves unemployed on the same day. Gemma would always be grateful to her for everything she had done for her. Gemma hadn't realized how utterly unemployable the trial had rendered her until after being made redundant.

Gemma lay in the bathtub and sobbed. The memories were too terrible. Time had not healed all.

Gemma still wanted to find happiness.

SPINNING

The weeks before she had met Grey had seen Gemma's life deteriorate even further. Her life was in a tailspin. She was broke. She was desperate. And she was scared. Terrified. What would become of her? She couldn't live with Poppy forever. Poppy needed to have her own life. Gemma was impeding her relationship with Brian (though neither of them would admit it). Gemma was nothing but trouble. She was a failure. Gemma no longer wished to even be alive anymore. Gemma wished she could just snap her fingers and disappear.

Violet's telephone call and invitation to meet a potential husband was unwelcomed by Gemma. She wasn't the type to marry anyone for money. She wasn't that type of person. It was insulting. What kind of woman did Vava think she really was? Gemma had married for love and only love. But upon reflection, what had that gotten her?

Gemma despaired at her future prospects. She was lost. It was despair and panic—even temporary insanity—that had driven Gemma to agree to meet the American.

REVEAL ALL
There was a gentle knock at the bathroom door.

'Gemmy,' asked Poppy. 'Are you alright? May I come in? I'm worried about you?'

Gemma quickly slid under the water and then shot back up. She wanted to wipe away all evidence of her tears.

'Come in,' replied Gemma.

Poppy opened the door and entered. She was wearing a white bathrobe. Her bare feet padded across the damp tiled floor and she then knelt down next to the large white porcelain bathtub. 'I'm here, Gemmy,' she said softly. Poppy then folded her arms and rested on the edge of the tub, her chin resting on her folded arms.

'I'm okay, Poppy,' replied Gemma.

'I heard you crying, Gemmy. Please talk to me.'

'I make a mess wherever I go, Poppy. I can't do anything right.'

'That's not true, Gem. You're a good person. You didn't deserve to have had any of this happen to you.'

Gemma looked at Poppy for a few seconds and then burst into tears again. She started sobbing uncontrollably. Poppy, shocked, reached out and hugged her. What was really wrong? Poppy wondered.

'Gemmy, please tell me what is going on. What happened to you? **What did Grey do to you?'**

**Grey.** There. That name again.

Gemma cried uncontrollably for several minutes. She fought to regain control of herself—to no avail. Okay. She had to finally tell someone. Tell Poppy. You can trust her.

'Poppy. The worst thing that can happen has happened to me,' said Gemma choking back tears.

Gemma was destroyed inside. Poppy could suddenly sense it. Gemma had hidden the damage well for a long time. Poppy wished she hadn't. Soon, she would realize why she had.

Gemma got out of the bathtub and with Poppy's help, put on her bathrobe and left the bathroom. They went into Poppy's bedroom and sat down on her bed.

Gemma then began to tell Poppy what had happened to her on her first night in Grey's house. At first Gemma spoke very slowly; the emotions were so painful. Gemma paused many times; each time breaking down into sobs. As the story continued, Gemma started to speak more quickly. She cried the entire time. Finally, she told Poppy the worst of it. Poppy broke down crying too. It was all too much for both of them. Grey had brutally raped Gemma; injured her; and broken her.

Poppy was devastated, too. No one should ever have to go through what Grey had put Gemma through. Gemma, gentle, kind, and good, had been destroyed by an animal. Poppy could only hold Gemma and let her cry; her whole body was trembling.

Poppy didn't know what to say. What could she say? What? She couldn't tell her that everything would be okay—because things would never be ok again. Nothing would ever be the same. Poor Gemmy; she had carried this secret with her for months, unable to tell anyone. It was overwhelming. It was crushing. It was the worst thing that could happen to someone, and it had happened to Gemma.

'Gemmy,' sobbed Poppy. 'I love you. I always will.'

### Gemma—London—Poppy

THE COUNTRY HOUSE

December 27, 2018

Poppy was emotionally drained. Gemma had finally broken down and revealed what Grey had done to her. Poppy was devastated. Gemma, the gentlest and kindest person she had ever known, had been left a hollow shell.

What now?

Poppy had spent the previous day consoling Gemma. They had spent the rest of the day in her room. Poppy had told everyone that Gemma had a bad flu and that she would take care of her.

Dinner had been brought to them, but neither could bring themselves to eat anything. Now that the door had been opened and the memory allowed to escape, a return to normality was impossible. Gemma had cried herself to sleep that night. So had Poppy. She had awoken the next morning exhausted.

Gemma was still asleep when Poppy finally crawled out of bed.

She entered the blue and white tiled bathroom and looked in the mirror. Her eyes were red from crying. She had dark circles under her eyes. She washed her face with warm water and then looked in the mirror once more—no change. She brushed her teeth.

She decided to take a quick shower. She would fill the bathtub with hot water for Gemma afterwards. As she shampooed her hair, she started to cry.

HOT BATH
Gemma woke up around 8am. She pulled herself up and looked around.

Poppy was sitting in a chair and looking out one of the windows of her bedroom. She was wearing her white cotton bathrobe. Her hair was wrapped up in a white towel. It was a cold and overcast day. The landscape was still lightly blanketed in snow.

'Good morning, Poppy,' murmured Gemma softly.

Poppy turned around and looked at Gemma. She searched for evidence of her current emotional state. Gemma stared blankly at her. This was not the Gemma she had known for the last 27 years. Poppy felt an ache well up inside her.

'Poppy. Could we visit the castle today? Just you and me?' asked Gemma softly.

'Of course, Gemmy. But first take a bath. I'll prepare one for you right now,' and Poppy stood up and walked towards the bathroom door.

'Thank you, Poppy,' replied Gemma softly.

THE CASTLE
They dressed warmly in wool trousers, cotton blouses, and coats. Poppy wrapped her soft Burberry scarf around Gemma's neck and shoulders. They put on their shoes and headed downstairs. The house was quiet. It seemed no one had woken up yet. The girls opened the front door; a blast of cold air hit them, and they exited, shivering in the frosty morning air.

They walked in silence across the snow-covered lawn towards the castle ruins. Poppy occasionally took quick glances at Gemma as they walked. She was still trying to gauge her emotions. It was overcast, the sky a combination of black and grey clouds. It was freezing cold. The snow crunched underfoot.

When they arrived at the castle gates, Gemma stopped and scanned the front of the structure. The air was crisp, refreshing. Gemma looked at Poppy blankly. She stared at her for a few moments and then finally spoke.

'Let's go up the tower.'

'Sure, Gemmy.'

The girls made their way across the snow-covered castle grounds and then entered the sole solid tower through a small wooden door. Poppy closed it behind them, and they both ascended the spiral staircase to the top floor.

Once there, Gemma climbed the ladder and pushed open the hatch. The snow on top of it slid off—half of it coming down on Gemma. She climbed onto the roof of the tower. Poppy followed.

When Poppy climbed out and onto the roof, Gemma was already leaning against the parapet and looking out across the snowy fields. Poppy approached her, her leather boots crunching snow underfoot.

'Poppy. I'm not going to let Grey ruin my life,' Gemma said as she continued to look straight ahead. 'I won't. I have so much in my life. I have you, my other friends, and Freya. I'm not going to let Grey rob me of everything. I still want to find happiness. I know I still can—if I don't give up.'

Poppy stood and listened in silence. She wanted Gemma to say everything she needed to.

'I can't explain my past actions. I didn't want to admit to myself what had happened to me. I didn't know how to deal with it. I…did…not…' and Gemma paused. She became very quiet for a few minutes.

Poppy wasn't sure if she should say anything yet. She decided to wait.

'I am strong, Poppy. Stronger than I ever realized. I want to be strong. I have to be strong,' and then Gemma turned around and faced Poppy. Gemma was pale. 'Thank you for yesterday, Poppy. I needed to tell someone. Thank you.'

Poppy could feel herself starting to tear up. 'I'm your friend, Gemmy. I love you.'

Gemma smiled faintly. 'I know, Poppy. Out of everyone, you are my truest friend. And you have always been there for me. I'm sorry the last three years have been so terrible. I have become an endless river of misery.'

'Don't say that, Gemmy. I have never felt that way. I only wish I could have protected you more.'

'Poppy, without you I wouldn't have survived any of it. I'm blessed to have a friend like you. Truly blessed.'

Gemma looked up at the sky and then looked down again and met Poppy's gaze. 'Poppy. Today, I'm moving forward. I am going to have a happy life. I'm going to work, make money, and buy a new flat—well, probably a rather small one. I'm going to find someone to share my life with. Someone kind and understanding. I'm going to marry someone. I was meant to be a wife. And, I still believe, a mother. Well, a godmother,' she said, **and Gemma smiled.**

Poppy moved forward and hugged Gemma tightly. She still didn't know how to respond to Gemma. Poppy remained silent.

While still being hugged, Gemma said, 'Poppy. Let's go back to the house. I'm famished.'

Poppy smiled at her. 'Sure. Would you like anything in particular for breakfast?'

'French toast. I haven't had that in *yonks,'* said Gemma in a Sloane accent, and she smiled once more.

### Gemma—London—Keeping Secrets

STOLEN GLANCES

Gemma had breakfast with Poppy's family and Brian in the highly polished wood-paneled dining room that morning. At Gemma's suggestion, French toast was served to the entire family, along with bacon, sausage, baked beans, fried Portobello mushrooms, and scrambled eggs. The French toast was fantastic. There was also regular toast with raspberry jam. All of it was served by the Croatian staff on the family's best porcelain and eaten with their finest sterling silver flatware.

Gemma seemed to have returned to normal. She chatted happily with the family, especially the twins, who had grown even closer to Gemma over the Christmas holidays. Poppy couldn't help but keep surreptitiously glancing over at her. Poppy was deeply worried about her. Poppy didn't know what to do. She wanted to tell her father, brother, and Brian what had happened, but she would do nothing without Gemma's express consent.

And then there was Grey. He was still very much in her thoughts. Poppy had not forgotten the Chaos bracelet episode in London. Also, his possible connections were also worrying. Gemma needed to go to the authorities and report him.

All of this swirled around in Poppy's mind. She didn't know what course of action would be best. Poppy could now sense that Gemma was in real danger. Grey was a violent predator, and a highly cunning one at that.

Poppy also struggled with how she should treat Gemma. She didn't want Gemma to feel awkward around her. She wanted to help Gemma…somehow. She decided that she would try to treat Gemma as normally as possible. Not pretending as if nothing had happened, but being the same positive and outgoing person Poppy naturally was. After all, that's

THE INSEPARBLE GANG OF HAPPY GIRLS

probably what Gemma expected—normality. At least, that's what Poppy hoped.

Eventually only Gemma, Poppy, and Brian were left sitting at the dining room table. Brian was tapping away at his smartphone when Poppy nudged Gemma. She looked at Brian and then back at Gemma. Gemma shook her head slightly. Poppy sighed.

COLD WEATHER

After breakfast, Gemma returned to her room and buttoned herself into a pair of dark grey lambswool trousers, put on a pale blue wool high neck jumper, a navy blue quilted Burberry jacket, and a pair of black leather walking shoes. She also put on a luxurious Holland and Holland fur hood made from coyote with a snood style neck. She tied the hood on with the black ribbon that was attached to it. That would keep her warm for the long walk.

Gemma looked in the gilt framed full length mirror that stood in one corner of Poppy's room. She looked like a posh Eskimo. Except true Sloane Rangers never used the word 'posh'—they instead used the term 'smart' verbally (even though they were thinking 'posh').

She was still slim and quite shapely. She always drew men's gazes, but how would they view her if they knew she had been a victim of, well, what Grey had done to her? Would men still want her? **Would any man want to marry her?** Gemma hadn't even considered any of this until she had finally broken down and told Poppy. And she knew that Poppy now viewed her differently, she could feel her quick glances and gaze continually resting upon her. Did Poppy really think Gemma **hadn't noticed?** How Poppy viewed her, Gemma wasn't sure. But she knew Poppy definitely viewed her differently now.

UNCERTAIN FUTURE

Here was the real question: Was Gemma now unworthy of marriage? Would she just be cast aside like a broken toy? Would Gemma spend the rest of her life alone? Why should she suffer for what someone else had done to her? She was the victim. She didn't want to become an object of pity. People distance themselves from the pitiful. They don't want to have to walk on eggshells all the time. No, it's easier for people to walk away.

'Have you heard about poor Gemma? How beastly. Poor girl. I think it would be best for everyone if she just went abroad.'

**Gemma didn't want anyone else to know what had happened to her.** It would devastate Freya if she ever found out. It would wound her very deeply; Gemma knew that. Violet would never forgive herself for introducing her to Grey. How would Vava treat her afterwards? She didn't think Violet would abandon her, but the relationship would be badly, horribly damaged. Gemma knew Vava would be consumed in grief—yes, Vava would be for sure. She definitely didn't want any of the men to know. Some of them might even go after Grey and try to kill him, but that would land them in prison. Gemma didn't want that either. She didn't want to destroy Poppy's family.

She knew going to the police was pointless. How would she explain that consensual sex had turned into a brutal rape? She had medical records of her treatment, but how would she explain to a jury why she had moved in with Grey the very next day and lived with him for three weeks? She had told people that they were engaged to get married (after he had raped her). How could she explain that to a jury? Would anyone believe her? Would people blame her? Would they ask her why she was in the bedroom of a man she had only met a few days before? How would she be able to make people believe her? Gemma didn't even understand why it had taken her so long to react to what had happened. Why had it taken her several weeks to even acknowledge *to herself* what had happened?

And the **scandal** that would follow would be huge. Everyone would know. It would be humiliating and devastating for Gemma. She felt awkward around Poppy now, and Poppy was understanding and accepting. How would others react to her?

Gemma's head was left spinning. She started to feel panicked. Breathe, Gemma. Breathe.

Okay. It's time to go for a walk. That will help you.

Gemma had always enjoyed taking walks. They calmed her and helped her clear her mind. Today, however, was different. No amount of walking could now calm Gemma down. Her mind was in turmoil. Gemma needed some time alone to resolve the issues swirling around in her head.

Gemma headed downstairs and out the front doors. She looked around. The castle ruins were on her left. To the right lay snow-covered farm fields just beyond the large house lawn. Beyond the fields, in the distance, was a small village. Gemma decided that today would be a good day to visit. She turned on her leather heels and started to walk down the road.

She started walking down the main road to the village, and after a few minutes of walking, she turned and looked back at the large stone country house on the hill. On the roof of the Victorian structure fluttered a large flag bearing the noble coat of arms of Poppy's family. That meant that the baron was in residence. The grey stone structure looked cold and imposing. No one looking at it at that moment would have guessed at the kindness and loyalty of the family who resided there. Gemma turned back around and continued to walk down the road towards the village.

It was a grey and overcast day. It was cold and occasionally a few flakes of snow would fall from the sky and swirl around her.

The snowflakes, caught in the wind, reminded Gemma of herself. She had felt helpless for the last three years; she had been carried along, whipped around, and thrown in random directions depending on whichever way the metaphysical winds moved her. Gemma had lost control of her life, and just when she thought she had regained it, she had been blindsided by Grey.

Grey. Him. Again. How would she escape him? What exactly was Grey up to? What did he really want from her? Grey must have realized that any hopes of continuing the relationship were hopeless. He had admitted that much himself. The change of heart Grey had apparently had didn't really surprise Gemma. She had expected it. That's why she had run out of the house on that final afternoon. She had fully expected Grey to try and stop her. He hadn't. But, now, it appeared that Grey had lost the internal battle with himself and reverted to his true nature. What did Grey ultimately want from her? Gemma breathed hard and continued to walk alone down the road to the village.

## THE SILVER BRISTOL

Gemma had been walking down the road for almost two hours when she heard a vehicle approaching. She looked behind her. In the distance she could see a silver Bristol motorcar approaching. She got off the road and clamoured up the small hill, the snow crunching under her leather heels. She stood at the top of the small hill and waited. The silver car slowed down as it came closer. Gemma looked carefully; Poppy was behind the wheel. The car came to a stop on the road in front of her.

'Gemmy! One of the staff told me they saw you taking off down the road. It's freezing! Get in! I'll drive you to the village.'

Gemma was cold and tired. She smiled and got into the silver Bristol. Poppy was wearing a navy blue cashmere sweater and her Burberry scarf.

'Thanks, Poppy. I think I was a bit too ambitious this morning,' said Gemma and Gemma smiled. She held her hands up to the heating vents and let the warm air warm her hands. She looked around the interior of the car. It was beautiful, all polished walnut and Connolly leather, a true English motorcar.

Gemma fastened her (recently installed and modern) shoulder belt and leaned back in the leather passenger seat. Poppy shifted the automatic transmission into drive and the car moved forward.

The Bristol hummed along the road at a slow pace; the roads had patches of ice here and there. Poppy was careful.

The silver Bristol prowled into the village, and Poppy parked the car next to the local pub. Poppy flashed her impish smile and said, 'We're here, Gemmy.'

The girls got out of the car. Gemma untied the black ribbon and pulled the coyote hood back and let it rest on her shoulders. Her glossy brown hair was now intermeshed with the fur hood. Poppy observed her: Yes, Gemma was still beautiful, and seemingly the same person she had always been.

Only she wasn't. Poppy was at a loss at what to do. She decided to be as much of herself as she could be.

'Brian is now out with James and Father. They are giving him the full tour of the estate today. He asked me to go with him, but I declined. I think the men in the family want to become more acquainted with Brian.'

'Now that he is joining the family, I think they want to make him feel welcome. They really like him. Brian had already spoken with them earlier and asked permission to marry me. Father and James teased him about Harrow. They told him that they would have to consider our engagement very carefully,' and Poppy laughed happily.

'James can be really funny sometimes. He pretended to argue against the proposal. They way Brian described it to me made me laugh out loud.'

'James has always been funny!' laughed Gemma. And then Gemma, thinking of the first day of the trial when James had held her hand as they exited the court under a barrage of photographers, smiled gently and said softly, 'And James is brave. Kind. And good. He is truly brave and loyal.'

Poppy smiled and then hugged Gemma. 'Come on, Gemmy. Let's get you a hot drink.'

THE GHOSTS OF OXFORD

The girls entered the pub together. It was around noon, and the pub was starting to fill up with the lunchtime crowd.

The owner, recognizing Poppy, showed her to a corner table near the fire place. Once comfortably seated, Poppy said, 'Gem, let's have lunch here. I'm famished. You must be tired *and* hungry after this morning's hike.'

'Sounds *marvellous*,' said Gemma. 'I haven't had pub fare in ages.' Gemma smiled as she looked at the paper menu.

The girls ordered lunch. The pub was filling up with a combination of permanent residents and Londoners who either owned houses in the village or were staying at one of the hotels in the Lake District for the holidays. By the time their food arrived, the pub was packed.

The girls were chatting happily when they noticed someone had stopped next to their table and was staring at them. The man appeared to be in his late 30s, slim, and of average height. He was dressed rather casually; he was wearing a white Oxford button down dress shirt, a blue quilted jacket, a grey wool scarf, and blue denim jeans. His brown hair was cut and combed like a City banker. He was rather average looking. He also looked familiar.

'Gemma?' the man said. 'Do you remember me?'

Gemma looked at him carefully. Why yes, she did remember him. 'Oxford. You were at Christ Church,' said Gemma cautiously.

'Yes. Let me make this easier for you. Gerald.' And he smiled. Gerald also acknowledged Poppy. Poppy smiled back at him. She also remembered Gerald.

Yes, Gerald. He had not only attended Oxford with George; they had also been roommates for three years. This was awkward for Gemma, but Gerald had always been nice to her. She hadn't seen him since Oxford. He hadn't attended the wedding. He had apparently fallen out with George just before the wedding. George had refused to say why. Gemma hadn't seen or heard from Gerald since.

Gerald had entered the army, and the last Gemma had heard, he was an officer in a Hussar regiment. Now, after a twenty-year absence, Gerald was standing before her.

'Are you here alone?' asked Gemma.

'No. Well. Yes. I mean, I'm staying with friends in the village. This is my first visit. I just walked over here to get a quick drink, and I saw you. I'm alone.'

Gemma smiled. 'Please join us, Gerald.'

Gerald sat down. He seemed a little uncomfortable, but his smile was friendly.

'What have you been up to, Geri?' asked Gemma.

'I was in the army for a few years, and then I left. Now I'm helping my father manage his farm. We have a farm in Cumbria. It's quite pleasant out here. I don't get to London that often anymore. How have—I mean. How are you, Gemma?'

Gerald had undoubtedly followed her downfall in the papers, and must have been fully aware of how badly she had fared. Gemma could feel how embarrassed Gerald was by his faux pas. She wanted to soothe his nerves, so she smiled and said, 'Much better, Geri. Really.'

'That's great to hear Gemma. Really.' And then Gerald seemed to wince. He had never been known for his conversational skills. He had never been charming like many of the other students at Christ Church. He had been the odd man out there. A middle-class background and manner had always singled him out from the rest.

Gemma smiled. Poor Geri. He was trying his best.

'Do you still live in London, Gemma?'

'Yes. I just moved into a new place in The City. I have a new job with an investment group.'

'That's great, Gemma.'

'So, do you like farming?'

'Yes, very much. It comes naturally to me. After the army, I enjoy the peace and quiet that the farm offers me,' said Gerald with a smile.

Poppy finally spoke. 'Gerald, if you have time, please come by the house for lunch one day.'

Gerald had been friends with both girls for almost three years. Gerald had been somewhat close to Gemma because of her constant visits to George. Poppy had also spent a considerable amount of time with Gerald. Both girls were undoubtedly curious about what had led to the break between George and Gerald, but neither wanted to bring it up. They were both happy to see him again.

Gerald looked at his watch. 'I'm afraid I have to go. I have to meet my friends.' He took out his wallet and handed each girl one of his business cards. 'Please call me whenever you like. If you ever visit the area, please feel free to stay at the farm with me and my family. Do you remember my parents? They met you once at Oxford.'

'Yes,' said both girls.

'Alright. Well. I have to go. Um. It was good to see you both again. Okay. Take care.'

And with that, Geri departed.

'Okay. Are you going to ask him what happened with George, or am I?' asked Poppy.

Gemma said nothing. Meeting Geri had unleashed memories of her (mostly) happy life at Oxford. Geri had been a part of it. Gemma remembered George. How happy they had been together, the golden couple. How could he have betrayed her?

'I'm curious, too, Poppy. I'll ask him when I get a chance.'

'He gave you his business card, Gem. He wants **you** to contact him.'

'He gave his card to both of us.'

'No. He was just being polite. He wants you to contact him.'

Gemma said nothing. She was deep in thought. So many things seemed to be coming full circle now. She was worried that George would reappear; that would be a nightmare. But, considering how her life had been going the last three months, it would not be that surprising.

Külli, the one person from Gemma's past that she hoped would contact her, almost certainly would not.

## Gemma—London—Enveloping Darkness

A BUSINESS MODEL

Grey sat at his desk in his Primrose Hill office. He was wearing a light grey suit, pale blue dress shirt, a white undershirt, a blue silk neck tie, and black leather shoes. He was suited and booted like a City banker today.

There were several envelopes and three small cardboard boxes on his desk. Grey was using a handheld loupe to inspect a precious gem that he was holding in his hand.

Grey had learned a lot about precious stones over the last two decades. He had also learned a lot about jewellery, and most importantly, he had a network of clients to whom he could fence stolen gems and jewellery to.

Grey never had any trouble finding buyers. When he had started selling his loot, the highest bidders were from the Persian Gulf and Russia. Now they were from mainland China.

The Chinese were a wily bunch, but they had more money than anyone else these days; and they wanted to flaunt it. And what better way to do that than display it on your wife? Yes, millionaires yearn for status and recognition—billionaires even more so.

In London, there were the rich, and then there were **the rich**. Grey had dealt with some of the richest people on the face of the Earth, and nowhere in the world were people more status-conscious than in London.

The British, that is, the native population, were almost entirely left out of the picture. The British no longer had any money. The real wealth in London was in the hands of foreigners. And London attracted the vainest people Grey had ever encountered.

Grey always used superlatives when he thought about his clients: the most ostentatious, the most extravagant, the gaudiest, the most tasteless, the greediest, the grossest, and the worst. Grey disliked most of his clientele; they were crass and vulgar. His clientele was made up largely of drug dealers, embezzlers, gangsters, hedge fund managers, and even corrupt dictators. There were some legitimately successful businessmen sprinkled in

266

among them, but they made up only a small percentage of his base.

Grey never sold gems or jewellery above board. That part of his business was made up entirely of stolen goods and was sold to the highest bidders through a network of people that had no direct links to him. That was the most lucrative part of his business empire.

The official and primary component of his business was art. Grey loved art because it was so easy to launder money through it. He could sell some of his paintings to fictional clients abroad that would pay him X amount of dollars, pounds, or euros, and then Grey could declare it on his taxes. It really was that easy. Grey laundered a certain amount of money, mixed in with his legit business deals, and he was in the clear.

Western governments were broke. They didn't care how people made money these days if you paid taxes. They didn't really ask too many questions. Just keep a low profile, and you'll be alright.

Grey was not extravagant. He didn't really care for luxury. He still wore dark khakis and blue blazers. Grey was American. He wasn't ashamed of it. And he had zero interest in becoming 'British' —whatever that meant, especially these days.

Grey was generous. He gave everyone in his gang a fair cut. His gang knew it, too. Grey's crew was extremely loyal to him because of that. Also, they had deep bonds going back to the wars they had fought in together. These bonds were strong, solid, and even unique.

A LIFESTYLE
Grey had more than enough money. He could retire right now if he wanted. Or he could go entirely legit and still make a good living. But Grey didn't want that. Grey enjoyed gangland way too much. Grey liked what gangland brought him: money, women, power, and most of all, excitement. Grey enjoyed the lifestyle.

A good combat officer has to like to fight. A good gangster has to like one overarching aspect of gangland: **power**. A CEO at a Fortune 500 company could become entangled in the court system for years in a dispute. In gangland, disputes could be resolved in a single afternoon. No lawyers, no judges, no courts—just brute force. Yes, why would someone like Grey ever want to go legit? Gangland was efficient. The smartest and the strongest survived and dominated. The weak were eliminated. It was kill or be killed, the Law of the Jungle.

Grey felt the biggest mistake that people made in gangland was becoming too greedy and too big. It's the tall poppies that get cut down. Stay low and you won't be noticed. Stand too tall and you're decapitated. Grey didn't want to take over and control London's gangland. He just wanted to steal as much as he could from those who did. And go unnoticed. Discipline and loyalty were required to pull it off. And Grey had both.

## GEMMA

But today, Grey had other concerns: Gemma. How would Grey bring Gemma back into his life? How would he convince her to be his wife? He wanted ~~a posh girl like~~ Gemma.

Grey had made a real mess this time. But Grey enjoyed a challenge. Grey had always risen to the occasion. And this time would be no different.

Grey was methodical. He planned out every step in advance. Like chess. Well, maybe. Grey didn't really play chess very well. He had always found the game rather boring. But, anyway, Grey was pursuing Gemma the way a general waged a war: he analyzed his opponent. He learned all that he could about them. He looked for weak points. (And he had found several of Gemma's.) And he attacked.

## ALONE

Grey had spent the Christmas holidays alone. Winter had decamped to Portugal, and Maria had flown to Lisbon to spend the holidays with her family.

Alone in the house, Grey was lost in thought. He wandered from room to room. Sometimes he would sit in the living room and stare out the window. He enjoyed people watching.

The blonde who drove the silver Volvo with the young daughter was someone he enjoyed watching more than anyone else.

She followed a regular routine. She would drive her daughter to kindergarten every morning, and she would usually return at around 9am. She would usually leave at around 11:45am, presumably to meet friends or perhaps even her husband for lunch. She would usually return at around 1:15pm. At around 3:20pm, she would drive off and pick her daughter up at school. She was usually back before 4pm.

Watching the blonde mother help her young daughter out of the car was of particular interest to Grey. He always imagined that Gemma would be doing that soon, but the daughter would be his. He wondered what color their daughter's hair would be. Grey watched as the blonde mother smiled and spoke happily to her young daughter. She would then hold her daughter's tiny hand and walk her to the front door of their house, which was located directly across the street from Grey's house in Primrose Hill on the other side of the narrow park.

Gemma, regardless of her feelings towards Grey, would love their daughter. Grey was sure of that.

Grey knew that first morning that Gemma would *never love him*. She would never forget what he had done to her. Grey would never win her heart. He knew that. He knew that. But—but—Grey really didn't care if Gemma loved him or not. *He loved her.* Grey would find a way to get her back, even if he had to drag her back into his life by her hair.

CCTV

Grey went downstairs into the wine cellar. The large wine cellar had been fully stocked by the previous owner. Grey had never drunk any of it. Grey didn't drink. He had Maria select wine, whisky, or brandy for his clients. Maria knew alcohol. He also allowed her to take a bottle home with her every Friday. Any bottle she wanted.

No, the wine cellar held another one of Grey's secrets: the surveillance room. Hidden behind a false wall, there was a long and narrow dimly lit room lined with TV monitors and computers, a desk, and two folding chairs. There were also shelves along one wall. On the shelves were numerous plastic containers holding USBs and even DVDs of video footage.

There was a German pistol on the desk. Two extra clips of bullets were next to it.

The previous owner, a Ukrainian oligarch, had more enemies than you could shake a stick at. He had installed hidden cameras in *every room* of the house.

Yes, cameras had even recorded what had happened between Grey and Gemma on that first night. Grey had never watched it, nor would he. He deleted it before he had flown to Croatia. Grey hadn't wanted any trace of his actions that night to exist outside of the human memory of the two participants. Grey always deleted video files showing evidence of his crimes. This event was just one more of them.

Grey scanned through the digital files. Ah, here were his favorite ones: Gemma serving him dinner. Gemma making and serving tea. Her mannerisms are what attracted him to her the most. She was unfailingly polite. She knew exactly how to serve tea or a meal. She was graceful. She was the daughter of the nobility. And she radiated it in her every move and gesture. She walked down the hallway like a panther. She glided up and down the stairs. Grey smiled as he watched the video footage.

Grey watched video footage of Gemma unpacking her clothing (what little she had) and hang it up carefully in the bedroom closet. Grey watched attentively as she spoke with Maria in her bedroom. She was telling Maria which items she wanted sent to the dry cleaners. Maria nodded and left.

Gemma then shut the bedroom door, walked over to the bed, and sat down. Gemma stared straight ahead for a few minutes. Then Grey watched the screen as Gemma started to cry. She laid back on the bed and covered her face with her hands and cried. Grey knew why. Grey wished he could go back in time and change things. But he knew he couldn't. It was pointless to even think about that anymore. What was done was done. Gemma had been damaged—by him. Grey regretted it. Not because he had hurt

Gemma, but because Grey had ruined the relationship.

It was difficult for Grey to feel much for others. His emotions were reserved for himself. Grey only regretted doing things to others if it caused *him* problems later on, but for no other reason really. Grey supposed he should feel guilty for what he had done to her, but it was truly difficult for him to do so. Grey surmised why: strong men cannot allow themselves to feel for others. That was weakness, and weakness was dangerous. An Achilles heel got you killed.

But still, Grey needed Gemma. Gemma had a grip on him that he could not fathom. Grey really didn't try to understand why he loved Gemma. He just did. And, that's all that mattered. Grey wanted her, and she would be his.

**Think, Grey**. Think hard. Your mind is as infinite as the universe. The answer is here. Think harder. Analyze, calculate, evaluate. **Okay**. There's an idea. That might just work. Yeah, that would work. Yeah. That's it. That will work. You're still the smartest person in the room, Grey.

And Grey smiled.

**END OF BOOK ONE**

CPSIA information can be obtained
at www.ICGtesting.com
Printed in the USA
LVHW091646141121
703308LV00003B/15